MINE

MINE

...The main house was dark. George knew he'd left a light on in the kitchen. Probably the bulb had burned out.

A reassuring beacon of light shone from the window of Marc's study in the guest cabin. The boy was writing late again. Marc's pup gave a half-hearted woof as he passed, and Pop grinned. What a monster that little fellow was going to grow up to be!

He'd better enter by the side door. There was a light switch just inside.

Pop stepped inside, turned on the lights and was hanging his down-filled jacket on a peg inside the mudroom when he became aware he was not alone. It was just a sensation in the hairs at the back of his neck. But the door to the basement gaped wide.

"Who the devil?" he muttered, reaching to close the door.

"Just me," said an unexpected but too-familiar voice from the doorway to the laundry area behind him.

Wheeling around, George stared into dark eyes filled with hatred. He had one split second of blinding disbelief and another of devastating comprehension before a sharp blow to the solar plexus knocked him backward down the cellar stairs and into total darkness.

PRAISE FOR MINE

"5 Stars!...Dee Lloyd is gifted with more than mere writing talent. She can see into people, love them just the same, and put that all together with skilled words. A charming read."

—Buzzy
Buzz Review News

"4 Stars!...From the first sentence in *Mine* I was drawn into the book by the suspense interwoven so skillfully into this love story. Dee Lloyd brought the characters to life, and I hope to read more of her books in the future."

—Jewel Dartt
Midnight Scribe Reviews

"An exciting and romantic mystery! This one will keep readers glued to the story."

—Detra Fitch
Huntress Book Reviews

"...Sparkles with imagination creatively lending a new twist to the age-old prospector's tale. Bravo Dee, for the wonderful word play and the joyful celebration of love. This reviewer truly looks forward to many more tales from the pen of this talented author."

—Cindy Penn
WordWeaving Reviews

"*Mine* builds in intensity and excitement to a fine, rip-roaring ending. Dee Lloyd offers pulse-pounding excitement leavened by a tender love story."

—Christine Janssen
Sharpwriter

"Dee Lloyd can always be counted on for fast-paced, exciting romantic murder mysteries. Fast becoming one of my favorite suspense authors, Dee writes strong, intelligent women who challenge the men around them. Her stories never fail to keep me on the edge of my seat to the very end, which comes far too soon!"

—Sue Waldeck
Road to Romance

"4 Stars!...Excellent...A delightfully written book that will sweep you away with the danger. Author Dee Lloyd has captured danger and betrayal, mystery and romance and intermixed it into a book that will not just keep your attention riveted but your fingers turning the pages. Definitely a book to relax and escape the day with."

—Tracy Eastgate
Tracy's Book Reviews

"Ms. Lloyd has constructed a taut, absorbing story, peopled with three-dimensional characters. She's definitely a woman to watch. I'll be looking forward to reading her future work."

—Catherine Witmer
Just Views Reviews

"Ms. Lloyd writes a wonderful contemporary romantic suspense that twists and turns and twists again! A definite Good Read!"

—Miriam M. Willis
Belles and Beaux of Romance

ALSO BY DEE LLOYD

Change Of Plans
Ghost Of A Chance
Ties That Blind
Unquiet Spirits

MINE

BY

DEE LLOYD

AMBER QUILL PRESS, LLC
http://www.amberquill.com

MINE
AN AMBER QUILL PRESS BOOK

This book is a work of fiction. All names, characters, locations, and incidents are products of the author's imagination, or have been used fictitiously. Any resemblance to actual persons living or dead, locales, or events is entirely coincidental.

Amber Quill Press, LLC
http://www.amberquill.com

All rights reserved.
No portion of this book may be transmitted or reproduced in any form, or by any means, without permission in writing from the publisher, with the exception of brief excerpts used for the purposes of review.

Copyright © 2006 by Dee Lloyd
ISBN 1-59279-724-5
Cover Art © 2006 Trace Edward Zaber

Layout and Formatting provided by: ElementalAlchemy.com

PUBLISHED IN THE UNITED STATES OF AMERICA

To David

*To Ann, Terry, Laura and Sharon
who remember H.J. Lloyd, the much
loved inspiration for Pop.*

*Enjoy!
Dee Lloyd*

PROLOGUE

George Haywood considered the last few lines he had written. He would tell Cadie the rest when he saw her in a couple of weeks. She could use some good news. He flexed his fingers, then printed neatly, "I love you, Midget." And signed it, "Pop." That nickname hadn't fitted his Cadie for years. She'd grown up to be a fine looking figure of a woman.

He sealed the envelope and tucked it into the leather book he used to log the core. He'd mail the letter in the morning. Flipping off the overhead light switch, he spun his old office chair around so he could stare into the glowing coals of the glass-fronted airtight stove that heated the shack.

He should be happier. Everything was going well. Maybe too well.

Too bad Cadie hadn't stuck it out at the School of Mines for another couple of years. Now that Pete was gone, he could use another mining engineer in the family. Still, the Banff School of Fine Arts had been the right place for Cadie. They'd be all right. At least, she hadn't married that smooth article she was engaged to last Christmas. *Thank the Lord!*

He looked over at the racks that held hundreds of long cylinders of rock that he and Marc had extracted from the property with the portable diamond drill rig. His weather-beaten face crinkled into a fond smile. Marc Banachek was a good one. When he'd turned up in answer to George's ad in the *Almaguin News,* George knew he was the man to live in the guest cabin and help him with the exploration. "Self-contained accommodation for a self-contained man." He'd been proud of the wording. And Marc had recognized himself in it.

He shivered. The cold of a subzero February night was beginning to seep into the shack. That's all it was. He and Marc and Cadie could handle whatever lay ahead. And soon, that other part of his life that had been so wrong for so long would be made right. There was a spring in his step as he left the core shack.

The main house was dark. He knew he'd left a light on in the kitchen. Probably the bulb had burned out.

A reassuring beacon of light shone from the window of Marc's study in the guest cabin. The boy was writing late again. Marc's pup gave a half-hearted woof as he passed, and Pop grinned. What a monster that little fellow was going to grow up to be!

He'd better enter by the side door. There was a light switch just inside.

Pop stepped inside, turned on the lights and was hanging his down-filled jacket on a peg inside the mudroom when he became aware he was not alone. It was just a sensation in the hairs at the back of his neck. But the door to the basement gaped wide.

"Who the devil?" he muttered, reaching to close the door.

"Just me," said an unexpected but too-familiar voice from the doorway to the laundry area behind him.

Wheeling around, George stared into dark eyes filled with hatred. He had one split second of blinding disbelief and another of devastating comprehension before a sharp blow to the solar plexus knocked him backward down the cellar stairs and into total darkness.

CHAPTER 1

Marc stared glumly out the large window at the white caps building up on the windswept waters of Nighthawk Lake.

So Pop's granddaughter was actually on her way, was she? That should be no surprise. She'd been on her way up here to Nighthawk three months ago when she'd had the accident that almost killed her.

Pop had told many fond stories about Cadie's stubbornness. Well, Marcus Banachek could be just as obstinate. She would find him right here until the end of the year. He'd told her lawyer so. He had also reiterated that Arcadie Haywood was damn well going to honor his lease, just as Pop would have. Besides, with the latest Ban Marcus thriller to finish for Wyeth and Burns before the end of September, he'd need privacy to write…and quiet. He'd make sure of that. He didn't intend even to speak.

Pop's little Cadie was not his responsibility. Besides, she didn't want him to look out for her or entertain her. She wanted him to vacate the guest cabin!

He muttered the crudest epithet he could think of. He was not going to go out of his way to pander to a grieving woman still recuperating from an accident. Particularly one as attractive as Cadie Haywood. It was no longer his duty to serve and protect. It had taken him a long time to accept how futile his best efforts in that direction had been. But he had learned.

Anyway, he'd never been a nursemaid. If Arcadie Haywood was well enough to get here, she was well enough to look after herself. He'd be polite and perhaps even help her get settled in. He owed Pop that much. Besides, she might know the results of the drilling. But nothing was going to jeopardize his freedom to do exactly what he wanted to do, when he wanted to do it. He'd earned that freedom.

He saved and closed the file and shut down the computer. The text on the monitor vanished. There was no point in trying to write any more this afternoon. Cadie's lawyer, with a few businesslike words of warning, had ruined his concentration.

"Come on, Lurch," he called to the huge black dog who was lying in the doorway.

In spite of his size, Lurch was still a pup, his legs still growing so quickly that he didn't seem to have them quite coordinated. He staggered eagerly to his feet and bounced in place like an angular basketball.

"Time for a long walk. We'd better take advantage of our peaceful male refuge while we have it."

Sunlight was breaking through the clouds and trickling through the white pine branches far overhead. Patches of pale yellow light danced in the sparse undergrowth. Tiny cones and long, waxy needles crunched under his boots. Marc breathed the warm, pine-scented air. This was a far cry from the sound of sirens and the smell of exhaust fumes.

Glad of the gangly black dog's company, he strode down the long driveway, then cut off along the worn path by the old log cabin and core shack. Lurch snuffled the ground loudly and crashed through the underbrush. Marc had to laugh at his energetic cavorting. He couldn't maintain his sour mood in the face of that much bouncing joy.

"And stop bumping into me, you ugly mutt," he shouted in mock fury as Lurch apparently misjudged the distance of one of his leaps and almost knocked him over.

He had never intended to get a dog; but Lurch had been hard to ignore, hanging around the kitchen door at meal time. Of course, once Marc had fed him, the homely mutt followed him everywhere. Before he knew it, he was the sole support of an already-ninety-pound dog who worshipped him and was growing before his eyes.

Lurch's possible ancestry had been a source of great amusement to Pop. Marc could still hear his deep belly laugh. "One of the summer people probably ditched him when the cute little puppy from the Humane Society began to show signs that his Labrador retriever mommy had got too chummy with a woolly mammoth," he would say.

"Look at those feet! You're going to have to build a barn to stable him."

Marc really missed the old man. They had known each other for such a short time. Only two years ago, Marc had answered his ad in the local paper. He never regretted it. The tall, stringy, old prospector with the keen hazel eyes and the strong handshake had accepted him for what he was and given him space to make his uneasy peace with what Marc knew was a cold, bleak world.

Marc hadn't pulled his weight in their relationship. Oh, he had done more than the minimum twenty hours a week of labor that Pop had made part of the rental agreement. He had worked alongside the older man, staking the claims, clearing the rough road for the all-terrain vehicles that would carry the disassembled diamond drill rig to the drill sites. Marc had actually done most of the heavy work with the drill. He hadn't, however, been able to bring himself to share Pop's dreams of finding gold. He didn't want any part of the inevitable disillusionment when those dreams crashed.

Instead, he had lost himself in the writing that saved his sanity. The characters he created were able to love, hate, seek revenge, even weep—experience all those emotions that lay rigid in the deep-freeze of his heart. More importantly, in his action-packed stories he could see that the good guys always won.

Over his objections, Pop and his son Peter insisted they give Marc a one-eighth interest in the claims in return for taking out the license that allowed them to stake additional acres. Nevertheless, he had stubbornly avoided the topic of the progress of the exploration. He should have showed a little interest. The old prospector had spent long hours in the drafty core shack wetting down the long cylinders of rock and poring over them with his magnifying glass.

While Pop was falling to his death, Marc had been less than a hundred yards away, writing happily about treachery and grisly murder. He hadn't heard a thing.

Chuck, the local Ontario Provincial Police officer, had seen no reason to suspect foul play. Marc had been the only person around that night and the only monetary tie he had with Pop was his interest in the probably worthless claims. He was even going to have to find another place to live by the end of the year. At the same time, neither of them was happy with classifying his death as accidental. However, they had been forced to accept the opinion of Pop's doctor, who felt a small stroke had caused the apparently healthy old prospector to fall to his death. No one would ever know why he'd been on the basement stairs when it happened.

That was another reason Marc refused to move away from the house. The whole situation made him distinctly uneasy. Not quite seven months after Arcadie Haywood lost her father to cancer, her grandfather had died. Then, three months later, she had narrowly missed being killed herself. No one seemed to be questioning those incidents, but Marc didn't like coincidences. Especially if the results of the drilling showed that the Nighthawk claims contained a large ore body.

The rock samples had contained enough gold for the local mining recorder to register the claims. He, Pop and Peter had celebrated the registration with high hopes and some very good whiskey. But during the week before he died, Pop had seemed more worried than elated by the results of the drilling. Marc had cynically assumed that the old man's dreams were collapsing. But the claims could be worth big money. And, if they were, there were probably greedy fingers ready to try to grab them. Unfortunately, people with greedy fingers didn't always have scruples about family ties.

Marc didn't know who would have inherited if Cadie had died in that car crash. Her Uncle Jack and his wife were the only family members at Pop's funeral last February. Marc had hoped at the time, that the lovely woman with the sad, hazel eyes wouldn't place too much trust in her loud, affable uncle.

Pop had been proud of his son, Pete, who taught at the Colorado School of Mines, a place even a cop who got his degree at night school had heard of, and of his little Cadie. But, for some reason, he had never mentioned his only surviving son. Then, there was that peculiar bequest to Jack of "the deed to a piece of moose pasture near James Bay that I am sure Jack will recognize."

Lord, Marc wished Cadie were homely or disagreeable. Maybe then he wouldn't feel so edgy about her arrival. She had barely spoken to him at the funeral, but when he closed his eyes, he had no trouble conjuring up her oval face with its pointed little chin and big, sometimes hazel, sometimes green, eyes.

He'd forced himself to live like a monk for the past two years, but Cadie's low, vibrant voice and small but definitely female body reminded his own thirty-six-year-old body it was still very much alive.

He could only pray that Arcadie Haywood prized self-sufficiency as much as her grandfather had.

He shuddered.

"A goose walking over your grave," Pop would have said.

Marc had no idea what that meant, but it sounded ominous.

"Come, Lurch," he snapped, then turned and headed back home.

He heard a car door slam. When he reached the driveway, he spotted a Jeep Cherokee parked in front of the house. The four-wheel drive vehicle wasn't what he expected a quiet bookstore owner to drive. What stopped him dead in his tracks, though, was the sight of Cadie in the clearing beyond the house. She was twirling around with her head thrown back in obvious delight. Her bare arms were outstretched and the sunshine caught the gold highlights in her windblown hair.

His breath caught in his throat. She was so lovely and full of life.

His abrupt stop put him directly in Lurch's path. The dog careened solidly against the side of Marc's left leg. Marc felt an excruciating jolt of pain and heard the snapping sound of his trick knee popping out as he crashed to the ground.

* * *

A few minutes earlier, Cadie had switched off the Jeep's engine and sat in silent contentment for a moment. The Cherokee's new car smell suited her mood. Four hours on the highway hadn't dimmed her eagerness. She was ready to begin her new, unfettered life. She grinned. The thought of herself as a free spirit was pretty funny.

The sprawling building that hugged the top of the rocky promontory seemed to radiate a quiet welcome. With its half-log siding and silvery, weathered cedar shake roof, the house almost blended into the landscape. If it weren't for the shiny red paint on the doors, window frames and the pillars of the porch, giving it a slightly irreverent air, it would be almost too solid and homey-looking.

The sunlit clearing beside it drew her like a magnet. She had spent so many hours sketching there a few years ago when both Dad and Pop were still alive. Leaving the car door open, she moved toward the bright, open space. As she stretched her arms out, as if to embrace the whole beautiful scene, her steps became a kind of dance. Spinning slowly 'round and 'round on the patchy grass, she dismissed the fleeting thought that a woman who was almost thirty must look a little weird cavorting like this in the sunshine.

Who cares?

She'd discarded all those concerns about living her life to please other people. This was the up side of being alone in the world.

Reminding herself to enjoy the moment, she twirled around one last time and stopped, wide-legged and slightly dizzy, to drink in the scene around her.

On the north side of the house, where the land dropped off sharply to the lake, the waves crashed on the headland just as she remembered. On the south, where it sloped gently to the sheltered beach, the water was calm and smooth. She held her breath and listened. Except for the rhythmic splashing of the waves, there was an almost tangible silence that seemed to cushion the house from the outside world.

She stretched her arms up toward the sunshine and swayed against the strong breeze that caressed her face and body. The mournful weight of the recent past slipped from her shoulders. Her fractures had healed, the ugly bruising had been replaced by a golden tan and her partner was running the bookstore back in Denver. Cadie felt free and alive. There were no unhappy memories here.

Today's drive had been easy. Her jaunty Jeep handled so differently from the low-slung station wagon that had plunged down the mountain only three months ago. She was going to enjoy wheeling it around the local bush roads looking for painting sites. Cadie was more pleased with herself than she could remember being in a long time.

A hoarse bellow of pain shattered her exultant mood.

Startled, she spun around to look down the driveway in the direction of the shouting. Just beyond the house, a man was being attacked by a huge black animal. She recognized Marcus Banachek immediately. His size and his thick shock of blond hair were unmistakable. He was cursing and trying to beat the beast off with his bare hands.

Without considering what she would do if the animal turned on her, Cadie picked up a fallen branch and ran toward them, brandishing the stick and shouting, "Get away! Get away from him!"

Her shouts blended with Marc's.

"Lurch, you maniac, down. I'm not playing. Drop!"

The animal stopped its barking and collapsed in a panting heap beside his master. Even lying still, its gaping mouth and big white teeth were impressive.

The fearsome beast was a dog. *His dog.* Cadie felt like a fool. Her heart was still pounding furiously and she had that stupid log in her hand. She wasn't actually afraid of dogs. She merely was more comfortable with cats and could never understand why anyone wanted to share house-space with a large, potentially vicious animal like this one. She tried to look nonchalant as she tossed the stick away.

Banachek's face was anything but welcoming. A lock of blond hair had fallen over his forehead and was hiding one of the eyes she remembered as cobalt blue. The eye she could see had chilled to the color of winter ice and his broad face was fixed in an intimidating scowl. He was so still he could have been carved of wood. For one hysterical moment, she was tempted to smooth the hair back off his forehead. She dismissed the urge as a momentary insanity in the face of finding a virtual stranger lying incapacitated at her feet.

Her eyes swept over the massive rest of him. Judging by the deep tan displayed by his short-sleeved shirt and denim cutoffs, he did not spend all his time indoors writing his violent novels about the greedy and the seedy. She caught her breath. One of his muscular legs was bent at an extremely awkward angle.

"Are you all right?" she ventured as she knelt beside him.

"No," he growled.

She could see his left knee was swelling already.

"I'd better put a splint on that before we move you," she said, getting to her feet. "I have a first aid kit in the Jeep."

He grabbed her hands. She gasped at the unexpected contact.

"Sorry," he grated out, not sounding at all apologetic. "Don't touch my knee. I know what to do for it."

"Can you stand up?"

"Yeah. Get me a strong stick to use as a cane. I can hop to the cabin from here."

"The house is closer."

His scowl deepened, but he bit out a grudging, "Right."

Not so much as a please, she fumed silently. She was tempted to tell him to get it himself, but the man was obviously in pain. Aloud, she said, "We'll get there quicker if you lean on my shoulder."

She should have been more insulted by the cool way his steely eyes deliberately assessed every inch of her perfectly adequate, five-foot-four-inch body.

"I'm stronger than I look," Cadie stated calmly, determined not to let him intimidate her. "Can we count on your hairy buddy to stay out of the way when I help you up?"

"Yes."

Marcus Banachek obviously did not believe in wasting words.

"Lurch," he said to the dog, "this is Arcadie."

"Cadie," she corrected, then smiled at how ridiculous that sounded.

"Actually, he can call me Arcadie if he wants to. I'd like you to call me Cadie."

Hard as it was to believe, she thought she saw an answering glint of humor in his eyes.

"Marc," he returned. Then ordered, "Let him sniff your hand." Hesitantly, she offered the back of her hand to the beast who looked as if he could swallow it whole. A yard of wet tongue swiped it and the thick rope of a tail wagged.

"Lurch, stay," Marc commanded. "Okay, Cadie, let's get moving."

He positioned himself so his good foot was solidly under him and allowed her to pull him up.

My, but he was big! He looked like every little kid's idea of a policeman—tall, strong, tanned, wholesome-looking. Not to mention unbelievably sexy, she thought. But not friendly.

"You're stronger than I expected," he said with a grunt as she hauled him to his feet. He put his left arm across her shoulders. "I'll try not to put too much weight on you."

She circled his waist with one arm and placed her other hand flat against his chest to steady him if he lost his balance. She could feel the heat from his well-toned muscles and the pounding of his heart against the sensitive skin of her palm. Her perverse imagination conjured up another absolutely improbable situation where she could hold his impressive body in her arms and feel his racing heart.

She felt her own pulse speeding up. What was wrong with her? Marc was a disagreeable man she hardly knew. She was acting as if her common sense had been confiscated at the border.

It didn't take long to get Marc to the house. With a minimum of help from her, he eased himself onto the large couch in front of the freestanding circular brick fireplace that dominated the big living room. While she quickly removed his heavy hiking boots, he leaned his head on the down-cushioned back and closed his eyes.

"Thank you, Cadie." His voice was an exhausted whisper.

She rubbed the spot on her shoulder where his hand had rested. She might not have been supporting much of his weight, but she was still going to have a bruise there to remind her of his firm grip. What she didn't want to remember was her body's unexpected response to the innocent contact. The surge of warmth that set every nerve in her body on alert was a new experience for her. She'd been engaged to Jerry, but his nearness had never made her uncomfortably conscious of his masculinity. Of course, Jerry had never exuded the raw virility Marc

Banachek did.

After the emotional wringer she had been through the last few months, she'd be wise to keep a safe distance from her taciturn tenant.

* * *

"Can I get you something for the pain?"

Cadie's voice was low and amazingly soothing. Her elusive scent reminded him of fresh spring flowers. Marc raised his eyelids enough to see concern in the gold-green depths of her large eyes.

"Yes," he said, conscious of how harsh and ungracious his own voice sounded. "About four ounces of scotch in a tumbler. No ice. It's in the cupboard over the sink in the kitchen."

She looked at him silently for a moment, then left without saying a word.

The woman even knew when to be quiet! He was in bad trouble. Even with the pain in his knee, during the trip down the driveway, he had been acutely aware of the smooth warmth of her bare shoulder under his hand. She must have noticed the way his heart was pounding when she had her hand on his chest. His long-dormant hormones had chosen a hell of a time to snap back to life.

When she had looked up at him to inquire how he was doing after they had covered about half the distance to the house, he'd had an irrational urge to slide his hand from her shoulder into her thick, gold-streaked hair and to kiss her until she was dizzy. He knew how her lips would taste as surely as if he'd been kissing her all his life. He hadn't done it. But, if he didn't get his mind off the taste of her, she was going to notice the tight fit of his cutoffs when she returned with the whiskey.

"Do you want it now?"

He opened his eyes slowly. Cadie was holding out the glass of scotch and staring at his misshapen knee.

"Just put it on the end table. I need you to do a couple of things first. I almost forgot I left Lurch on the 'Stay' command. All you have to do is go to the door and call, 'Lurch, okay. Come.' The 'okay' releases him. The 'come' calls him. You'd better duck, though. He comes like a bullet."

"He's...big," she said. She was no longer the fierce, little Amazon who had come to his rescue flourishing a big stick.

"Don't be afraid. He's a big marshmallow." He hadn't meant to sound so gruff. The woman needed reassuring. It was not her fault he was attracted to her. He tried to soften his voice.

"Just say 'easy' when he gets near and then 'drop.' He has too much energy but he does try to please."

Cadie leveled her shoulders and walked stiffly to the door.

"Leave the door open," he called to her. That way, if Lurch looked as if he might knock her down, Marc could at least holler at him.

She called the dog and bravely stood her ground as he approached at a gallop.

Marc held his breath.

"Easy," she said firmly.

Lurch sidled up to her, tail wagging fiercely, and licked her hand all the way to the elbow.

"Drop," she said. She turned to grin at Marc when the dog collapsed on the porch.

"Stay," she said jauntily.

When she returned to him, leaving the dog on the porch, she had a delightfully smug smile on her face.

"I can't believe he came when I called."

Every thought that went through her mind showed in those expressive eyes. Why hadn't he met her ten years ago? Well, he hadn't. Even if he had, he probably would have been looking past her at some tall, busty redhead anyway.

"Well, I'm going to give you another chance to be in control," he said, poker-faced. "I need your help to put my knee back in."

"No, thanks," she said, shaking her head. "You need a doctor for that. There must be a hospital or a clinic in the area."

"No need. I've done this before. Lots of times when I was playing football and a couple of times since. Just face away from me, swing your leg over mine, grab my ankle and hold on tight. You can do that, can't you?"

Her dubious expression told him how resistant she was to the idea. "It sounds barbaric. I'm not one of your locker room buddies."

No question about that. Marc looked at her long, slim legs and swallowed hard. He could see why she might view placing his fairly hairy leg between her thighs as too intimate. However, he knew it would bring him a certain amount of relief from the pain. His determined gaze held her wavering one until she gave him a grudging nod.

"It's against my better judgment," she muttered.

"First," he said, "I'd better down a little anesthetic."

He drank the whiskey in one large gulp.

"God, that's awful," he gasped. "Come on, honey. Time to climb aboard."

He reached over and placed his hands on her waist and turned her away from him. Cadie's back distracted him for a moment. She had one world-class derrière. The rest of her was just fine, too. She wasn't tall, but her legs were long and slim, her breasts just the right size to fill a man's hand. Cadie looked at him over her shoulder.

"Well?" she said. She glanced almost fearfully at the light coating of curly blond hair on his leg. Then, she blushed. Her lips looked soft and as if they needed kissing. This was nuts!

Marc tore his eyes away from her mouth. What was happening to his mind? It must be the liquor hitting his bloodstream. Get serious, he told himself. He had drunk the scotch to kill the pain, not to lower his inhibitions.

"Okay, swing your leg over and grab my ankle. Now hold on tight. Don't let go for anything. We're going to do it…"

He placed his right foot against her buttocks and pushed hard. "Now!" he gasped.

The momentary pain was excruciating, but the damned knee did snap back into place.

When Cadie scrambled back beside him, she gave him one long, searching look.

"I'll be right back," she said before she dashed into the kitchen.

He could hear her emptying a tray of ice cubes. In seconds, she was back with a glass of water and an ice bag she had improvised out of a hand towel. She placed the ice gently on his swollen knee.

"I have some leftover pain killers," she said, on her way out of the room again. "My purse is still in the car."

"You don't need to do that," Marc said to empty air.

His mouth twisted into an ironic smile. He had been agonizing about whether or not he was duty-bound to look after Arcadie Haywood. Now he was the one who needed help. He was going to have to stay off his feet for a while—probably two or three days. He cursed under his breath. The last time this happened, he recalled the doctor had insisted he keep the leg elevated for a week. Then he had to refrain from putting any weight on it for another ten days. However, maybe he could avoid seeing Wilf about this.

"Blast! Now I'll have to coax Vi to come in for the next couple of weeks," he thought aloud.

*   *   *

As she entered, carrying her purse and one of her suitcases, Cadie overheard him. *Who's Vi?* Of course, a man like Banachek would have a woman who would be happy to come in to make him comfortable. Why should that bother her? He was nothing to her. He was her late grandfather's tenant. But she was ridiculously glad he wasn't eager to call the unknown Vi.

"Bad habit talking to yourself," he said sheepishly when he saw her. "I guess I spend too much time alone."

"Take these," Cadie said. "They'll help."

He looked at the tablets she had placed in the palm of his hand.

"I'll be fine," he muttered. "I'll just rest here a little while. I'm feeling better already."

* * *

She had unusual eyes. There was a narrow rim of dark gray around the green and gold fire of the iris. He had never seen eyes quite like them. Right now they were locked on his with grim determination.

"The water glass is right beside you. Take them."

He didn't have the energy to fight her. He swallowed the tablets.

"You should be able to get a bit of rest now. I have to unload the Jeep and unpack my bags. I'll be back in a couple of hours to help you to the guest room." She gestured toward the room beside the one that had been hers when she'd visited Pop.

"Thanks, but my own place is just over there. I'll be fine. I just need to close my eyes for a few minutes."

"We'll see how you feel when I come back."

* * *

She was damned bossy for a complete stranger.

Cadie started toward her room, then paused. "You don't have to…go anywhere now, do you?"

She was blushing again.

"No," he said, unable to suppress a half grin that made her color a little more. "I'm okay, but thanks."

It was a long time since he had met a woman who blushed. As he watched her quick retreat, his grin softened. He could still see the grim determination on her face as she ran to his rescue with that branch. It was just his luck that Pop's little Arcadie was turning out to be one hell of a woman. She was enough to stir the ghosts of dreams that had long ago shriveled to dust. Too bad he had nothing left to offer to a woman like that.

Somehow he had to get her out of here—out of his life.

No one knew how completely the bad guys had beaten him. His sudden decision to leave the force had caught his fellow officers by surprise. In the fifteen years he'd been with the Metropolitan Toronto Police, he had gained an enviable reputation because of the high conviction rate of his arrests. It was common knowledge he was being groomed for promotion, but two years ago, he had resigned. He couldn't stomach the brutal world he worked in any longer.

When he left, he had been the leader of an investigative team that had tracked down the perpetrators of several highly publicized serial murders. The last had been particularly offensive. It had involved the murder of children. When he had looked into the expressionless eyes of the killer, the emptiness there had shaken him.

He had seen traces of that same hollowness in his own mirror. He realized, with horror, that every time he forced himself to stifle his own revulsion or compassion, he was hastened the day he would wake up to find that he, too, had become a monster incapable of human emotion.

The final straw came when the killer had been set free because a piece of crucial evidence had been declared inadmissible in court. Marc had come home early, sick at heart, to find Val, the woman who had been sharing his condo and his bed, sharing that same bed with Willy, his long-time buddy.

He should have been filled with pain and rage. But he was not. He hadn't been able to care that much. The farm boy who had been determined to help the weak and the unfortunate, was gone forever. That naïve boy had believed his motives were pure and noble, but Marc had learned the hard way that everyone was self-serving. He could see now that he'd only yearned to be admired and respected. He hadn't realized that nobility, like loyalty and love, was a myth.

That moment, he decided to quit the force. He could live on the investments he'd made with his share from the sale of the family farm and what he got for the condo for quite a while, if he was careful. Taking with him only the notes for his police novel, he escaped to Chartwell Falls.

He did believe that moments of happiness were possible, but they were rare. Sometimes, in the peace of the forest, serenity slid into a man's soul; then there was the solid satisfaction of achievement. These were dependent only on yourself.

He no longer trusted women. Men were no better. Everyone had an angle. Except Pop—except that old man with his uncompromising honesty and his big heart. Unfortunately, the hollow, self-centered man Marc had become had let him down.

He rubbed his eyes. One thing he knew for sure. He wasn't going to touch another drop of scotch while Cadie was here. It had taken two years to develop this bland detachment. It had been too hard-won to allow his suddenly rampaging hormones to destroy it.

The accident with his knee served him right. He'd been so caught up in the illusion of beauty and joy and grace that he'd allowed himself to come smack up against painful reality again.

As the painkillers took hold and he drifted off to sleep, he was vaguely aware of the scent of lilacs and the sensation of having a feather-light comforter tucked around him.

* * *

Cadie moved away from the over-sized sofa and the over-sized man on it.

"So much for non-interference in each other's lives," she thought disgustedly.

Elsie would be beside herself with glee if she knew what had happened. Cadie remembered the skeptical twinkle in her best friend's blue eyes when Cadie had insisted she was simply going to ignore Marc's sexy presence.

Elsie! She had promised to call her the minute she arrived. And what she could use right now was a dose of Elsie's cheerful common sense. Elsie's I'm-just-a-fun-loving-redhead-with-nothing-more-on-my-mind-than-the-next-man-and-the-next-party act fooled a lot of people. However, many of them discovered that it was costly to take her at face value, especially when she was representing a client. She was a smart lawyer and a true friend.

She also, apparently, was waiting by the phone.

"Cadie!" she exclaimed. "You finally got there. Didn't the dealership have the Jeep waiting for you? Williams swore he'd have it ready for you."

"Everything went like a dream, Elsie," Cadie assured her. "I'm a little later than I expected because my tenant had a little accident and put his football knee out as I was arriving. It took a while to get him settled."

Elsie chortled. "So you have the gorgeous hunk at your mercy. And you'll probably have to devote some time to nursing him back to health. I feel sooo sorry for you."

"Stop it, Elsie. You know I don't want to have anything to do with any man right now. This is just going to make it harder to get him to move out right away."

"I still say Banachek is just what you need. You deserve a prime male specimen after that toad, Jerry. Go for it!"

"Did you talk to the realtor about selling Dad's house?" Cadie pointedly changed the subject.

"Yes. He's getting right on it. But your Uncle Jack called me today and insinuated you had put your real estate dealings in his hands."

"Not in this life," Cadie told her. "He's determined I'm going to let him sell Dad's house and this property at Nighthawk Lake and move to Florida to recuperate near him and Aunt Rose."

"What a great guy," Elsie drawled. "Of course, there's nothing in it for him."

"The more I see of him, the better I understand why Pop refused to see him when he turned up a couple of years ago. Dad tried to play peacemaker, but all Pop would say was, 'I told Jack thirty years ago I didn't want any part of him. I see no reason to change my mind now.'"

"What exactly does he do for a living?"

"All he ever says is, 'Buying and selling in Florida. Among other places.'"

"Well, that pins it down." Elsie paused. "How's the bod holding up after the long flight and the day's drive?"

"Couldn't be better. I'll call you again in a day or so. Right now I'd better unpack and try to get Banachek to the doctor."

"Pay attention, Cadie. Marc Banachek would be perfect for you. What could be better for a woman who owns a bookstore than an author?"

"Will you forget that?" The only reason she'd read the first Ban Marcus bestseller was that she made it a rule to read at least part of every book she sold. She'd been compelled to read it to the end, but she'd found it repulsive. She didn't like being forced to share emotions and scenes that raw. "The fact he writes ugly books about the seedy and greedy doesn't make him appealing to me. Besides, he's going to ask his girlfriend to come and look after him."

"Oh." Elsie sighed. "If that's the way it is. Anyway, you can enjoy the view. You take care. I'll let you know the minute I have any word on the house."

Cadie replace the receiver slowly. She really did not want to have to deal with Marc Banachek or his injury. She wanted him gone.

The worst part of having him laid up with a bad knee was that there was no way he could look for another place. He was just going to have to stay in the guest cabin for a while longer. She refused to consider the possibility he might have to stay in the main house.

First, I have to convince him to see a doctor. Then figure out how we're going to manage if he can't walk! she thought, shaking her head at the unfairness of fate. Whoa! Not true.

There was no we. Marc was not her responsibility. Vi, whoever she was, would have to come to look after him.

Her eyes were drawn back to Marc's sleeping figure. His rugged face looked almost vulnerable without its frown.

"He's about as vulnerable as a wounded grizzly," she whispered to herself. "Don't forget that, Cadie. And he's moving out soon. You'd better hope."

CHAPTER 2

Soon after the gnawing ache in his right knee woke him, Marc became aware he wasn't going to be able to put off getting to the bathroom forever. But he'd be damned if he was going to ask Cadie to help him to get there. He wished good old motherly Vi were here.

He spat out a heartfelt curse. The nearest phone was in Pop's den, almost twenty interminable feet away. He didn't care if he had to crawl on his belly, he was going to reach the bathroom on his own. Then he had to call Vi.

He pushed the comforter aside and swung his legs off the sofa. Grasping the padded arm, he placed his feet on the floor, and hoisted himself onto his right foot. Then, gradually, he tried to ease some weight onto his left one. He bit back a cry of pain. This was not going to work.

"Are you trying to wreck your knee completely?"

He turned to see Cadie standing behind him with her eyes flashing green fire. She did not waste any time talking, but put her arms around his chest and yanked him off balance so he toppled back onto the sofa almost on top of her. When the sharp jolt of pain had passed off, he realized Cadie's arm was behind his back and his shoulder was pressed against the softness of her breast.

The sensation of Cadie struggling to extricate her arm made him forget his other problems for a moment. He knew that special chemistry could explode between a man and a woman, but he hadn't realized the reaction occurred independently of a person's will.

"Move!" Cadie said, more crossly than he thought necessary. "My arm is trapped."

"You're awfully bossy for a little woman," he complained as he leaned forward so she could free herself. After all, she was the one who'd pulled him off his feet. Unfortunately, he ruined the effect by letting a crooked grin escape. "I haven't heard so many orders since I left the force."

"I'm not a little woman," she retorted. "You're a giant. I haven't been called short since I grew five inches the year I turned fourteen."

She straightened up, obviously stretching to her full height. He figured she had to be—at most—five-four or five.

"And don't ask me why I think it's important to try to prevent you from making a permanent cripple of yourself," she grumbled, tucking her blouse back into the waistband of her shorts. "What were you trying to do?"

"Get to the phone," he snapped. "And to the can."

"Which do you want to do first?"

"Phone."

"I'll bring it to you," she said, meeting the full force of those marvelous stormy eyes. She waved a warning finger. "Don't you move."

* * *

What a rude, unpleasant... Most of the crude expressions Cadie had learned from her fellow students during her two years at the mining school resounded through her mind as she went into the study to get the phone. She rejected them all. *Clod!* Yes, she liked that. A clod of earth was coarse and totally lacking in feeling or sensitivity. And absolutely without appeal.

"Your phone, Mr. Banachek," she said, her voice dripping icicles. "I hope you're planning to call the doctor first."

"I know what he'll tell me."

The stubborn clod was not going to give in gracefully.

"'Keep that knee immobilized and the weight off it for a few days.'"

"I'd like to hear it from him."

She stared him down.

"All right. I'll call Wilf Raeburn."

It took less than a minute to complete the call.

"His nurse tells me Wilf is still at the clinic and will wait for us there," he said. "Would you lend me your shoulder again for a minute?" His face like a storm cloud, he pointed to the washroom off the study.

"I'll call you when I'm ready," he dismissed her at the door.

Cadie felt a wave of compassion for his embarrassment. She suspected he was a lot more comfortable in the role of giving assistance. When he emerged from the washroom, she moved toward him and, wordlessly, put her arm around his waist. He looked down at her as if he wanted to say something, but just shrugged and draped his arm over her shoulder.

"Let's go," he said. "I'll call Vi when we get back."

After he hopped to the Jeep, still parked in front of the house, she drove him in silence the twenty miles into Chartwell Falls. Although she did her best to avoid the bumps and potholes in the road, out of the corner of her eye, she could see him clenching his jaw with every jolt.

A lean, dark-haired man who, she assumed, was Dr. Raeburn, met them in the parking lot as they pulled to a halt. He opened the door of the Jeep, looked at Marc's knee and, after one curious glance at Cadie, waved her out of his way. With the ease that obviously came from experience, he assisted Marc into the clinic.

"You appear to have done quite a job on that joint," he said.

"Yeah," Marc said. "Lurch crashed into me and my trick knee went out. Cadie held my foot while I straightened it. It's not too bad now."

"I'm not a big fan of do-it-yourself medicine," Wilf commented dryly as he helped Marc hoist himself onto the examining table.

He turned to Cadie and gave her a swift once-over that she was sure had taken in all her vital statistics.

"You must be Arcadie Haywood."

The smile that lit up his pleasant face said plainly that he'd been waiting for her to come and liven up his drab existence. She suspected it was a smile that got a lot of use. The signal those heavy-lidded brown eyes were sending was definitely not a wistful and lonely one.

"Cadie," she corrected with a smile of her own.

"I'm Wilf Raeburn. I'm glad to meet you. Vi mentioned you might be arriving soon."

She supposed that, in a town the size of Chartwell Falls, everyone knew everyone else's business. Certainly everyone appeared to know Marc's friend, Vi!

Wilf's long, capable fingers moved swiftly over the swollen knee.

"Well, Marc, I can't see that you've created any further damage putting it back in place," he admitted. "But we need an x-ray of that knee. The lab is closed now, so you'll have to come back in the morning. This shot will help with the inflammation, and I'm putting a padded plastic sleeve on the knee. Its only function is to keep your knee straight for the time being. The velcro straps are adjustable. Don't try to tighten them."

The scowl on Marc's face was, if anything, growing darker.

"I'm sending you home with crutches," Wilf continued. "For the next couple of days, use them only when it's absolutely essential. The rest of the time, I want you flat on your back to let those tendons and ligaments heal. There's only so much abuse a knee will take. From the look of this, I suspect you've gone back into too many games with this one frozen. Football?"

"Mostly," Marc growled

"You're going to be at the house, Cadie?"

At her nod, he smiled approvingly. "Good. Put ice on this joint. Most of the swelling should go down in twenty-four hours. He's going to object and want to take the splint off. Don't let him do either."

"Cadie won't be with me for the next twenty-four hours," Marc told him. "I'll be at the cabin."

Wilf gave them both a long look, then shrugged. "Well, you'd better consider imposing on your neighbor until you can get someone to come in. It's going to be at least ten days before you can put any weight on that leg."

"Marc can stay in the guest room until he can arrange for some home care," Cadie said, accepting the inevitable. "I'll see to the ice for a day or two—if it's necessary."

"Call me if you have any trouble. I'll pop around in a day or two to see how you're doing." Wilf gave Cadie a broad grin that offered both sympathy and friendship. "Both of you."

"I'll be fine," Marc said. His expression became even grimmer when Cadie said Wilf would be welcome any time. "You don't have to put yourself out on my account."

"If you want to avoid surgery, you'd better obey orders," Wilf warned him.

They left the office with a requisition form to have the x-rays done and a prescription for pain killers. Cadie dashed into the pharmacy across the street, had the prescription filled and picked up a couple of ice bags.

When she climbed back into the Jeep, Marc was sitting in the passenger seat with his eyes closed.

"We should stop at Vi's on the way home to see if she is available for the next little while," he said.

Even in the dim light of the street lights, his drawn face showed how much the pain had tired him.

"Why don't you call her when we get home?" she asked as she pulled out into the light traffic.

It was almost eight o'clock and she hadn't eaten since she had pulled off the highway for a coffee and carrot muffin on the way up from Toronto at about eleven o'clock that morning. She was exhausted and hungry. Marc must be, too.

"That would probably be a good idea," he said with a yawn. Then his eyes snapped open. "It's Wednesday, isn't it? She'll be at bingo anyway. She never misses a Wednesday night. I'll have to try to catch her later."

At the end of her emotional and physical tether, Cadie gripped the steering wheel. She was on the verge of tears. She didn't care if the unknown woman named Vi was Marc's current or his ex-lover. She wanted her, or somebody, to come to the house and take over. She didn't want to cope with Marc in close quarters. Everything about the man rattled her. Maybe they could get a nurse to come in tonight to deal with his injury and care.

"Let's see how you feel after you've had something to eat," someone with a voice very much like hers offered. "We can manage tonight and you can call her in the morning."

"Oh, she'll be at the house at eight o'clock tomorrow morning anyway. Thursday is one of her days. Mondays and Thursdays."

"Every week?" Cadie couldn't come straight out and ask what Vi's duties were.

"Pop and I never messed our places enough to need them cleaned more than once a week. The other day she cooks and does laundry."

Cadie suddenly liked Vi a lot better.

The jolting of the gravel road did not seem to be affecting Marc as much as it had on the way to town. That probably had something to do with the shot Wilf Raeburn had given him. She saw him tense though when they drove onto the long, pot-holed driveway to the house.

She'd left a light on in the living room and in Pop's study at the front of the house, but, as they rounded the curve to come into view of the house, it seemed to be ablaze with light.

Marc swore under his breath.

"What is it?" she asked, pulling up in front of the wide steps that led to the verandah.

"Nothing," he muttered.

*   *   *

But it wasn't nothing. When their headlights hit the front of the house, he could've sworn he saw someone duck out of the light around the dark corner of the bedroom wing. If his damned leg had been working properly, he'd have hit the ground running and caught whoever it was and found out in short order why he was skulking around the property.

It was too late now. The moon had not yet risen and the night was black. The intruder could amble down the dark beach path and circle back to the road without danger of being noticed. Marc didn't mention it to Cadie. He could see no point in making her nervous. Anyway, what he saw could simply have been the shadow of a tree moving in the freshening breeze.

"Where's Lurch?" he wondered aloud, just as the dog galloped up to the Jeep from the direction in which Marc thought he had seen someone disappear. It had probably been the dog's shadow he'd seen. Lurch was a pretty good watchdog. If there'd been a stranger, he would have barked. But why would the dog have been moving into the woods, away from the vehicle bringing his master home?

Cadie went directly into the kitchen and he followed her.

"I didn't turn this light on when we left. It must've been on all day," she said pointing to ceiling light fixture.

She was rummaging in the refrigerator as she spoke. "Could you eat a ham and cheese omelet and toast? That's about what I'm up to cooking right now."

"Sounds perfect," he said. "I'll owe you a meal. I have a couple that I don't ruin. Pop and I used to share dinner now and then. It broke the monotony of microwaved frozen dinners."

He sat down on one kitchen chair and put his foot up on another. Cadie was a pleasure to watch. Her slender hands worked quickly as she grated cheese and beat the eggs for their omelet. She had lost weight in the six months since the funeral, but she had lost none of her independent attitude. She held herself rigidly, refusing to give in to the fatigue she must be feeling.

"You must be tired out after your flight and your long drive from Toronto," he said, looking at the faint dark smudges under her eyes. "I appreciate all you've done for me. I'll try make it up to you somehow."

When she grinned at him unexpectedly, little flashes of gold flared in her greenish eyes. The first time he'd seen her, he was attracted to her, but when her face lit up like this she took his breath away.

"Just put up with my bad temper," she said. "When a painting doesn't work out the way I want it to, I turn nasty."

She pulled a face probably intended to make her look evil. It only made her look like a mischievous child.

"When I get ugly and snarly, remember that you owe me one."

He couldn't imagine her ever looking ugly to him, but he didn't comment or return her smile. Wooden. That's the way he wanted her to think of him—wooden, unemotional, maybe even a little dense.

* * *

Cadie turned back to the stove. *Well, so much for trying to make him forget his sore knee by amusing him.* He really was a clod. A sexy clod. But a clod.

Cadie watched him as he made quick work of his omelet and whole wheat toast. He ate with total concentration. His large, square hands used the knife and fork methodically and without any wasted motion. His eyes were focused directly on his plate. She didn't know what to make of him. Of course, he might be concentrating so hard because he was on the verge of falling asleep in his chair.

But when he turned his attention to her, she had the feeling his penetrating blue eyes could see every hidden thought in her mind. The force of his gaze caused a tremor of excitement or fear to race through her. This man was dangerous. She wasn't sure if even the new free spirit she'd decided to be could cope with him.

Raising her hand to cover a yawn she couldn't hold back, she said, "We'd better get you to bed before I fall asleep on you."

She saw an amused glint in Marc's eyes and glared at him.

"I'll fill the ice bags and attach one to that fancy gizmo on your knee," she forged ahead. "I'll set my alarm. Three o'clock should be about right for another pain killer and a fresh ice compress."

* * *

He shook his head. There was no way he was going to have her hovering around him in the night. Those eyes that reminded him of the sun-dappled forest were going to invade his dreams as it was.

"No," he said a little too forcefully. "You've had too big a day to disturb your rest for me. I'll sleep on the day bed in the study. If you fill the two ice bags and put one in the freezer of the little refrigerator in there, I'll be fine. It's only a few feet from the day bed."

"Fine," she said.

* * *

She wasn't going to argue with him, but neither was she going to lie awake listening for him to lose his balance and wrench his knee again while he coped with his crutches and tried to retrieve the ice bag from the freezer at the same time. She found sheets and blankets in the linen closet and navy blue silk pajamas still in their package in the bottom drawer.

He grimaced when he saw them. "I'll wear the tops tonight in your honor, but I'll save the bottoms for when I can get both legs in them."

Obviously he was used to sleeping in his underwear or in nothing at all. The picture of that tanned and muscular body sprawled naked on the white sheets she had just spread on the day bed flashed through her mind. This was a dumb time to develop an erotic imagination! Hadn't she just decided not to think about Marcus Banachek?

"I'll give you a few minutes to get into bed and I'll be back with your medication and the ice," she said, retreating as quickly as possible from the scene her own mind was creating.

In fact, she was moving so fast she almost tripped over her empty suitcases in the middle of the guest room where she was planning to sleep. She was glad she'd left the light on.

Wait a minute. She distinctly remembered turning off the bedside light when she finished unpacking. And she had put the suitcases in the corner out of the way. Swiftly, she opened the top drawer of the dresser to check her small jewelry chest. Everything was there—her pearls and gold chains and the emerald dinner ring and pendant that had been her mother's. She couldn't tell if anyone had been through her clothes; she hadn't put them away too neatly in the confusion after Marc's accident. Well, her few pieces of jewelry were the only things she had brought were worth stealing and they were still there.

Shaking her head slowly, she picked up her traveling alarm and set it for three o'clock.

* * *

By the time Marc finished washing himself as thoroughly as he could standing on one foot and leaning on a crutch and had pulled on a fresh pair of boxer shorts and the pyjama top, he was damp with perspiration. When he got back to his bed, he literally fell into it.

He did not hear her light step on the carpet and was lying with his eyes closed when he caught the light scent of lilacs.

"Sit up for a minute," she said, in her soft voice that seemed to wipe away all the irritations of the day.

She handed him his tablets and a glass of water. He took them, while she busied herself with attaching the ice bag to his splint according to Wilf's instructions. For a split second, her fingers brushed against the hard muscles of his thigh.

The contact hit him like a crackle of static electricity. The sharp intake of Cadie's breath told him that she had felt it, too. He felt her quickly pull the bedding up under his chin and turn off the light beside the day bed.

"Good night, Marc," she said over her shoulder as she left. "Hope you can get some sleep. I've set the alarm for three o'clock."

CHAPTER 3

Cadie awoke to the heavenly aroma of coffee and frying bacon. When she stretched experimentally, a tender spot on her shoulder reminded her sharply of the big man who had reluctantly leaned on her to steady himself. In spite of the adrenaline pumping as hard as it had since her rude welcome to Nighthawk Lake, she had slept quite soundly. Even being jolted out of bed by a strident alarm at three a.m. to change the ice pack on Marc's knee had not kept her from falling right back to sleep.

Marc. What an enigma he was! He wasn't friendly, but once or twice she had seen a glimmer of warmth, maybe even vulnerability, in his eyes. She had no trouble seeing the incisive and depressing Ban Marcus in him. Yet, he was also the man who had the sense of humor to call his dog Lurch. He piqued her curiosity. If she had any wits at all, she reminded herself, she'd stick to her decision to avoid him.

That coffee was calling her. Marc wasn't likely to be up and making breakfast. It was probably the mysterious Vi.

Since she'd left both doors between her bedroom and the kitchen open in case Marc needed her in the night, she could hear the sound of water running in the kitchen and the muffled sound of voices. Pop had certainly soundproofed this place. He always said he wanted family to visit, but he didn't want to hear them moving around. That would make it easier to forget Marc was in the house when things got back to normal—whatever normal was.

Right now, for the first time in months, she was hungry. She was even ready to face Vi—and Marc—for a cup of coffee and some of that fragrant bacon. After a quick shower, she pulled on an old Colorado School of Mines sweatshirt, jeans and faded red deck shoes and made her way to the kitchen.

Marc was seated in the same chair he had used for their supper last night. When he saw her, the relaxed smile faded from his face.

"'Morning, Cadie," he said, before turning to the well-upholstered, older woman standing by the sink. "Violet, my love, I'd like you to meet Arcadie Haywood. Vi Wheelwright is our housekeeper, Cadie, and a godsend."

Vi greeted her with a shy smile. "Hi, Ms. Arcadie," she said. "Can I get you some breakfast?"

"Oh, please call me Cadie. I've never quite forgiven my mother for calling me Arcadie. When I was born, she'd just finished writing a paper on pastoral poetry and thought it was a beautiful name. Please make it Cadie."

"All right, Cadie. And you just call me Vi." She gave Cadie a smile that had lost some of its shyness. "But I kind of like Arcadie. Don't you, Marc?"

"One of my all-time favorite names," he said, a hint of a smile softening his granite features. "Vi tells me she's free to come in every day if we want her. She can't live in, but she'll stay from eight to four every day but Sunday. We can work out a schedule so she can do whatever you want her to do here at the house, too. What do you say?"

What could she say? Marc was going to need help over the next few days, and she was determined not to get more personally involved with it than she had to. Unfortunately, it didn't make sense to have Vi dashing back and forth between the house and the cabin. And Marc should have someone within hearing distance during the night. There was only one solution.

Cadie took a sip from the mug of black coffee Vi had poured her.

"Every day for as long as you are willing to come, Vi," she pronounced, "if your coffee is always as good as this."

Vi accepted her praise with a little smile and a one-shouldered shrug. "Don't see why I shouldn't," she said.

"But I think Marc should stay here in the main house for the next few days," Cadie added.

"Out of the question," he stated.

She met his stormy blue eyes. She should be more relieved he didn't seem to want to have anything to do with her either.

"The day bed in the study is pretty handy to everything. It doesn't make sense for Vi to rush back and forth between the two buildings, when the whole point of having her here full time is to make sure you have help when you need it. Besides, this kitchen is much better equipped than the one in the cabin, if I recall."

"We'll bring your computer over and set you up fine," Vi contributed. "If you stayed here, Marc, I'd feel better about helping Cadie get settled in."

After a moment's thought, Marc conceded reluctantly. "For a day or two. If it'll make your life any easier, Vi."

"Well, that's that then." Vi turned her attention to Cadie. "I brought a basket of field tomatoes from home and I'm just making a couple of toasted bacon and tomato sandwiches for Marc. Would you rather have some eggs and hash browns?"

"One of those wonderful-smelling sandwiches sounds great," she replied, sitting at the far end of the pine plank table from Marc.

She looked at Marc's leg on the chair beside him. An ice compress covered the knee.

"So," she said, trying to sound as if she started every morning with a large man in her kitchen, "how's the knee this morning?"

"The swelling's going down," he muttered, not moving his eyes from the joint in question.

Silence fell. And lay there.

However, Cadie barely had time to work herself into a decent panic about the situation she'd invited when Vi served her breakfast. It was the best B and T sandwich she'd ever tasted. When her eyes widened in appreciation, Marc actually grinned at her.

"A local man smokes the bacon himself," he told her and took another bite of his own sandwich. "How about joining us for a cup of coffee, Vi? We can make our plans for the day."

Vi tucked a wisp of gray hair back into her tidy bun and sat down beside Cadie.

"I feel as if I know you, Cadie. George used to talk about you all the time. I want you to know I sympathize with your loss. I miss him, too. He and I…" She blinked rapidly and swallowed before continuing, "and my husband, Sam, go back a long way."

She turned to Marc. "Speaking of Sam," she said, "he's back. He blew in a few days ago and asked me to see if you wanted him to put a couple of loads of gravel on the driveway. He said George told him he wanted it done in the fall."

Marc gestured toward Cadie.

"It's Cadie's house," he said.

"If Pop thought it should be done, go ahead," she decided. "Is there anything else your husband should do before the snow flies? I'm hoping to use the old log cabin as a studio so we can keep the smell of turpentine and oil paint out of the house this winter. Would your husband have time to do some renovations?"

Marc's eyes narrowed. She could feel his annoyance that she intended to stay. Well, he'd have to live with it.

"I could talk to Sam, but I can't guarantee how long he's going to be around," Vi said. "You'd be better off with my son, Luke. He's the carpenter."

There was a warmth in Vi's voice when she mentioned her son that had been absent when she referred to her husband.

"Would you mind asking Luke?"

The conversation turned to Vi's duties for the next couple of weeks. In spite of Marc's annoyed protests that he wasn't a child, Vi agreed with Cadie that making sure he followed doctor's orders would take a lot of her time and energy. In addition, she would cook for them and do as many of the other housekeeping chores as she could fit into the hours.

"We'll have to get moving soon if we're going into the Falls for your x-rays this morning, Marc," she said as she began to clear the table. "Good thing I brought the Buick today. It's a big, old car and the front seat should push back far enough to give Marc some leg room," she explained to Cadie. "I usually walk. The farm's less than a mile away if I take the shortcut along the beach."

When, not too much later, the old sedan left for town, Cadie breathed a sigh of relief. She was finally going to get some of the privacy she had come so far to find. To be fair, she didn't think Marc would inflict himself on her if he had any choice. When his leg was healed, she'd make sure he looked for another place to live. Even if he stayed on in the cabin until the end of the year, she'd probably only see him in passing once or twice a week.

As for this morning, she had some chores to face before she could allow herself to scout for painting sites. To begin with, if she didn't clear Pop's things out of the master bedroom right away, she never would. It would be too easy to leave the stamp of his personality on the room and turn it into a kind of shrine. She could just see Pop's reaction to that!

She had to be sensible. Pop's room was larger and brighter than the one she was in. The access onto the flagstone patio through its sliding glass doors would be handy in good weather. She could see herself spending a lot of time in the open area that filled in the L between the bedroom wing and the main part of the house. From one of the redwood loungers, she'd have a good view of the length of the lake.

Cadie put her empty coffee cup in the dishwasher, then headed for the bedroom. Vi had emptied the dresser drawers, anticipating that Cadie might want to use them, and had left Pop's clothes folded tidily into boxes to be sorted through. The closets and the shelves of the bedroom and his study were just the way he had left them six months ago.

She started with the clothing because it was going to be the most difficult. Working quickly, she put most of Pop's clothes directly into containers to go to Goodwill. She checked the pockets and put any papers she found in a pile on the dresser. All she saved for herself was Pop's Black Watch winter jacket and a floppy leather hat. She put aside another wide-brimmed hat for Marc, in case he wanted it as a memento.

Then she began removing the dozens of framed photographs of family and scruffy-looking groups of grinning prospectors from the walls. Those, she put in another box to decide about at a later date. The only thing she left on the walls was a little oil sketch painting of the old log cabin. It was very rough and amateurish. It was also the first oil she had ever done.

"Oh, Pop," she sighed. "I wish I'd told you more often how much I loved you."

A minute later, she discovered she had been staring unseeingly at the glass case that contained what Pop had called his "rock collection." Actually, it was an excellent display of precious and semi-precious stones. What on earth was she going to do with that?

As tears began to fill her eyes, she turned away. Suddenly, she wheeled back and stared at the case. Pop had had this case for as long as she could remember. He had even brought it to Golden twenty years ago when he had come to help her father to look after her when her mother died. Cadie was familiar with the shape and color of every specimen, but she'd never seen the pieces in such a haphazard display. Pop had been a stickler for order. Each stone had always been set squarely above its printed label.

Now the case looked as if someone had tipped out all the stones and then tossed them back at their velvet-lined nests by the handful. A half dozen had come to rest against the inside frame of the box and been left there. The case was too heavy to have been jostled and upset accidentally.

More upset than the discovery warranted, Cadie couldn't bear to look at it. She felt almost as if some part of Pop had been violated. Feeling like a coward, she picked up the small box into which Vi had put the contents of Pop's top dresser drawer and rushed down to the kitchen with it. Maybe the big airy room with its crisp yellow curtains and gleaming appliances would lighten her spirits.

She was about to sit down at the large pine table when she heard a plaintive whining outside the glass doors that led to the patio. A black beast with soulful brown eyes and a lolling tongue was staring longingly at her. When he caught her attention, he began to wag his great hairy rope of a tail. For some reason, Lurch looked more lonely than intimidating to her this morning.

She thought of her first sight of him leaping around his fallen master. Had that been less than twenty-four hours ago? The dog looked as if he needed company as much as she suddenly did. He shouldn't have to suffer because Marc had played too much football and wasn't available to walk him. She slid the glass door open slowly.

"Stay!" she said, as if she knew what she was doing.

The tail beat the deck faster.

"Okay," she said, suspecting that she was taking her life in her hands. "Would you like to go for a walk?"

Lurch obviously would. She had to laugh at his ungainly efforts to be appealing.

"Let's go then." She stepped out into the sunlight to join the dog.

* * *

Meanwhile, Lurch's master was slumped in the passenger seat of the old Buick taking advantage of the fact Vi didn't indulge in conversation while she was driving. Ever since they'd left Chartwell Falls, he'd been trying to figure out how to deal with living in close quarters with Cadie.

She wasn't what he had expected. Of course, he remembered her understated, bred-in-the-bone beauty from his glimpses of her at Pop's funeral. He had looked at the lovely, sad-eyed woman from a distance, much as he would a beautiful painting. Viewing women that way prevented the disillusionment that inevitably followed by getting to know them. Besides, she'd had lots of friends milling about her, as well as her over-protective uncle.

But she was no clinging vine. His mouth twisted in an ironic smile. Last night, when they had returned from the clinic, he'd noticed the shadows under her long-lashed, hazel-green eyes and had watched her bite her lower lip to keep it from trembling with the fatigue to which she'd stubbornly refused to give in.

This morning, even after getting up to change his ice pack at three o'clock, she'd managed to look fresh and spunky and unbelievably sexy in her old sweatshirt and jeans. Marc blew out a long, unhappy breath through pursed lips. He'd thought the past couple of years had proved he didn't need a woman in his life; of course, he hadn't been living under the same roof with a spirited female straight out of the dreams of his younger, more naïve days. He groaned silently. He had to make sure that, as long as she was at Nighthawk, he continued in the role of polite, antisocial stranger. Arcadie Haywood deserved a whole man.

The insulating cocoon he had spun around himself shielded him, not only from the world's horrors, but also from its wounding warmth. Even at family gatherings, he'd become merely an observer, not able to take part in the warm exchange of affection. He had nothing left to give.

Wilf had sure turned on his best smile for her last night. *Yeah, someone like Dr. Wilf Raeburn might be right for Cadie.* Not an ex-police detective who'd had every spark of human warmth burned out of him.

This was all idle speculation. An outgoing person like Cadie wouldn't tolerate the isolation of Nighthawk Lake for long. He could hope.

None of that, however, excused being rude. Any neighbor would offer his help with the task of disposing of Pop's personal property. It would be small payment for everything she had done for him yesterday, and he owed Pop at least that much.

"Well, here we are, Marc," Vi said, releasing her tight grip on the steering wheel and turning off the ignition. "Wait there. I'll go around to your side and hand you your crutches."

Marc had already opened his door and levered himself to his feet when he caught a glimpse of Lurch tearing around the corner of the house at top speed. Right behind him was Cadie.

"Lurch," she shouted. "Drop."

When the dog instantly collapsed in an ungainly heap, Cadie hooted with glee. "Good heavens! He did! Lurch, stay!"

Her laughter was too infectious to resist.

When she reached the car, he released his free hand from the frame of the car door and, impulsively, extended it toward her. With the same lack of hesitation, she stepped into the curve of his arm and gave him a little hug.

"What a relief!" she said. "I thought we were going to have a rerun of yesterday. And we'd be on our way back to the clinic."

Laughing with her and returning her hug seemed completely natural. She fit against his chest as if she'd been designed for him. He made himself ignore the fact that her friendly touch sparked a totally inappropriate tightening in his lower abdomen.

"Congratulations, little one," he said, "but he obeys me, too, you know. I haven't given him into your total control."

* * *

She would have found anyone else calling her "little one" patronizing, but she felt an unreasonable surge of pleasure at the unexpectedly friendly tone in Marc's voice.

He pointed to the big dog, still flat on the ground, wagging his tail and inching along on his belly.

"Right now, you are putting a real strain on his training. You'd better release him."

As casually as if the brief contact had not sent her pulse rate into the stratosphere, she turned away from his loose embrace. When she gave Lurch the command he had been waiting for, he leapt to his master's side and accompanied him into the house. Cadie hung back, trying hard to snap herself back into her not-overly-friendly-neighbor mind set.

While Vi shepherded Marc back to his bed in the study, Cadie headed reluctantly for the kitchen and the cardboard box containing the contents of Pop's top drawer.

When Vi returned, she was smiling with some satisfaction. "I gave Marc his medicine and put ice on his knee. He's already half asleep," she said. "You're ready for a coffee, aren't you?"

Without waiting for an answer, she went speedily about the business of getting the coffee.

"No muffins this morning. Lunch is in less than an hour." She paused in her staccato monologue when she noticed the box on the table. "What's all this?"

"Some of Pop's stuff," Cadie said, with an embarrassed shrug. "I've boxed his clothes to give to Goodwill or the church group, unless you know anyone who could use them. I did as much as I could, but the bedroom started to get to me. This looks like the contents of his top drawer. Would you mind going through some of it with me?"

Vi patted her arm awkwardly.

"Sure." She reached into the box and turned a tarnished silver pocket watch over in her hand to read the inscription. "'July, 1957. Dora, Jack and Peter.' You'll want to keep this, Cadie. Your grandmother must've bought it just before she died."

She had never seen the watch before. Come to think of it, she had seen very few mementos of the grandmother who had died before she was born. She put the timepiece to one side and reached for a slide rule in a worn leather case.

"I definitely want to keep this old slide rule. Pop kept it with him all the time. He didn't believe in calculators."

"I didn't realize George was the kind of man who would keep such a bunch of junk," Vi said fondly, holding up a ring of old keys. "Look at this tarnished tie clip. And a souvenir key chain from the Calgary Stampede. Here's a box of cufflinks I'll bet he hadn't worn in thirty years.

"Nothing in this wallet except an expired driver's license," she went on, as she sorted through the contents of the little carton.

Cadie was engrossed in a small envelope of snapshots. "I don't recognize any of these people, Vi," she said, fanning out a handful of them and passing them across to her.

Vi was suddenly silent.

"I never imagined he'd have kept that all these years," she said, staring at the black-and-white photo of a smiling dark-haired girl in a white one-piece bathing suit.

She turned it over. In a round girlish hand were written the words, "To George, forever yours, Violet."

"I was seventeen when I wrote that," she said thoughtfully. "All I wanted in the world that summer was to marry George Haywood. But he was ten years older and insisted that we wait a year until I'd finished school. When he left me to go prospecting in Northern Quebec, I was so mad at him that I married Sam. George was right. I was too young."

She breathed a deep sigh. "That's water long under the bridge, girl. A year later, George married Dora. She was a widow with a five-year-old son, your uncle Jack. She made George a good wife. He adopted Jack and she soon gave him a son of their own, your father. Here's a snapshot of George. Can I keep these two?"

"They really belong to you."

The two women sat in silence for a minute.

"Well," Vi said briskly, standing up and brushing imaginary crumbs off her skirt, "do you want to get on with clearing the bedroom?"

They made short work of the rest of the boxes and carried them out to the garage. Cadie refused Vi's offer to sort through the shelves of books with her. Before she could return to the bedroom alone, Vi stopped her.

"About your grandfather and me." She hesitated and then plunged on. "You may hear gossip, Cadie. But don't believe it. George and I cared about each other and he knew what kind of marriage I have, but he was too honorable a man to sleep with another man's wife.

"When he moved back here and built this house, he was good to us. He gave Sam a lease to graze cattle on his land for almost nothing. He insisted it gave him some kind of a tax break to call it a working farm. And he hired me to look after his house.

"We never talked about our feelings, but we knew they were there. Seeing him two days a week for the last ten years made them the happiest years of my life. I wanted to be sure you knew the truth," she said.

Both women had tears in their eyes when they parted.

Cadie went back to the master bedroom and looked around her. The only evidence that remained of the decade Pop had lived in this room was the display case holding the rock collection and the shelves where he kept his technical mining books and his favorite collections of humorous essays and short stories. Cadie spotted a well-worn copy of Thurber's hilarious reminiscences about his family. Her hand stopped just short of the shelf.

Someone had been rummaging through the books. They looked as if they'd been taken off the shelves and replaced hurriedly. From the time Pop had come to live with them when Cadie was nine years old, they had made of game of doing the dusting together. She knew he always lined books up so their spines were all the same distance from the edge of the shelf. These books were not. Several had even been re-shelved upside-down.

It made no sense at all. There were no rare books among Pop's collection. There were no missing papers for anyone to search for. Pop's will had been straightforward and had been left with his lawyer in Denver. All his holdings had been listed methodically. Nothing was missing. What would anyone have been looking for in his library? Judging by the way that the rock specimens and the books had been put back, the search had been rushed. That seemed to eliminate Vi and Marc. Either of them could have searched the house at leisure any time over the past few months.

*   *   *

Cadie spent the next few days flipping through Pop's books, searching for notes or marks in the margins, in the hope that whoever did this had missed whatever he'd been looking for. However, she found nothing. About all she learned was that her grandfather had been interested in a fascinating variety of topics.

Vi proved to be a godsend. With her in charge, Cadie had no need at all to see Marc during the day. Once the two women had dragged a stand with Marc's computer on it up to the day bed, he seemed content to spend his days there writing. Then, although he and Cadie shared the evening meal which Vi had prepared, they did not indulge in much conversation. Of course, they were left on their own at night. All it meant, though, was that Cadie left the connecting doors to the central part of the house open so she could hear him if he needed her help.

On the surface, they were mere acquaintances, who happened to be sharing the same shelter. However, even though they had as little to do with each other as possible, Cadie found herself terribly aware of the air of quiet male strength that seemed to surround him like a force field. Any room seemed to come alive the moment he stepped into it, and she was having trouble explaining to herself the pleasure that surged through her at the sound of his low voice.

It was a good thing he was so grimly determined to keep his distance from her. She'd been too battered emotionally by the events of the last year to be able to weather a relationship with what Elsie had automatically recognized as "a real man." Since the morning of their impulsive hug, he hadn't touched her. It was rare he even met her eyes. It was for the best.

Unfortunately, she had no control over their nightly encounters in her dreams. Unlike the vaguely remembered shadows of an elusive golden lover that had surfaced when she awoke back in Colorado, she remembered the details of these fantasies with embarrassing clarity. There was no question of the lover's identity now. She was exasperated by the perversity of her unruly mind. Her determination to squelch her erotic daydreams about Marc only seemed to focus her subconscious more directly on him.

She felt like a schoolgirl with her first crush. Sometimes, when they were doing something as innocent as serving their dinner or setting the table, she would find herself staring at his firm lower lip, or his muscular thigh, or the way his pants stretched over parts of his anatomy that she had never actually seen outside of her steamy dreams. The memory of the uninhibited liberties she took with his body in those vivid dreams made her face burn. She was sure Marc must often wonder what was the matter with her.

Wilf Raeburn's visits provided a welcome diversion. He dropped by a few evenings "to ride herd on Marc," but stayed around to chat with her over a cup of coffee in the big cheerful kitchen.

On the Wednesday evening that marked the end of Cadie's second week at Nighthawk Lake, Wilf joined her in the kitchen.

"I don't often have the chance to relax with such an attractive woman, Cadie," he said, pulling out a chair across the table from her.

Although he was a born flirt, who probably brightened the lives of a good many of the single women of the area, his visits gave a much-needed boost to her ego. She'd never had any illusions about her looks, but when she discovered that Jerry's proposal had been inspired more by her father's modest estate than by any attraction to her she realized she must be even plainer than she'd thought. Wilf was only being friendly, but she enjoyed his compliments anyway.

As his melting brown eyes gazed into hers, he reached across the pine table and brought her fingers to his lips.

"Beautiful!" he said, reaching with his other hand for one of Vi's oatmeal cookies that Cadie had put out for him.

"Mmm," he said around a big bite, "homemade cookies. My life is so full of so many wonderful temptations. Instead of trying to convince you that I'm the best catch in the Near North, maybe I'll see if I can steal Vi from Sam. I don't think he appreciates her talents the way I do."

Cadie laughed. "You'll have to line up behind Marc. He's a great fan of those same talents."

"Actually, pretty lady, maybe tonight is the night you should accept my on-going offer to run away together. That way you might avoid the mood your friend Marc is in after my examination."

"Is his leg worse?" she asked anxiously.

"No, No," Wilf assured her. "His knee is healing as well as could be expected, but I think he was hoping I'd have better news for him. He has just about run out of patience with babying that knee."

* * *

"You've got that right, Doc," Marc said evenly from the doorway. His powerful arms took his weight easily as he swung into the room on his crutches.

"I've decided to rejoin the world. You got any wood you want chopped, lady? Trees you want felled? Fresh doctors you want slugged? Anything you want done, I'm ready. Just think of me as your healthy, belligerent, big brother."

He could not believe he had said that. It was nothing to him if Wilf wanted to sit in the kitchen and flirt with Cadie. He was shaken by the intensity of his irrational determination to keep her from falling for the doctor's famous bedside manner. It was not in the least brotherly.

"I'm not being fresh." Wilf grinned at him as he reached for another cookie. "I'm being charming."

Cadie put a mug of coffee in front of Marc without asking.

"Thanks," he said. "I see I made it here with only seconds to spare if I'm going to get any of Vi's cookies."

"I'm leaving soon," Wilf said easily.

"You don't have to rush away on my account." Marc was feeling a little self-conscious about his rudeness.

"I'll only stay long enough to ask if Cadie wants to go to the Stone Ridge Inn with me on Friday night. Would you like to, Cadie? It's one of their seafood nights. They have a special way with Arctic char and king crab," Wilf tempted.

"I'd like that," she replied. "I haven't had a seafood dinner since…for months."

* * *

She had been going to say since the weekend before she had broken her engagement to Jerry. She realized, with relief, that all that memory evoked was a slight feeling of distaste.

"Great!" he said. "I'll pick you up at six-thirty if that's all right with you."

He made a great show of kissing her on the cheek as he rose from the table.

He paused at the door. "Don't forget, Marc. Only a little weight on that leg for brief periods. Don't try to move around without your crutches for another two or three days," he said. "And leave your mighty ax in the woodshed, Paul Bunyan. I don't want to have take a scalpel to that knee of yours. Friday, then, Cadie."

He left with a wide grin and a wink at Marc.

*   *   *

"What's the joke?" Cadie asked.

"I have no idea," Marc replied with feigned disinterest.

He was not going to acknowledge Wilf's adolescent taunting. He would have to make clear to the good doctor that he was not in competition with him for Cadie. He had not dated anyone local in the two years he had lived here and he was not about to start now.

The unexpected sound of the telephone eliminated the need to explain any of that to Cadie.

CHAPTER 4

"Katie?"

The mispronunciation of her name told her the caller was Jack Haywood. There was no point in telling him again that her name was Cadie with a D.

"Hello, Uncle Jack. Are you calling from Florida?"

Leaning against the kitchen counter, she raised her shoulders in a resigned shrug at Marc.

"No, honey, I'm calling from Toronto. How are you managing up there in the wilderness? Are you feeling all right?"

"I feel great," she replied. "How did you know I was here?"

"Oh," he said, with a heavy teasing note in his voice that set her teeth on edge, "I have my sources. Will you be ready to head back to civilization soon? You know your Aunt Rose and I would love to have you spend the winter with us in Lauderdale."

"Not this winter, Uncle Jack."

"We'll see how you feel when the mercury drops to forty below zero." His laugh blasted over the line. "I've got some great news for you. I've just been talking to a man who is very interested in buying the claims your granddad staked last year. His offer is way above market value."

He named a figure that raised Cadie's eyebrows, but did not change her mind. She pasted an artificial smile on her face as if to soften her words, even though her uncle could not possibly see it.

"Uncle Jack, this is my home now, and I'm not interested in selling it or having the landscape torn up by some mining company."

"I understand how you feel about your Granddad's place, girl, but those are highly speculative claims. And this man is prepared to pay you big money. You're not going to find anyone else fool enough to believe in Dad's pipe dream of finding gold in that kind of terrain. Pete must have taught you, sweetie, that you find gold in veins of quartz, not in the mix of rock you're sitting on."

"It's probably the deal of a lifetime, Uncle Jack, but you're going to have to tell your prospective buyer I'm not interested in selling."

"Honey, slow down and think."

His voice was becoming louder. She could envision his heavy jowls getting red with the effort of getting her to see reason.

"This is probably your only chance to make this kind of money on that land. Pass this up and all you're left with is a mile of lakefront in cottage country that's too far from the city to be worth much and a couple of hundred acres of bush and mediocre grazing land. Use your head. Sell the place and you can live anywhere you please."

Cadie found herself twisting strands of her hair into tiny corkscrews as she ran out of patience. In another minute she was going to be rude.

"I like it here," she said. "I'm sorry, but I can't talk any more right now. I have company. Thanks for the thought, Uncle Jack. Good night."

"He just doesn't give up!" she exploded as she replaced the receiver and returned to the table.

"Maybe he has the mistaken idea you're as sweet and pliable as you look," Marc said into his coffee cup.

She could wish for a more complimentary assessment. Cadie looked at the unsmiling man dwarfing the captain's chair at the end of the table, his tanned forearms leaning on the gleaming knotty pine.

"Then he's not very swift, is he?" she shot back.

There was a flash of something that might have been answering fire in his cold eyes. She was tempted to tell him exactly what she thought of his own disposition, but she bit her tongue.

Why was she letting his opinion get to her? His lease would be up in a few months and he would be out of her life. That thought wasn't as attractive as it had been. She couldn't help being affected by the deep sadness and disillusionment she sensed in Marc. Someone should show him the world was not such a dreadful place.

What was she thinking of? Believing they could change a man's sour outlook on life was a trap women have always set for themselves.

Cadie didn't need that kind of grief.

"Uncle Jack probably also believes," she couldn't help adding, "that, because I make my living painting pictures and selling books, I don't understand the real world. Believe me, my world has been plenty real."

His expression remained wooden, but something in the way he inclined his head encouraged her to talk to him. She would be smarter to say good night and retreat to her own room. But she needed information that Marc might have.

"Marc," she began, "neither Dad nor Pop ever spoke much about the claims you helped them stake here on the property. I know they found enough signs of gold to get the claims registered. What else can you tell me about them?"

"Not enough," he replied. There was sincere regret in his rumbling voice. "I just provided the muscle your grandfather needed to clear enough of a road to transport the diamond drill. Then I helped him run the drill and cart the core back to the shack. When we signed the rental agreement on the apartment, he made the weekly hours of labor a condition of the lease."

With a rueful look at his leg and an apologetic grin, he added, "I guess I owe you a rain check on this week's labor. Or, probably, I should just double the rent."

"No need. I'm sure I can find something for you to do when you're fit again."

She saw the fleeting twinkle in his eye and looked away.

Marc went back to her original question. "Pop spent a lot of time logging diamond drill core samples. Most of the time, I had the impression he was happy with the results, but he didn't tell me what they were. I'm afraid I never believed the gold was more than an old man's dream."

Cadie nodded. "I thought the exploration was mainly an excuse to get Dad to fly up here now and then."

"Could be," Marc said. "And I know Pop got a kick out of the idea that, after prospecting over most of the north country and the Rocky Mountains, he might finally have found the pot of gold at the end of the rainbow right here on his own land."

Even though she shared Marc's overall assessment, Cadie rushed to her grandfather's defense.

"If Pop was able to get the claims registered, there had to be a good chance there was enough gold here to be profitable. There's what's called the 'prudent man rule' that the mining recorder has to follow. He has to decide whether a reasonably cautious man would be justified in investing his labor and money with a 'reasonable expectation' he could develop a mine on the property. Of course, I have to admit, they're often wrong."

"I should've realized something like that when your dad and Pop were so pleased to get the claims registered."

"Pop was good at what he did." It was important to Cadie that her grandfather had Marc's respect as well as his affection. "He never found gold, but he located more than his share of other minerals. He made a lot of money around Marmora and in Alaska. And, unlike most prospectors, he invested it smartly. We thought he'd retired for good when he built this place. Then he called Dad to come out to do some aerial surveys with him."

"Your grandfather was maybe the finest man I ever met," he assured her. "But I don't have a lot of faith in dreams coming true. Vi mentioned one day that Sam was sure Pop was wasting his hard-earned money on the drilling. He said no one looked for gold in this kind of rock. I guess that's when I got the idea that maybe Pop was getting old and your Dad was humoring him."

"So you weren't even curious enough to check on the results of the drilling?" Cadie didn't try to keep the disbelief out of her voice.

"I should've shown more interest in what Pop was doing. I was just too self-centered. He needed someone to talk to now and then, but most of the time, I was too wrapped up in my first book," Marc admitted.

He was a hard man to read, but when he raised his eyes, Cadie thought she saw a plea for understanding in their blue depths.

"I gather," he went on, "your uncle seems to think you should get rid of the claims for whatever you can get."

"He's too eager."

He met her eyes in silent agreement. Jack Haywood's hard sell bothered him, too.

"Anyway, he's pushing me so hard to let him make a deal for the property that I'm beginning to suspect there's something big in it for him." She frowned. "I remember Dad and Uncle Jack talking one evening in our kitchen in Golden a couple of years ago. My uncle was fascinated when Dad mentioned the electromagnetic survey he was doing with Pop. He kept him talking long after I went to bed. Do you think it's possible Pop really did find enough gold to mine here?"

"Anything's possible," Marc said.

MINE

* * *

The timing of Pop's death still bothered him. *Damn it.* Marc had been so "self-contained" he'd been oblivious to what was going on around him.

"I don't know anything about your uncle," he could not help adding, "but you're right to be cautious about trusting him...or anybody right now."

He could see she was relieved he shared her reservations about Jack Haywood.

"Pop wouldn't even talk to him," Cadie said. "I don't know what it was Uncle Jack did, but Pop never forgave him for it."

She paused for a moment. "You know, in theory at least, it's possible Pop did find gold here. For years he talked about the big ore body that was discovered at Hemlo, north of Lake Superior, in the early eighties. He said it revolutionized geological theory about the kinds of rock formations where large veins of gold could be found.

"At Hemlo, they found a layer of gold-bearing rock ten to fifteen feet thick almost three hundred feet below the surface. Because the ore body was sandwiched between an upper layer of sedimentary rock and a lower one of volcanic ash, Pop said experts saw no reason to doubt the existence of gold anywhere in the Canadian Shield."

"The night Pop died he mentioned you'd spent a couple of years at the school of mines," he said. "I wonder why he didn't discuss the exploration with you."

"I wish he had. Even his lawyer in Denver doesn't have any results of the core analysis beyond what they submitted to the mining recorder. The claims were listed among his assets in the will. That's all. I hoped I might get a clue from the notebook he logged the core in, but I haven't come across it in any of his papers."

"When I got back from the funeral," Marc said, "it crossed my mind that his log book might be something you'd want to see. I was pretty sure he kept it in the core shed or in the old log cabin that it's attached to. But I wasn't able to find it. If you think I'd be of any help, I'd be glad to look through his things with you. The log book is pretty distinctive. It's a narrow, leather-bound, red ledger-style notebook."

* * *

He had searched the old house and the shed! Had he also rummaged through the book shelves and the rock collection?

But Marc had lived alone near the house for the past six months. He had the skill and plenty of time to do the kind of search she could never have detected.

"I've already sorted through the bedroom and the study. If there had been a notebook there, I'm sure I'd have found it." She hadn't meant to sound so abrupt. "I wonder…"

Marc's vivid blue eyes were fixed on her. She hated this indecision. Was she going to trust him or not?

"I wonder if that's what they were looking for in Pop's bedroom," she finished quickly.

Marc stiffened. The shadow of the man he thought he had seen disappearing around the side of the house as they returned from the clinic flashed through his mind.

"When?"

"I don't know, but somebody took Pop's books off the shelves and put them back in a mess. Not the way Pop would have left them," she said.

Marc recognized the familiar prickling sensation he got when the first piece of evidence backed up one of his hunches.

"Did you touch them?"

"I'm afraid I looked through all the books pretty carefully. I was more interested in finding out what they had been looking for than in who had done it," she admitted. "But I didn't touch the rock collection. Come, I'll show you."

Someone definitely had made a quick, amateurish search of the room. Marc was positive Pop never would have left his collection in the shape it was in. It was obvious the person who'd done it was more interested in speed than in keeping the search secret.

"This is the way they got in," he said, pointing to the fitting that should have held a metal bar to secure the sliding glass door leading to the patio. "It wouldn't take a minute to disconnect the bar early in the day," he said, "and toss it out onto the patio. Later, he could slide the doors open and walk right in. He probably waited until I had turned my lights off in the cabin for the night."

"I did look at the latch," she said, "but I didn't see any sign of a break-in. I never thought of checking for a security bar. Why would anyone want the log book?" Cadie asked, then answered her own question. "Unless they didn't want me to know the results of the drilling so I'd sell the claims for less than they're worth."

"I wish you'd called the police when you discovered this, Cadie. I suspect you and Vi have smudged any fingerprints the searcher might have left. I wonder if he found the book."

"If this was done before I got here, he's still looking for it."

She told him about finding the light on and the suitcases that had been moved after they got home from the clinic the night she arrived.

The uneasiness he had felt ever since Pop's death returned full force. "Why didn't you tell me?"

He had to ask, but he knew why. Cadie was too independent to admit she was nervous about spending her nights alone in the bedroom wing, half-expecting the intruder to return. He resisted the urge to take her in his arms and assure her that he'd see that no one invaded her home again.

The brief hug they had shared thirteen long days and nights ago had made him wary. If he held her again, he knew he'd have to satisfy his curiosity about what it would be like to kiss Cadie Haywood. Over the past few days, he'd caught her looking at him as if she was wondering the same thing.

"You had enough problems that night," she said.

"Yeah," he said, looking her squarely in the eye, "and I could've been connected with the person who did the searching. Even if I was in no shape to do it myself. Smart girl, Cadie. Don't trust anybody."

"I'm trusting you now," she snapped. However, she didn't sound positive he deserved that trust. "Will you help me look for the log book in the morning?"

"Sure," he said abruptly, still smarting a little that she could suspect him of snooping through her things. "Do you want to start with my cabin?"

"Let's save that for the last," she offered. "I'd like to give the core shed another going over. It seems to be the most logical place."

"Right after breakfast," he promised. "It might be smart, Cadie, not to tell anyone else what you noticed. I can't think of a reason why the intruder would come back," he added hesitantly, "but I'd sleep better if we left the doors open between your bedroom and mine for the next few nights so I could hear you if you called."

* * *

"I'd sleep better, too," she admitted grudgingly. She resented the rush of gratitude she felt at his offer.

He took a half a step closer and, for a split second, she thought he was going to draw her into his arms, but she was mistaken. It was probably for the best. But she could have used a hug.

"There are several companies in North Bay specializing in electronic security systems that alert the police if someone is trying to break in. At the same time, they make enough noise to scare away most intruders," he suggested instead.

"That would be overreacting, wouldn't it?" she objected, hoping it was the truth.

"Give it some thought." He turned on his one good heel to begin the awkward journey to his own part of the house. "Good night, then."

* * *

Several hours later, something startled Cadie awake. There it was again. She should be able to identify that elusive flicker of sound. *Oh, Lord!* It was the whisper of fluttering wings. She lay rigid. Yes, this time she felt a definite breeze on her cheek as the creature flew low over her bed. Unreasoning terror gripped her. The familiar nightmare where she was trapped in a dark place while flying things attacked her was happening in real life.

Suddenly, outlined in the pale beam of moonlight that slanted through her window, she saw two winged shapes. *Bats!* Powerless to control the screams that tore from her throat and echoed in her head, she yanked the sheets over her face.

"Marc! Marc!" she sobbed as loudly as she could.

First, she heard his thudding feet as he came through the house at the dead run. Then, through the sheet, she saw he had switched on the overhead light.

"Cadie!" he said, pulling the sheet from her clenched fingers. "What's wrong?"

She had never seen anything more welcome than the solidity of his bare chest and his broad shoulders. When he opened his arms, she hurled herself into them, and pressed her shuddering body against him. Her fingers sought the warm flesh of his back and gripped him tightly. Her reply was slightly muffled because her cheek was so tight against his chest.

"Bats," she told him when she found her voice. "At least two...I saw them against the window." She shivered again. "I know they're harmless, but they terrify me. Anything with wings. I can't go into a house where people let their pet birds fly free."

* * *

"They're hiding now," he said, gentling her with slow, circular strokes on the smooth skin of her shoulders and back. Cadie stopped shuddering, but her arms were still clenched tightly around him. Her full breasts were flattened against his chest. Her choice of nightwear surprised him. He would've expected to find her in practical pajamas, not this tempting scrap of peach satin that hung on narrow straps and barely covered her from her breasts to her knees.

Her nipples were hard as little pebbles. Were they reacting to the coolness of the room and her fright or to his touch? He wanted to continue holding and stroking her, until the comforting embrace inevitably grew into passion. His stroking fingers were inching closer to the sides of her tempting breasts.

Heaven help him, he was on the verge of taking advantage of her fear. Making love had been the last thing on Cadie's mind when she had called his name in terror, however, her sobbing cries had fit into his dream. As they had every night since she arrived, he and Cadie had been making unbelievably beautiful love together. Released from the tight control he clamped on it during his waking hours, his libido had been running wild in his dreams. His dream-Cadie was a willing and eager partner in every one of his erotic fantasies.

At the moment her real voice had called to him, they had almost reached the peak of their lovemaking, and Cadie had been crying out for him to enter her. He had leaped from his bed, aroused and more than a bit confused, to rush to her side.

Finally wide awake, he realized the woman in his arms was not his midnight lover. But as he smoothed the hair from her forehead, it seemed natural to press a tender kiss on the top of her head.

"It's all right, Cadie," he said. "I'm here and I'll get rid of the bats for you."

* * *

Cadie felt the chill leaving her body. Marc's soothing hands were inducing the most delicious warmth. She wanted to snuggle against his broad chest just a while longer, as if she belonged here in the safety of his embrace. She realized she didn't, but she couldn't pull away from his comfort too suddenly. She'd do it in stages.

"I'll be fine," she began, as she tipped back her head to look at him.

Marc's cobalt blue eyes seemed to have taken on an even darker hue and held a softness that surprised her. She felt herself raising her head to meet the tantalizing lips descending toward hers. It was as if some force stronger than willpower was pulling them together.

It seemed an eternity before they touched. His lips met hers tentatively, then began to rub slowly back and forth. The friction of his warm, smooth lips and the slightly rough stubble of his beard against her face stimulated an unsettling need. When the tip of his tongue tasted the corners of her mouth, Cadie, who had resisted any open-mouthed kissing, even from her ex-fiancé, found herself opening to him and even experimentally touching his tongue with the tip of hers. He surged inside as if an emotional dam had broken.

Cadie moaned and clutched at his shoulders while he made love to every surface in her mouth. His tongue explored the smooth linings of her cheeks, the arch of the roof of her mouth, even the sharp edges of her teeth, stoking the fire that burned low in her abdomen. Her tongue instinctively darted and flirted, and her body writhed against him as if, of its own volition, it sought to merge with his. When they came up for breath, Marc realized he had both hands on her rounded buttocks and was holding her intimately against his rock-hard erection.

"Oh, my God, Cadie!" he said, in a voice rough with emotion. "Cadie."

His voice brought her to her senses and she began to pull away from him. The moment she did, he released her and shifted his weight so there was some space between their pelvises. He raised his hands to place them on either side of her face.

"No," he gasped. Her eyes had become dark and unfocused with passion. "Stay here with me just a minute more."

He swallowed hard, then placed a gentle kiss on her forehead.

Confused, almost stunned, by the violence of her response to his kiss, Cadie remained still. When Marc wrapped his arms around her and held her quietly to his chest, she could feel him struggling to regain control. She lay there against him, her breath ragged, wanting him to hold her forever and, at the same time, wondering how on earth she was going to come away from this with any dignity at all.

When she was able to control her voice, she said, with a weak grin, "When I say thank you for coming to the rescue, I don't fool around."

*   *   *

Marc kissed her on the nose. If that's the way she wanted to handle it, he would pretend nothing special had just happened. But he knew differently.

Kissing Arcadie Haywood had rocked him back on his heels. Her kiss had revealed an unexpected and untutored passion that had reached out to him and almost got by his defenses. He must not let it happen again. The woman presented a frightening threat to his hard-won peace of mind.

"Something distracted me for a moment there, but you may have noticed I haven't done anything about my rescue yet." He was trying to find a playful tone of voice. "Why don't you go to my room, climb into my bed and try to get back to sleep? I guarantee there are no flying mice in my room. I'll get rid of yours and bunk in here for the rest of the night. In the morning, I'll pick up another security bar and install it for you. Deal?"

"Deal." She paused. "I know this sounds silly, but would you get my robe out of the closet for me? That door has been partly open and the bats could be lurking in there. Don't you dare laugh, Marcus Banachek!"

"Would I laugh at the woman who rushed to defend me with only a stick for a weapon when I was being attacked by a ferocious hairy beast?" he asked, handing her the white robe.

He did, however, wear quite a wide grin as he escorted her from her bedroom across the dining room and the kitchen into the study. Not daring to remain to see her safely into his bed, he retrieved his crutches and hurried back to Cadie's room and her unwelcome guests.

In the more than two years he had lived next door, there had never been one bat inside, let alone two of them. How had they gotten into Cadie's room? She had not dreamed them. He'd spotted one of the little creatures perched on top of the curtains. Needless to say, he hadn't pointed it out to Cadie. It should be easy to shoo them out with the badminton racket he'd picked up from the racks in the mud room where the outdoor equipment was kept. The bats' radar would pick up only the rim and the webbing would not harm them if they connected with it without too much force.

In a very few minutes, he had the two tiny tree bats winging gratefully off into the darkness. He checked around the patio for the missing metal bar, but had no luck finding it. For the next hour, he inspected every inch of the bedroom. There was not a crack or opening that even a mosquito could get through.

Someone had played an unpleasant joke on Cadie. Perhaps he hadn't known how violently she would react to it. Perhaps he had. Marc would ask Cadie in the morning who might know about her fear of flying things.

He looked at the bed where he had held her in his arms. He had been unprepared for the kiss that had almost carried both of them away. She'd tasted so sweet, had clung so tightly, it had taken every bit of his considerable willpower to control the arousal that had begun with his erotic dream.

He had needed the isolation of Nighthawk Lake—even with its lack of female companionship. But abstinence had not been as difficult as he had expected it to be. For him, sex had been simply an entertainment, an enjoyable release of physical tension. He had always been able to keep part of himself cool and detached.

However, tonight, holding Cadie, his almost uncontrollable need to merge with her soft satiny flesh had frightened him. The sixth sense that used to warn him of physical danger when he was on a case was flashing every signal it could. The message it was sending was that making love with Arcadie Haywood could make a shambles of his newly acquired serenity.

His body stirred again at the thought of Cadie's eager response to that kiss. What he'd seen in her fascinating hazel eyes could not be confused with relief or gratitude. She had been in the grip of the same desire that was driving him. He sat on the edge of the bed for a few minutes with his head in his hands, then he breathed a heartfelt sigh and turned off the bedside light. What was left of this night promised to be long and uncomfortable. His knee was throbbing, too, from the workout he had given it in his dash to Cadie's room. He only wished all his discomfort was physical.

He suspected Cadie was in more trouble than she could handle alone. The intensity of his need to protect her could not be anything else but the primitive instinct of a man to keep his woman safe.

A snort of sardonic laughter escaped him. So far, he had kept her safe from two terrified little tree bats someone had put in her room.

Like a kid who keeps probing a sore tooth with his tongue to see if it still hurts, he let his mind drift back to Val. His relationship with her had been a different thing altogether. She had been Willy's new partner. Tall, redheaded, street-wise and ambitious, he had liked her wise-cracking sense of humor. Together, they had found temporary release from the pressures and tedium of their jobs, sharing some good laughs and, when their shifts permitted, nights of enjoyable and energetic sex.

However, they had refrained from burdening each other with their troubles. In retrospect, he saw that he and Val had been two solitudes who had shared his condo for a while. Val had not needed him. He certainly had never felt this disturbing compulsion to protect her.

And when he had surprised her with Willy, he had felt nothing. Nothing at all.

He'd treasured that lack of emotion and the invulnerability it provided. Cadie's very presence threatened that pleasant numbness. Against his will, she had rekindled a spark of human feeling in him. To say nothing of the fire her kiss had sent raging through his blood. Neither kind of warmth had a hope of lasting more than a few weeks. He would be a fool to begin a relationship doomed to disappoint both of them.

However, if he continued to live under the same roof with her, he wondered how long he'd be able to resist kissing her again.

CHAPTER 5

Cadie awoke to the ominous sound of heavy machinery growling and crashing outside her window. Unfamiliar men's voices shouted curt commands. She jerked upright and stared around her. She couldn't place those blue-and-white curtains. Then she remembered. She was in the study, in the day bed where Marc had been sleeping. The whole scene where she had made such a fool of herself came back to her with a sickening thud.

She had been on the verge of hysteria because of the bats and had thrown herself at him. It could have been worse. He could have accepted what she was so obviously offering. But, instead, he had been very kind before sending her off, like a little girl, to the safety of his room.

Kind! She could at least be truthful to herself. Under no stretch of the imagination could anyone ever describe the kiss that had totally demolished her as "kind." It had been hot, sweet and overwhelming. His gentle touch had been comforting at first, but once she opened her mouth to him, they had both seemed helplessly caught up in a whirlwind of runaway sensation. The sensible Arcadie she had been for the whole of her adult life had been transformed into a wild and wanton woman, desperate for Marc's lovemaking. If he had not stopped, she would have eagerly spent the night in his arms.

She shook her head. She had never before experienced that kind of desire. Even now, her breasts ached to be crushed again to his hard chest. What had happened to her usual self-control? When she'd made the decision to give free rein to the emotional torrent she'd felt building up inside her, she'd only contemplated allowing herself more artistic freedom.

Apparently, I've been keeping a lid on more than my painting style, she thought with an ironic smile.

For Heaven's sake, she was not sixteen. She was almost thirty years old. Old enough to get into a cool shower and collect her thoughts. Somehow, in a very few minutes, she was going to have to face Marc.

From the racket outside, it appeared the men had begun to work on the driveway. Perhaps the noise and confusion would provide sufficient distraction to cover her embarrassment.

* * *

When Cadie stepped cautiously into the kitchen, she found Vi alone, slamming pots and cupboard doors. Her usually cheerful face looked peeved.

"'Morning, Cadie," she said, as she poured her a mug of coffee. "As you can hear, Sam has started on the driveway. What can I fix you to eat this morning?"

"Nothing right now. I'll make myself a piece of toast later."

Cadie took the coffee out to the wrought-iron table on the patio just beyond the kitchen's sliding glass doors. She hadn't asked if Marc had already eaten. She could only hope.

The house was built on the highest point of the bluff. About fifty feet to the left of where she sat was a sharp drop to the sparkling blue water. On the other side of the house, out of sight from the patio, was the sloping path to the sheltered, sandy beach.

The pungent scent of the white pines was drifting down as the heat of the morning sun released the aromatic oils from their long, waxy needles. As she rested her head on the padded back of the deck chair, Cadie tried to let the sun's warmth relax her tense muscles. Here, in central Ontario, every single summery day in September was a found treasure. Cadie hadn't expected to be wearing denim shorts and a sleeveless blouse outdoors in this part of the world at this time of year.

It was no good. The racket from the grader and the gravel truck was making it impossible to sit there and enjoy the morning. Annoyed, she stomped back inside.

"My eardrums couldn't handle it," she told Vi as she reentered the kitchen.

Her timing couldn't have been worse. Marc was entering the room from the direction of the study. When he saw her, he smiled stiffly. She met his eyes for a moment. He appeared to be as apprehensive about her reaction to their passionate embrace as she was about his. When she returned his smile with one that was hesitant, but not unfriendly, his face relaxed a little.

"Was the Great White Hunter's night mission successful?"

"It certainly was," he replied. "After a wild chase," he went on in his best cop-reporting-the-incident voice, "the two fierce animals were captured and released unharmed into the wild."

Vi was looking at them as if they were speaking a foreign language. "What fierce animals?" "Come off it, my little dumpling." Marc laughed at Vi's bewilderment. "You must've noticed that Cadie and I switched bedrooms last night. You gave me a very odd look when I came into the kitchen from the wrong direction this morning."

Vi gave his backside a swat with the tea towel she was holding. "I did wonder what you'd been up to, you rascal. Then, when Cadie came out of your room, I gave up wondering."

Vi's indignation when they told her about the invasion of the bats was almost comical.

"This house was solidly built and properly caulked. And George made sure it was kept in good shape. There are no holes for vermin to get in here. I don't understand it," she spluttered.

"I couldn't see where they got in, unless someone put them in Cadie's room to get a rise out of her," Marc agreed calmly. "But they were there, large as life."

Vi snorted. "Can't see why anyone would pull a trick like that."

Cadie shuddered. "I don't know who'd find it funny. I've always been terrified of things flying in the house. I remember, when I was a child, running screaming out into the pouring rain in my nightgown and bare feet because a bird had fallen down the fireplace chimney and flew out of the fireplace at me. But no one around here would know about that."

"I seem to remember George mentioning that," Vi said. "He used to talk about you a lot."

"That's true enough. Some of the stories I know would surprise you, little one," Marc said with a teasing grin.

At that moment, a short, stocky man in his early sixties appeared at the glass doors to the patio. His overalls and work boots indicated he was one of the workers involved in spreading gravel on the driveway.

"How's chances for a glass of cold water, Vi?" he said, taking off his baseball cap.

"Cadie," Vi said, "this is Sam. It's his crew who are tearing up your property this morning."

Vi fetched him a glass of water, which he began to drink standing on the patio outside the kitchen door.

"Come in and sit down, Sam," Cadie said. "It's nice to meet a friend of Pop's."

"He was a good man, your grandfather." Sam Wheelwright sat down and wiped the perspiration off his balding forehead with his forearm. "My boy, Luke, and I helped Marc here, and your dad with the staking last summer, you know. There was a lot of heavy brush to clear from the side lines of those claims."

"Did you work with Pop often?"

"Sure did," he said, putting down his empty water glass. "George and I shared a lot of things over the years," he added with an odd twist to his mouth.

Vi took his glass away without looking at him. "Marc was just saying that Cadie found bats in her bedroom last night."

"Well, that's the kind of thing you have to get used to if you're going to live in the country, girl," Sam said. He apparently did not share his wife's surprise.

"Yes," he added in a thoughtful voice, "it was sad to see your grandpa losin' it near the end. He used to be a real smart man."

He shook his head sadly. "A real smart man," he repeated. "It was hard to see him pour all that money down those diamond drill holes. Couldn't talk to him, though. He had it fixed in his head that there was gold here. Well, I'd better take some water out to my two helpers or we won't get your road fixed today. Nice to meet you, Miss Cadie."

Cadie watched him close the french doors quietly behind him. "Did everyone think Pop's judgment was slipping, Vi?"

"Sam sure did. Don't know about anyone else. George seemed just as keen as ever as far as I could see."

"Pop had all his wits about him, Cadie," Marc assured her. "Your father had enough confidence in him to help him with the surveys. We still don't know what the drilling results showed. He could've been mistaken or he could've been waiting to tell anyone what he'd found until he got a second opinion."

He pushed his chair back from the table. "Come on, Cadie. Let's get away from this unearthly racket. We can save the core shed for another day."

He stood up and reached for his crutches. "See? I'm even using the equipment this morning. Do you need anything in town, Vi? I moved the pick-up out onto the road before Sam got started this morning."

"We could use some milk and a dozen eggs," Vi told him.

"This is a perfect chance to go into town to buy some brushes and canvasses." Cadie gave in to the temptation to spend the morning with Marc. "I've done a few charcoal sketches, but I'm itching to start painting."

As Sam had barely begun to spread the loads of crushed stone that had been dumped near the house, there was only a small area of freshly graded gravel for Marc to struggle over on his crutches, but he complained loudly about honoring his promise to use crutches he didn't need.

"And look at the cause of it all over there. He's not even hanging around to see if I make it to the road."

Lurch was eagerly performing his few tricks for Sam who was rewarding him with large dog biscuits.

"Man's best friend," Marc mocked fondly. "It's all tummy love."

* * *

Cadie was glad to leave the noise and dust of the road work behind them. At the same time, she was grateful for the distraction it had provided. Now that they were alone in the quiet cab of the pickup, however, Cadie felt the embarrassment crowding in on her.

"Marc," she began, "about last night—"

"Last night," he interrupted, "had to happen."

He pulled off the highway into the parking area for one of the public beaches. He switched off the ignition, and, taking her shoulders deliberately in his big hands, he turned her to face him.

"We'd both been wondering what it would be like. And you were frightened. It just seemed natural to me to kiss you. If you're going to tell me you're sorry it happened, don't... Say anything," he finished lamely.

"I'm not sorry," she said quietly. "We've been thrown together. We were curious. And the chemistry is certainly there. But, living in the same house or even next door..." She raised her hands in a helpless gesture. "We can't let it happen again."

* * *

He grinned with relief. She was too honest to pretend nothing had happened, but she saw the problems that getting involved would create. A small ridiculous part of him wished she weren't being so sensible about it.

"You're right," he said. "Together, we're combustible. You and I could start a major forest fire, little one."

She looked as unhappy about it as he was.

"Oh, hell," he said, sliding his hands up into her hair and tilting her head up for just one last taste of her lips.

Last night's kiss had been no fluke. The short, sweet joining of their lips told him that. They pulled apart simultaneously and stared, startled, at each other.

"This is not a good idea," Cadie said. "I'm out of my depth here. You'd soon find out I'm no match for you."

"I don't understand."

"You would expect me to be..." She blushed and turned away.

He cradled her chin in his hand and turned her back to face him.

"Cadie?" he said softly.

"Last night, I was frantic about the bats. That must be why I behaved so strangely. I'm not usually that responsive." Her voice was barely audible.

He stared at her.

"I'm a cold fish," she blurted out defiantly.

She wasn't joking.

"Do you really think what happened between us last night—and just now—happens every time I kiss a woman? Believe me, Cadie, it was a first for me. I've never felt as if I'd been struck by lightning before. It was you."

He couldn't believe he'd said that. He was supposed to be cutting off their budding relationship, not coming on to her. But, surely, Cadie couldn't really believe that garbage about being cold. She was the sexiest, most exciting woman he'd ever met.

The unhappy cast of her eyes and the self-deprecating twist to her lips told him she was serious. Some inept idiot had done a real number on her self-esteem. Cadie deserved better. She was a warm, beautiful woman, and he had to convince her of how attractive she was. He ignored the voice of his better judgment. He'd just have to be sure things didn't get out of hand. It might even help to pay his debt to Pop.

He almost laughed aloud at his attempt to rationalize his attraction to Cadie. He'd become pretty good at fooling himself lately, but he couldn't quite make himself swallow that.

"I understand why you're cautious," he found himself saying. "You've been through a lot in the last few months and I came up here to do a bit of healing myself. But please don't reject our friendship before we've even begun to explore it. Neither of us wants to get involved in anything serious, Cadie, but I do want to get to know you better."

* * *

Cadie's automatic reaction was to wonder what Marc hoped to gain from her friendship. Jerry's single-minded crusade to get her to give him control of her inheritance before the wedding had made her wary of men who pretended to find her attractive. But Marc was nothing like Jerry. His kisses were certainly in a different class!

He held out his hand. "I think we could be friends. Good friends."

"No more kisses," she cautioned.

"We'll hold off on the kisses. I promise."

She put her hand in his. "I could use a friend," she said, knowing she wasn't being totally honest with him. She was afraid that she wanted more from him than friendship.

"Well, friend," he said, "I don't think the stores open for another half hour. Shall we take a short stroll down the beach? You can tell me about growing up in the Front Range of the Rockies. The only time I was ever out west, when I went for Pete's funeral, I didn't even get to see the mountains except from a distance."

As they walked slowly along the hard-packed sand for about a quarter of a mile, Cadie told him about being raised by her father and Pop in the Denver area.

"I always knew they loved me and did their best to understand me and my need to paint. Luckily, I was pretty much of a tomboy and loved going off into the bush prospecting with them when I was growing up. I've done more camping than the average woman," she said with a grin.

Marc listened to her low, sexy voice and tried to blame his frustration on the difficulty of using crutches on a beach. He didn't want to admit that trying to be Cadie's platonic buddy was never going to work.

As she walked slightly ahead of him with her bare feet in the water, he tried to pretend he didn't notice her long, shapely legs and nicely rounded hips. Now the breeze off the water was flattening her light cotton blouse against her breasts. He concentrated on keeping his eyes on her face. The wind was lifting the blond-streaked bangs that usually covered the still-pink scars on her forehead.

He hardly noticed the scars on her forearms anymore, but the sight of the ones on her face jolted him. If she had hit her head just a touch harder, he might never have met her. His fingers itched to smooth away the long strands of light brown and gold hair that kept blowing across her face. With every minute that passed, he wanted more and more to gather her into his arms and kiss those dreadful scars. From there, his lips and fingers would roam over every beautiful inch of her.

"Damn these crutches!" he exploded.

* * *

Cadie felt a rush of guilt.

"I should've realized that walking on the sand would be hard for you," she said. "We can sit on those large boulders over there until you get your second wind."

"It was my idea," he reminded her. "And I'm not tired, just fed up."

They sat side by side in the sunshine, watching a family of ducks placidly feeding in the reeds as the early morning sun glinted on the water.

"Did you grow up in Toronto?" Cadie asked, after a while.

Marc laughed. "Farthest thing from it," he replied. "My parents had a fairly large acreage on the Niagara Peninsula. We grew peaches and pears. It was a great place to grow up." His face softened when he mentioned the farm. "My sister Eva and I worked around the orchards after school and in the summer, but we couldn't wait to get away to the bright lights when we graduated from high school.

"Eva studied nursing at one of the big training hospitals in Toronto. When I graduated a few years later, I joined the Metropolitan Toronto police force."

"Do you often go back to visit?" Cadie asked.

"Nothing there to visit," he replied. "My parents were both killed when their truck hit a patch of black ice on the highway about six years ago. Neither Eva nor I wanted to take over the operation of the farm, so now it's part of a subdivision. The money came at a good time for me. The interest on my half gave me the chance to change careers."

"Is your sister still in Toronto?"

"Eva, her husband and my two nephews moved to Arizona a couple of years ago. I haven't seen her in a couple of years, but I said I'd go out to visit them this Thanksgiving."

MINE

Cadie looked away. This would be the first Thanksgiving she would be truly alone. Last year, she and Pop, still reeling from the loss of her father, had tried to find something to be thankful for. This year, he, too, was gone.

Marc looked down at her with a sheepish grin. The hard lines of his face had relaxed and his eyes were a deeper blue than the September sky. She wondered how she could ever have thought he was unapproachable.

"Eva has always referred to me as 'the clam' because I don't talk much about myself or what I'm doing. She wouldn't recognize me this morning. Why didn't you stop me?"

"I was interested," she said simply. "Are you hungry? With all the confusion, I didn't get around to having breakfast this morning. Right now, I'd kill for a warm muffin and a cup of coffee."

"That I can provide," he said. "By the time we get back to the truck, I'll be ready to get off my feet, too. These crutches don't behave well in the sand."

"I was surprised to see you using them this morning."

The reminder of his dash to her side during the night brought a vivid memory of her huddling, needy and terrified, in his arms. She turned to him suddenly. "You didn't do the knee any damage, did you?"

"No," he assured her. "I'm sure it's healed, but I'll go along with Wilf's orders for another two days because I can't afford the time for an operation if I'm wrong."

* * *

Until he found out who had been messing around with Cadie's things, he didn't want to leave her alone in that isolated house.

A few minutes later, they were entering the family style restaurant where Chartwell Falls people seemed to congregate for morning coffee. As they headed toward the only empty booth, they almost collided with a dark haired man who was sliding out of the one in front of it.

"Luke Wheelwright," Marc greeted him. "Just the man we wanted to see. This is Cadie Haywood, George's granddaughter. Your mother suggested she see you about doing some renovations."

"Oh, yes," Cadie said eagerly. "Vi said I should speak to you about converting the old log house into a studio. Do you have time for a cup of coffee right now?"

Cadie probably would have recognized Luke without the

introduction. He was a little taller than his parents, but had inherited Vi's round face and Sam's stocky, muscular body. She estimated he was probably in his early forties, although he had quite a bit of silver mixed in his dark hair. His shy smile reminded her of Vi's the morning she had met her.

Luke would like nothing better, he told them, than to put some big windows in the north side of the old log cabin and help her to convert it into a studio.

"I seen you drawing out by Loon Lake a couple of times," he said. "It's going to be too cold for that pretty soon. I'll get over to your place next week to get a start on the cabin. I've always liked that old building."

After Luke left them, they dawdled over their coffee and warm carrot muffins dripping with butter. They were in no rush to get back to the noisy chaos that surrounded their home that morning.

"Pardon me." The booming bass voice came from the wiry little man standing apologetically at the end of their booth.

"You don't know me, Ms. Haywood," he went on in his amazing voice. "My name is Vic Tyler. I have a real estate office a couple of doors down the street. I got a call this morning that you might well be interested in. Do you think you could spare a few minutes to drop by the office today?"

"I can't think what we'd have to discuss," she told the smiling man with the shrewd eyes.

"I'm pretty sure you'll find what I have to tell you important to you."

"Can we find the time after we finish our shopping, Marc?"

"Sure. That heavy machinery is probably still crashing around and raising dust at home."

"Good. See you shortly then." Vic Tyler left as quickly as he had appeared.

Their shopping took very little time. A person could walk from one end to the other of main street in less than five minutes. Cadie discovered the little crafts store that took up a corner of the florist's shop was amazingly well-stocked with artists' supplies.

"I got tired of going to North Bay for my own paints," explained the owner, a dark, angular woman of about Cadie's age who had introduced herself as Betty Tibbs. "Some of my pictures are hanging at the Almaguin Art Center down by the highway. They aren't great art, but the tourists seem to like them. Maybe you should think of joining the Art Guild. We'd all be glad to see you. Lord knows there aren't many of us under fifty."

She looked out the window and saw Marc swinging along on his crutches toward them. When he caught sight of Cadie and smiled, Betty winked at her and sighed. "And there sure aren't any men like your friend. He doesn't paint, by any chance?"

"Not that I know of," she said picking up her parcels. "I'll be talking to you again soon about joining the Art Guild."

When they got to the truck, Cadie put her purchases in the lockup, along with the security bar Marc had picked up.

"I'll install that for you as soon as we get back to the house," he said. "We don't want any more uninvited guests."

The meeting at Vic Tyler's office was brief. Marc offered to wait in the truck, but went along when Cadie suggested he join her. Mr. Tyler appeared at his office door the moment his secretary announced them.

"Thanks for coming," he said, offering his hand to Cadie and ignoring Marc. "I want to offer you my sincere condolences, Ms. Haywood. George was highly respected around here."

Cadie murmured her thanks as he indicated she be seated at one of the two chairs facing his large polished desk. Marc took the other.

"I knew him back when he was still scratching around for his first big find. Did quite a bit of prospecting myself when I was younger—up north of Timmins, and near George's find around Bancroft, then up in Bachelor Lake. I always seemed to stake my ground near the big strike, but not close enough." His laugh was big and obviously practiced.

Although the expression on his pixie-like face became serious and businesslike, he could not keep the excitement out of his voice when he got to the point of the meeting.

"I received a call from Sandor Green's office this morning." He paused, looking for recognition in Cadie's face. "The president of NorthAm Mining Corporation? Oh, I was sure from something he said that you'd already had contact with him."

Marc looked puzzled, then he raised his brows in silent question.

"Not with me," Cadie said.

Vic Tyler beamed at them both. "Well, Mr. Green has made a most generous offer, considering the current state of the market, for your house and acreage on Nighthawk Lake."

He named a figure slightly larger than the one her Uncle Jack had mentioned.

"But my property is not for sale, Mr. Tyler," Cadie told him. "I have no plans to put it on the market."

"Mr. Green led me to believe you were expecting his offer."

"I've never heard of him," Cadie said, rising from her chair. "But you can pass on the information that I have absolutely no intention of selling my house. You do realize," she added, "that only surface rights are included in the deed. No mineral rights."

"Yes," he said with a frown, "it did strike me as odd that Mr. Green did not mention the claims George staked on the property."

He rose and shook Cadie's hand. "Even if you are not considering selling at the moment, Ms. Haywood, I'd give it some thought. This is a hard country to live in year 'round. There are no Chinooks to take the curse off the winter the way there are out west. Just a deep freeze from November to May. And it's not as safe as it used to be in the off-season. We've had a rash of break-ins the last couple of winters."

He shook his head and gave a smile probably intended to show he had her best interests at heart.

"It's a lot of money to give up for a summer place. I could find you another nice one for a quarter of what Mr. Green is offering for yours. You'll never get another offer like this one."

As they left, she promised to let him know if she ever changed her mind. However, once they were in the pickup on their way back to Nighthawk, she couldn't get his last statement out of her mind. The words reminded her of Uncle Jack's when he called about the offer he had received for her claims. Had that offer been from NorthAm Corp. too? She mentioned her suspicions to Marc.

"That could be. NorthAm Mining Corporation," Marc mused. "Until Vic Tyler mentioned the name, I'd forgotten all about it. I got a phone call from a guy who could've been Sandor Green not long after Pop died. He said he was representing NorthAm Mining Corporation and that they wanted to buy my share in the claims. I told him I wasn't interested."

He had realized at the time that his attitude toward the claims was not logical; in fact, it was ridiculously sentimental. But the time he had spent staking those claims with Pop Haywood had been too short and too important to him. He couldn't bring himself to sever that last tie with the old prospector for money he didn't really need. Besides, something about Sandor Green had put him off. It was interesting that NorthAm's name had surfaced again.

When they arrived back at the lake, the driveway was deserted. Because the equipment was still there, he deduced the workmen had gone on their lunch break. Luckily, before leaving, the men had spread the gravel evenly enough for Marc to get the pickup to the area by the front door that had been graded and rolled hard. When he turned off the engine, the only sound was the light breeze whispering in the pine trees and the single loud call of a blue jay.

The look on Cadie's face as she gazed up into the sunlight filtering through the towering white pines that lined the drive made Marc catch his breath. She was feeling it too. Until now, he'd experienced the healing power of the shimmering silence only when he was alone. Somehow, this sharing made him feel linked to her in a way that even kissing her had not.

That realization destroyed the sense of peace completely.

* * *

Blissfully unaware of Marc's moment of panic, Cadie picked up the bag of groceries and the art supplies and headed for the kitchen. Marc grabbed the purchase he had made in the hardware store and followed. Wondering vaguely where Vi was, Cadie began to put the milk and eggs away.

"I'll attach this security bar for you and be back in a minute," Marc said over his shoulder, as he swung away on one crutch, carrying the long box over his shoulder.

She watched the muscles of his back working underneath his shirt with an appreciative smile. It was beginning to seem natural to be going about the everyday business of living with him around.

She had barely closed the refrigerator door when she heard him shout her name. The urgency in his voice sent her running.

When she reached her bedroom, she saw Vi lying unconscious on the floor. Her face was streaked with blood. A large area of the hooked rug that her head rested on was dark with it. Marc knelt beside her, pressing a face cloth to the side of her head.

"She's been shot," Marc said, "but her pulse is strong. Call Wilf. And the O.P.P. Tell them to get Chuck Fournier out here."

Cadie reached Wilf's office nurse who assured her crisply that she would get Wilf, Chuck and an ambulance on their way to Nighthawk Lake immediately. Then Cadie covered Vi with the down duvet from her bed and began chafing her cold fingers.

Her thoughts were whirling. How seriously was Vi injured? And why had she been shot in Cadie's bedroom? If someone wanted to kill Vi, why did he choose this house to do it in? Why would he have risked shooting while the property was teaming with workmen? Did the gunman know Vi was alone in the house?

Marc stopped his pacing and was examining the smaller of the bedroom windows.

"She was shot from outside, Cadie," he said, indicating the two small, circular holes in the window pane that looked out across the clearing to where the wooded path to the beach began. "From the size of the holes and the lack of starring in your window, I'd imagine he was a little distance away. At least as far as the edge of the clearing."

She looked where he was pointing and saw the bullet holes in the center of the window. Then her eyes widened with horror as the significance of his words struck her. Vi was not necessarily the intended target. This was Cadie's bedroom.

"He couldn't have known it was Vi in here!" she whispered.

Marc crouched down beside her and put his arm around her shoulders. "We'll find him. Whoever is doing this," he said, pressing his lips gently on her forehead.

It was at that moment, as Cadie was raising her lips to be kissed, that Vi chose to stir.

"Oh," Vi moaned as her eyes fluttered open. "My head hurts."

The pupils of her eyes were huge as she stared at them blankly. She raised her hand to the makeshift bandage Marc had fashioned out of a towel.

"What's this?" she cried. Then she noticed the blood on her dress and on the rug. "And all this blood?"

Marc was trying to calm Vi and tell her what little he knew about what had happened when an ambulance and a police car pulled into the driveway, sirens still screaming.

"I'll let them in, Marc."

Quick as she was, Cadie had not quite made it to the door when two large men in the dark blue uniforms of the Ontario Provincial Police burst into the front hall. Wilf Raeburn and two paramedics were right behind them.

"She's in there." Cadie pointed toward her bedroom.

Wilf wasted no time with greetings but tore past her to Vi's side and dropped to his knees.

"Good. You're conscious," he said, as he began to unwrap the blood-soaked towel from Vi's head. "Now, Vi, let's take a look at that head wound."

While Wilf was examining his patient, the senior half of the

Chartwell Falls O.P.P. detachment identified himself to Cadie.

"Sergeant Chuck Fournier, Ms. Haywood," he said.

"Cadie," she responded automatically.

He glanced over her shoulder at Marc. "I understand you've had a shooting."

"We just got back from town and found Vi unconscious, Chuck," Marc said. "I haven't had a chance to look at anything beyond the bullet holes in the window."

Chuck Fournier was a stolid-looking man with a receding hairline of dark hair. Marc knew the bland expression on his square face was deceptive. During the brief time they'd been rookies together in Toronto, he had learned there was an active and observant mind at work behind that placid face.

As he asked Marc and Cadie a few questions about their activities that morning, he wandered around the room. His dark eyes missed nothing. He stopped by the window to examine the bullet holes, then crossed the room to dig a bullet out of the wallboard opposite.

"Could be a twenty-two," he said under his breath. He turned and stared out the window at the woods on the other side of the clearing. "He must've come up the path from the beach."

Joe Miller, the young officer who had come along with Chuck, called to him from the hall outside the bedroom door.

"I found the other one, Chuck," he said, indicating a slug on the carpet up against the baseboard.

As he walked across the room, Chuck took tweezers and a small plastic bag out of his pocket. He carefully picked up a little piece of metal that still had some of Vi's blood adhering to it and put it in the bag.

Wilf finished winding a bandage around Vi's head and got to his feet.

"You may not think so right now, Vi, but you're a lucky woman," he said. "From what I can see without an x-ray, that bullet cut a long graze along the side of your head. It's only natural that you feel stunned right now. You have a concussion and you've lost quite a bit of blood. I'm going to have the ambulance take you into the hospital in North Bay to be monitored for a day or two."

Vi's lips thinned for a moment. "If you say so," she agreed reluctantly. "Will you let Luke know what's happened, Doc?"

Wilf assured her that he would, then told Chuck he could ask her a few questions while the paramedics were getting her onto the stretcher and attaching the I.V. he had requested.

"But keep it short," he said.

"The last thing I remember," Vi told them, "was coming in here to change the linens on Cadie's bed. Look at them now." There was a trace of quite normal exasperation in her voice. She pointed at the still neatly folded but blood-splattered sheets and pillowcases scattered on the hardwood floor.

"And your grandmother's hooked rug," she wailed. "That blood will never come out."

"That should be the least of your worries, Vi. It's not your fault you happened to be in the wrong place when somebody decided to use my window for target practice," Cadie told her.

Now that the police and medical people had arrived and taken over, Cadie was finding it hard to keep her voice steady.

"Funny time to choose to fire a gun," Chuck Fournier muttered. "With two occupants who could come back at any time, a housekeeper moving around the house, and three men working outside."

He turned to Vi. "Do you know what time you came in here, Vi?"

It was a few seconds before she answered, "It must've been about eleven-thirty. I was thinking I'd have time to make the bed before I started on lunch."

"So the men were still working outside," Chuck prompted.

"Yes, they were still crashing around out there. Sam had just come in for another drink of water. He was letting the boys run the backhoes. They were going to dump one more load of gravel before lunch."

"That's enough," Wilf interrupted. "She's told you all she knows. I want to get her up to the Bay right away."

As they were leaving, Marc commented, "The sound of the truck dumping its load of gravel would cover the rifle shots."

"By all rights, that room should've been empty," Chuck muttered. "Why would anyone in his right mind decide to fire at the window of an empty bedroom in the middle of a day? Why wouldn't he wait until there weren't all those people around."

All the time that Wilf was checking Vi and Chuck was examining the room, Marc had been sitting on the arm of Cadie's bedroom chair with a firm, reassuring grip on her cold fingers. The warmth of the large hand that engulfed hers was the only thing that seemed real to her. Everything else had a nightmare quality to it. She was an inoffensive seller of books and an unknown painter of rugged landscapes. People did not search through her belongings or loose bats in her bedroom.

And she certainly did not find women who had been shot in the head bleeding on one of her grandmother's hooked rugs!

The cold shock of disbelief was gradually being replaced by justifiable anger.

"What makes you think he's in his right mind?" she snapped at Chuck. "This is by far the most dangerous stunt he's pulled, but it's not the first one. I don't know why, but there's somebody around here who is out to make my life a nightmare."

It all poured out. "He broke into my bedroom and rummaged through Pop's books and rock samples; he went through my luggage the night I arrived while I was taking Marc to the clinic; last night, he let bats into my bedroom. Now he's shot poor Vi. He could've killed her. Or me."

Marc squeezed her fingers more tightly.

"What's all this?" Chuck marched over to the bed and sat down on it.

"Start at the beginning," he said, taking a notepad out of his pocket. "When exactly did you arrive at Nighthawk Lake?"

"Maybe we should start earlier than that," Marc interrupted. "We should tell Chuck about the car crash you barely survived."

"When was that?"

"Early last May. But that has nothing to do with any of this," she protested. "It was an accident."

She didn't want to reopen that chapter of her life.

"It could've happened to anyone. I was setting out to drive across the country to spend some time here. But I had only got a few miles from home when some drunk driver in a van forced my station wagon off the road. When my wheels hit the gravel shoulder, I lost control." She swallowed. "The wagon landed halfway down the mountain."

"It was sheer luck you couldn't fasten your seat belt and were thrown free of the car before it exploded," Marc finished for her.

Cadie stared at him and frowned. She had not told him any details about the accident.

"How did you know that?" she asked.

"I read it in the Denver paper, Cadie." Marc looked annoyed at her suspicious tone. "Pop had a subscription that hasn't run out yet. There was a big article about your miraculous escape. The anti-seatbelt nuts used the accident to stir up a lot of controversy about the fact your faulty seat belt saved your life. They have to make a big deal about the exceptions to the rule."

"It was an accident," she repeated stubbornly.

"The paper didn't mention the results of the police investigation," he persisted. "Did anyone ever tell you what they found when they examined your car at the scene?"

"All I know is they never found any trace of the van. I was unconscious for a few days while the investigation was going on. When I came to, I guess nobody wanted to bother me with the details."

It was all she could do not to shriek at him to leave her alone.

"I'm going to have to ask you some questions you may not feel like answering, Cadie," Chuck said calmly. "Let's start with, how long was it after your grandfather's accident that your car was forced off that mountain road?"

CHAPTER 6

Chuck was dead right about her unwillingness to rehash the distress of the last year. It had taken every bit of gumption she possessed to conquer her depression after losing her grandfather so soon after her father's death and the end of her unfortunate engagement. The fact the healing process had been sapping most of her physical strength made it even more difficult for her spirit to recuperate.

She could handle this, too. She only hoped she could avoid mentioning the details of the fiasco with Jerry. She didn't want to admit in front of Marc how gullible she had been. She could almost hear Pop's scratchy voice telling her to stop feeling sorry for herself. She straightened her shoulders and lifted her chin.

"The accident happened about three months after Pop died," she said, in answer to Chuck's question.

It had taken that long for her to finally face the fact she would never see Pop again. The memorial service in Golden had allowed all his friends to pay their respects. The trip to Nighthawk Lake was something in the nature of a private pilgrimage. She'd decided it was about time she accepted how foolish it was to be angry at him for dying and leaving her all alone. Every day since she'd arrived she'd been able to say a bit more of her personal good-bye to him here in the country he loved, at the site of his last dream.

"Detective Banachek seems to think there might be some question that yours was an accident."

"Detective Banachek wasn't there!" she said, trying to keep the lid on her temper. "And there's no reason for anyone to want to harm me."

The bullet holes in the window pane mocked her. Obviously someone thought there was.

"It's Marc Banachek," Marc said with a scowl. "I haven't been a police detective for almost two years, Chuck. If I sound like a cop, it's because I don't believe in coincidences any more now that I'm a civilian than I did when I was on the force."

There was the sound of loud voices from the front of the house.

"What do you mean I can't go in there? My wife is the housekeeper. And I'm working here today. The boys and I just got back from lunch in town." A note of apprehension crept into in the rough voice. "Where is Vi?"

Chuck Fournier got to his feet in a hurry and met Sam Wheelwright outside the open bedroom door. Joe had a firm grip on Sam's arm.

"It's all right, Sam." Chuck waved Joe aside. "Vi's had a bit of an accident. Doctor Raeburn had the ambulance take her to the hospital in North Bay. But don't worry. She's going to be fine," he assured him.

Sam's ruddy face blanched. "What kind of accident?" he asked.

"Somebody fired a couple of bullets through the window of Ms. Haywood's bedroom."

"My God," Sam gasped. "Vi."

"One of the bullets just grazed her head. She's going to be fine," Chuck repeated as he steadied the older man. "Come with me to the living room. We can sit down there."

He turned to Cadie and Marc. "Just relax for a few minutes. I'll be right back."

"We'll be in my study," Marc informed him.

Cadie was glad to leave her bedroom with its blood-soaked rug. As they passed through the kitchen, Marc picked up some crackers and cheese and two cans of cold beer.

"I'm sure I can't swallow a thing," she told him when he sat her at his desk and placed the food and drink in front of her.

"You don't have to enjoy it," he said. "Just get it down."

She would normally have resented his bossiness, but seeing the concern in his eyes, she complied with his brusque order. The first bite of aged cheddar tasted surprisingly good and the light beer took away the dryness, if not the tension, in her throat.

"Do you think this could have anything to do with the offer from NorthAm that Vic Tyler told us about this morning?" she asked.

"It's possible."

Marc took a long pull at his beer, then set it down firmly. "Someone is determined to get you out of here one way or another. Unless you get an offer for the property from someone else, we have to assume NorthAm has something to do with it."

"The bats last night. The shots this morning. Whoever it is seems to be getting anxious," Cadie said, shaking her head in disbelief. This couldn't be happening to her.

"But those shots were never intended to hit anyone," Marc said. "It isn't as if the gunman was shooting from the dark at someone he could see in a lighted window. Nobody could have expected Vi to be in your room and he couldn't have seen her to aim at going by the distance those bullets came from. The shots were meant to be a threat you'd have to take seriously."

* * *

Pop's odd statement Cadie was going to need someone in her corner who was tougher than Elsie Watson leapt into his mind. The old man had foreseen this. Why couldn't he have been more specific about the danger he was anticipating?

"Cadie, just before he died, Pop was concerned you might run into some serious trouble if anything happened to him. Do you know what he was talking about?"

"Pop said that? I don't know what he could've been thinking of." She laughed ruefully. "Back home, I don't have time to get into trouble. Every minute I don't spend at the shop, I spend painting. It must have something to do with the claims Pop staked on this property. The trouble started when I came here."

"Except for your accident," Marc stated.

"Marc, you're reaching."

The flash of fire in her hazel eyes reminded him vividly of Pop in one of his irascible moods. Cadie had inherited more than her spunk from George Haywood. There was no point in trying to push her. He'd back down for now, but he needed her to talk to him about several things. Her relationship with her business partner was one of them. The terms of her will was another.

His confused feelings for Cadie made him reluctant to broach the topic of her broken engagement, but he didn't like the timing of that either. He couldn't stand the thought Cadie had planned to be married last Christmas, but he wondered if the reason for the split-up had anything to do with her current problems. He had more than one motive for probing that sensitive topic. He couldn't afford to consider her sensibilities for long. It would be the height of stupidity to ignore someone who sent messages with a gun.

* * *

"I'm trying not to overreact," Cadie said, fighting to keep her voice steady. "This last year has been a nightmare that I'd just as soon forget. But someone is doing his best to frighten me. What makes me boil is he's succeeding. If you really think there may be a tie in to the crash, I'll see what I can do about getting the details from Colorado."

She was hoping against hope Marc would say that wouldn't be necessary, but he simply looked faintly apologetic and said, "Anything we can find out about your accident could be important."

"All right," she said. "As soon as Chuck leaves, I'll call Elsie. She can be pretty persuasive. If she talks to the police officers who handled the investigation, she has a better chance of getting them to cooperate with her than we do."

His smile told her he approved of her decision.

"I hate not knowing who is doing this to me."

"We'll get to the bottom of it," he said as Chuck rapped on the open door of his study.

"Sam's off to North Bay," Chuck told them. "Joe is checking out the area where we figure the gunman must've stood. I'm going out to join him. We want to take advantage of the few hours of daylight we have. Do you mind if I come back in the morning for our talk? I'm going to need some background from you, Cadie, but I want to have enough time to do it right."

It was phrased as a question, but Cadie knew that there was no way he was going to allow her to put off the interview.

"Fine," she said. "About nine?"

"I'll be here," he replied.

"Do you want some help with the search?" Marc offered.

Considering the thickness of undergrowth and the porous pine needle floor, he knew how small the chances were that, even with three men covering the ground, they would find any traces of the marksman.

"Another pair of eyes can't hurt," Chuck accepted.

"I'll meet you outside," Marc told him. He turned to Cadie. "After we're finished out there, why don't you and I go into town to get something to eat?"

"We don't have to do that." Cadie was quick to reject the idea of facing the inevitable questions or, at the very least, curious stares. "I'll rummage around in the kitchen and find something for us to eat, if you're not too particular."

"If you're sure you feel up to it," he agreed and left her peering into the freezer.

She put some chicken pieces in the microwave to thaw, then steeled herself to go to her bedroom. Much as she dreaded facing the state of her room, she had to change out of her blood-smeared clothing. She took a bucket and a couple of large plastic trash bags out of the pantry and prepared herself to tackle the unpleasant task.

It had all been cleaned up. The blood-soaked hooked rug and the sheets were gone. The floor had been washed. A wave of warmth filled her at Marc's thoughtfulness. The plastic trash bags he had taken from the pantry had not been intended to cover footprints or whatever else they found outside, as she had thought. He must have come directly here. She smiled. No matter how hard Marc Banachek's exterior was, he couldn't hide the gentle, considerate man who lurked inside.

* * *

The sun was very low in the sky by the time Marc returned. Cadie was in the bright, warm kitchen, leaning against the counter, talking on the telephone. Her cheeks pink and her eyes bright, she smiled a greeting at him. She had changed into some kind of a soft-looking pale green outfit that covered her snugly from head to toe and made her almost too enticing to resist. A delectable aroma was emanating from an enameled iron pot simmering on top of the stove. A pie was cooling on the counter and the thick pine board table was set with bright red place mats she'd found somewhere. Cadie continually amazed him.

"Great, Elsie! That's a load off my mind," she was saying. "No, I don't see why I can't be there for the closing on October eighth."

She motioned to Marc to sit down and mouthed that she was almost finished.

"No, I don't want a party. Just lunch with you and Doris, as usual. I'm serious. There's nothing special about this one. Thirty is just another number." She laughed. "Maybe you're right. Anyway, if you notice anything at all unusual in the police reports, please fax me a copy. Marc has a machine. Would you? It's not too much trouble? I'll get the fax number from him and send it to your office tomorrow. See you in three weeks, then. No, really, I'm fine."

So Cadie had acted already on her promise to call her lawyer friend.

Reluctant as she was to reopen that chapter of her life, she was good as her word. At least, about this she was, he hedged.

He stopped himself. Don't be a fool, Banachek, he told himself. Dreams of finding a truly loving woman died even before the situation with Val. Even if Cadie turns out to be as special as she seems, you're not the kind of man she needs. You don't even want to be.

"That was Elsie. She'll get on to the state police in the morning," Cadie said, as she replaced the receiver. "Did you find anything helpful out there?"

The tense lines that had been absent when she was talking with her friend pinched the corners of her eyes.

"Joe did. Well, not exactly helpful," he qualified. "He found an old twenty-two-caliber rifle pushed under a fallen birch tree. I remembered Pop had a rifle and a shotgun on a gun rack in the old log house. We found the shotgun on the rack. The cradle for the twenty-two was empty."

"I remember that rifle," Cadie told him. "I'm surprised Pop still had it. He used to hunt partridge with it before he gave up hunting. He said the partridge had a better chance with a twenty-two than with a shotgun. I made a terrible fuss over a dead rabbit he brought home about twenty years ago. and I don't even think he ever touched the gun again after that."

"Anyway, unless the gunman left fingerprints," Mark said, "we haven't learned anything about the man's identity."

"We keep saying 'the man,' but it could just as easily be a woman."

"It could," Marc agreed. "Quite a few women around here learn to shoot as kids."

He moved to the stove and lifted the lid on the pot.

"What smells so good? Mmm. Chicken."

"I found some packages of legs and wings in the freezer and plenty of vegetables in the crisper, so I threw together a chicken stew," she answered as she put a pan of packaged rolls into the oven. "I can't take credit for the apple pie. It's one of Vi's frozen ones."

After Marc washed up, he made a quick call to the hospital in North Bay.

"Good news," he told her after he hung up. "The nurse on her floor tells me Vi's condition is good and she's resting comfortably."

Cadie's disturbed night and the strain of the day had brushed faint shadows under her eyes again. Marc wished their agreement allowed him to kiss away the tension, but he settled for draping a friendly arm around her shoulders.

"Come on, little one," he said. "Let's put the whole ugly situation out of our minds for a while. I'm looking forward to that chicken stew."

The vain hope he would find Cadie lacking in even one little thing faded. Marc had to tell her truthfully that the meal was one of the most delicious he could remember. When she threatened to jeopardize his cookie supply by telling Vi what he had said, he found himself joining her in the first wholehearted laugh he'd had in months.

They fell back into the easy relationship they'd enjoyed for a while on the beach that morning. Cadie told him her plans for the studio Luke had promised to build in the log house and about the growing market she had found for her paintings amongst the customers at her bookstore. When they went on to talk about their different tastes in reading, Cadie realized they had never talked about Marc's books. He spent a lot of time writing in his study, but always managed to deflect her questions from the subject of his work.

"You tricked me into reading your first novel, you know," she told him.

He raised a quizzical eyebrow.

"*Heart Beat.* Can you tell me honestly you didn't choose that title to fool someone who was looking for a romance novel?"

"Not guilty. The cop's name was Heart," he protested, laughing. "Not exactly a romantic hero, though, was he?"

"He could've used a little compassion in his soul. And I would have liked him to find something or somebody worth caring for. But, in spite of that, I have to admit you are a talented storyteller. I'm usually put off by that kind of grim realism, but I couldn't put the book down until I finished it. I recommended it to quite a few of my customers."

"I hope you encouraged them to buy the hardcover."

Her praise pleased him. He had been steering conversation away from his writing because he'd suspected she would be repelled by his graphic descriptions of horrors he had seen and his first-hand knowledge of the darker side of humanity.

For months at a time, Marc had lived inside the twisted mind of a serial killer until he knew him so intimately he could predict his next thought. That lead to the arrest...and the experience carried over into his books. Even when a reader knew the story he was reading was fiction, the intimate probing of that kind of evil was pretty strong stuff. In her paintings, Cadie focused on beautiful strong images. She was as ruthless about cutting out the ugliness in a scene as he was about making sure that it was not ignored. Given their opposite artistic points of view, he was relieved she was able to appreciate his skill. But he wished she could admire what he was trying to do.

"I only present the facts, Cadie. Violence isn't glamorous. I can't gloss over the horror that's out there. I have to describe the true picture."

There was a long silence while he waited for her comment.

* * *

"But it isn't the only true picture." For some reason, she needed to convince him. "There are all kinds of facts. There are children who are molested. But there are also millions more children who are surrounded by love. I want to read about the ones who are loved. I know there are too many scenes of blood and filth in the world, but there are scenes of incredible beauty, too. I edit the ugliness out of my paintings because I hope I can show people how to focus on the bits of beauty they can find everywhere."

His tolerant smile was annoying.

"I'm not saying there's no validity in your cynical view, but it is lacking balance. Beauty and honesty and love do exist, too," she said with all the huffy superiority she could muster. His smile was getting to her. "You think I'm incredibly naïve."

"No, I don't," he answered quickly. "It must be comforting to think the way you do."

Well, that was the best she could expect from Ban Marcus.

After they rinsed the dishes and put them in the dishwasher, Marc lit a fire in the circular red brick fireplace in the living room. With Marc slouching at one end of the sofa, his feet on the coffee table, and Cadie sitting at the opposite end with her stocking feet on the cushion between them, they quietly watched the dancing reflections of the flames in the gleaming copper dome suspended above the fire. Cadie tried to convince herself that Marc's strong physical appeal didn't have to get in the way of their friendship.

The only awkward moment arrived when it was time to go to bed. Cadie yawned and said she was going to try to get some sleep.

"I don't like the idea of you spending the night alone all the way at the other end of the house," he told her.

Then he laughed when she stiffened and her smile faded.

"I'm not trying to put a move on you, Cadie," he assured her. "I just would sleep better if your bedroom were not so isolated. After what happened there today, perhaps you should sleep in the spare room in my cabin. Or maybe, until we find out who is harassing you, I should move into the guest room next to yours," he suggested.

Much as she dreaded leaving the reassuring warmth of his company, she didn't know how much sleep she'd get with him in the next room. It was going to be hard enough to live by the unspoken rules of the platonic friendship they'd agreed on.

"You've been wonderful today, Marc. Oh, I didn't even thank you for the cleaning job you did in my room this afternoon. But I can't impose on you any more. If I moved, I'd only have to move back sometime. And who knows how long it is going to take to catch whoever is doing this?"

She swung her feet onto the floor and started to get up.

"I'm not going to give that sneak the satisfaction of driving me out of my own room," she raged on. "And I have a feeling he'll know."

It was the recognition someone was always watching her that was the final straw. Fighting to be strong and self-sufficient, trying to refute the evidence she had an unknown enemy, and struggling to resist her attraction to the big man who was obviously worried about her safety was more than she could manage. All the fight drained out of her.

When Marc saw the tears glistening in her eyes and muscle in her jaw tensing with the effort to keep her lower lip from trembling, his arms reached for her. In one smooth motion, he lifted her onto his lap. He held her against his chest and breathed soothing noises into her silky hair.

Surrounded by his strength and his warmth, Cadie gave in to her tears. With every breath she took, his musky, clean scent comforted and excited her. The tang of the outdoors and the smoke from the fire he had been tending clung to his sweater. His big hands stroked her back, and, vibrating under her ear, his low. indistinct words rumbled in his chest.

"That's it, Cadie, love," he murmured as her shoulders began to shudder with sobs. "Let it all out. Scream if you want to. It's no disgrace to cry. Not many people could've handled what you've endured the way you have. Lean on me for a while."

*   *   *

Cradling Cadie in his arms felt so natural Marc could not feel even a twinge of regret for his impulsive offer to watch over her. Although she had come to the end of her emotional tether, she was still struggling not to be dependent on him. Perversely, that made him more determined to keep her safe.

He let himself enjoy her softness and warmth and the honesty of her need for his embrace. She had stopped sobbing, but she still clung to him. He couldn't explain it, but holding her this way was as soothing to him as it seemed to be to her.

He was acutely aware of the soft breasts that were pressed against his chest. It was all too obvious she was not wearing a bra and the pliant flesh of her hips in the light cotton pants was molding itself to a vulnerable part of his anatomy that was stiffening against her tempting softness. He could tell himself that his reaction was the result of his long period of celibacy, but that did not explain the confusing emotions he was feeling. Never in his life had he experienced this compulsion to protect a woman.

At the same time, the fierce, primitive urge to strip off her clothes and stake his claim by plunging his aching arousal deep inside her was almost more than he could handle. He swallowed hard. He was not going to take advantage of her when her defenses were down. He was not even going to allow himself to kiss her goodnight.

Well, he thought, looking at her rosy lips that were still wet with tears, perhaps they could share a little kiss without allowing it to get away from them.

The little kiss he pressed to her temple became a line of little kisses that followed the track of a tear down her cheek to the corner of her mouth. Then Cadie turned her parted lips to meet his and the kiss could no longer be called little.

She tasted of wild honey and smelled of lilacs. A man could never get enough of tasting and nibbling this sweet flesh. He slipped his hands under the soft material of her shirt and took the weight of her breasts in his hands. Her nipples were hard against his palms. He raised the shirt and flicked his tongue across one taut nipple.

* * *

Cadie gasped. The sensation shot like a jolt of electricity to the moist ache between her legs. She had never known she could burn like this. When he began to suck gently, she knew she was in danger of losing all control.

"Cadie. Cadie," he murmured hoarsely.

He spoke her name like a lover. *A lover!* A stab of shame brought her out of the beautiful sensuous fog. She had thrown herself at him again. Had she lost her mind entirely? She placed her hands on his shoulders and pushed him away.

"No, Marc," she gasped. "I'm sorry."

When his eyes, dark with passion, met hers, she could see he was struggling for control. Then the too familiar impassive mask descended over his features. Firmly, with an air of resignation, he pulled her shirt back down with a snap.

"You're right, of course," he said, as she slipped off his lap and stood in front of him, wishing she could disappear. "It would be a major mistake."

"Yes." Cadie's voice was less firm than she would have liked. "It won't happen again."

"We'll have to chalk it up to experience," he said flatly. "Well, come on. I'll check out your room before you go to bed."

She wished she had the courage to say she could do it alone, but she couldn't, so, in spite of her acute embarrassment, she followed him. Keeping their distance from each other and doing their best to avoid eye contact, they examined every corner of every room in the sleeping wing and every latch of every window.

"I'm taking Lurch out with me to check the property. Leave the door to your room open and I'll put him in with you for the night when we get back."

Cadie nodded her agreement.

* * *

Without bidding her good night, Marc left her. He was furious at himself for getting carried away like an inexperienced kid; however, he could not follow his natural inclination and isolate himself in the privacy of his cabin. He was going to have to bunk down on the living room couch so he could hear her if she needed him. He muttered an oath. It was going to be a very long night.

Thank the Lord Cadie had had the sense to stop their lovemaking before they had gone too far. What was wrong with him? If he needed a woman that badly, surely he could find one who would complicate his life less than this one. He had let the domestic picture of Cadie, flushed from the heat of the kitchen, and the tantalizing aroma of the supper she had prepared for him turn his brain to mush.

Then to have been enough of an idiot to kiss her again! Cadie's delectable body was off bounds for now and forever. He would act as her bodyguard, but, he vowed, his investigation of her problems was going to be as businesslike as possible.

Lurch was lying on the patio just outside the kitchen doors where they had left him on guard. Uneasily, Marc remembered the shadowy figure Lurch had apparently ignored the night Cadie had arrived. It must have been someone the dog knew well. That narrowed the field considerably.

Although the night passed uneventfully and he heard nothing from Cadie's room, he got very little sleep. Every little night sound awakened him. He spent most of the night up prowling around the house.

He had the coffee made and was standing at the stove, frying bacon, when Cadie made her appearance in the kitchen. Lurch was at her heel. The dog had taken Marc's assignment to stay by her bed as a command to remain within inches of her. When she tried to let him out the kitchen door, the dog looked to his master.

"Okay, Lurch," he said. Then, giving Cadie only a quick look over his shoulder, he added a muttered greeting.

* * *

She returned it and poured herself a cup of coffee.

"As long as Vi isn't cooking for us, we don't have to have all our meals together. I mean"—she hadn't meant to sound so rude—"we might as well have only our evening meals together. That is, unless we happen to meet in the kitchen at other times."

Good Lord, she was babbling like an insecure teenager.

"I'd be willing to cook every other night, if you would," she concluded, more forcefully than she intended.

"Sounds good to me." He didn't lift his eyes from the eggs he was scrambling. "That would give me some solid chunks of time to spend at the computer. I haven't been able to get much writing done lately."

They ate together, but conversation was stilted. When Chuck arrived a few minutes early, Cadie was relieved to see him.

"Do you mind if Marc sits in on this?" he asked. "It would probably save time."

She could think of no reasonable reason to object to his presence.

Chuck was nothing if not thorough. By the end of the first half hour, Cadie wondered if he was ever going to stop asking picky questions. They covered the topic of her father's legacy and the fact she was just now in the process of selling the family home. She told him about the business she and Doris had started four years ago.

"Yes, Doris and I are the beneficiaries of each other's insurance policies and we have an agreement that, if one of us dies, the other has first chance to buy the other half of the business at a nominal price."

"Who inherits the rest of your property?" he asked.

"I haven't actually got around to making a will. I was going to do it at the same time as my ex-fiancé, Jerry, and I drew up the prenuptial agreement, but as it turned out, none of that happened."

To her relief, Chuck had the grace not to ask any questions about Jerry.

"You received a second inheritance when your grandfather died." He was relentless on the subject of what she owned.

"Pop's will was clear-cut. I'm sure you've seen a copy of it." She was losing patience. What did this have to do with the harassment she'd been subjected to since she arrived here?

"As a matter of fact, I did get my hands on one," he said blandly. "The only thing that's not clear is the value of the claims staked on this property."

"So far, I haven't been able to find any information about that in his papers," she told him.

Chuck raised one eyebrow.

"Pop was sure he was going to strike gold," she continued, "but it's doubtful he did. He'd have told me. Just this week, though, I received an offer on the claims through my uncle, Jack Haywood. Somebody thinks they're worth something."

Chuck wrote for a while on his notepad, then turned to Marc to question him on his involvement in the staking. He was frankly incredulous about Marc's lack of interest in the success of the venture.

"You were given a percentage of the potential profits and you say that you didn't bother to find out how the exploration was panning out? Not many men would be unconcerned about finding gold."

"I guess I didn't take the possibility seriously."

Chuck looked dubious, but he dropped the topic.

"So, Cadie..." Chuck pursed his lips and whistled silently, "who is your next of kin?"

"I guess it's Jack Haywood. But he has nothing to do with this," she stated firmly. Her uncle might be capable of trying to take advantage of her ignorance of the real estate market, but she knew in her bones that he would never hurt her. "He's in Toronto," she protested.

Chuck nodded, but did not comment.

Changing the subject again, he said, "I've been in touch with the

Colorado State Police. Their records state only that you were seriously injured in a single vehicle accident. There was no mention of foul play. The record did show your station wagon was too badly damaged when it exploded on impact to tell much from it. No one else saw the van."

He looked at her uncomfortably. "I don't have the manpower here to assign anyone to keep an eye on you. It's a good thing you have an ex-cop staying in your house. I hope you're not planning to move back out to the cabin anytime soon, Marc. And I'd be a lot happier if the two of you weren't spending the nights so far apart." He flushed. "I mean, your bedroom is at the opposite end of the house from the study."

"Chuck's right," Marc said, looking distinctly unhappy about having to agree. "If you needed me in the night, it would take me a long time to get to you."

"The study is not that far away," she argued.

"It's your choice," Chuck said quickly. "I have no authority to tell you how to live. Just be sure to keep your eyes open and call me right away if anything else happens. Joe and I will stop by any time either of us is in the area."

After Chuck had made his exit, Cadie wheeled on Marc.

"I don't need a babysitter," she said through clenched teeth. "In spite of the scene I made last night, I'm perfectly capable of looking after myself. And I like the isolation of my own room."

"Don't make this into something it's not, Cadie. Do me a favor. If I'm going to get any rest before this is cleared up, you're going to have to agree to have Lurch spend the night in whichever room you are sleeping in and let me bunk in the room next door. I don't want to spend another night wide awake on the living room couch," he said gruffly. "Make up your mind. Will I be in your guest room or will you be in mine? Let me know when you decide."

When he strode back toward his own room, she noticed he had left his crutches behind. She was too annoyed with him to call him back.

She had never met anyone so arrogant and full of himself. What made him think he had to look after her? She had been running her own life for almost ten years and no one else had ever hinted she was not capable of doing it.

Perhaps, she thought with a flash of honesty, that was because she had never been under this kind of attack before.

Marc returned, looking no more agreeable than he had when he left.

"I forgot the crutches. I don't need them, but I told Wilf I'd use the damned things for one more day."

*   *   *

He looked at Cadie's flushed cheeks. He didn't know if she was more embarrassed or angry. He figured angry. She certainly didn't look receptive to any more advice, but he had an uneasy feeling someone was growing desperate to get her out of the way. The picture of Cadie lying wounded in Vi's place that flashed through his mind made his blood run cold.

"I suggest you make a will right away, Cadie. Even a handwritten one will do until you get to a lawyer. All you need is a couple of witnesses to your signature."

The brilliant green fire in her eyes told him that he had been right about the anger.

"Maybe leave everything to your favorite charity," he risked adding. "And send a copy to good old Uncle Jack."

"Uncle Jack has been very kind to me since my dad died," she exploded. "We have no proof he's involved with any of this."

"We have no proof anyone is involved," he said. "But someone is and your uncle has the only motive that comes to mind."

"You're wrong."

There was no point in arguing. He turned away and headed for the study. He could feel her staring at his back as he moved away from her, all too aware the damned crutches didn't add to his image. He couldn't help but grin at the less-than-heroic picture he presented.

Just before he closed the study door behind him, he called, "It's my night to cook. Let me know at dinner which of us is moving."

CHAPTER 7

Cadie suddenly remembered this was the night she was having dinner with Wilf Raeburn. She almost called after Marc, but stopped herself. It would serve him right if she and Wilf just breezed out the door as Marc was putting the finishing touches on a meal for two. He needed to learn she was not subject to his orders.

She suppressed a shudder as she entered her bedroom and began to change into her painting clothes. Although there was no trace of the blood that had been spilled on the floor, she was intensely aware of the location of every splash of it. The knowledge that, if the bullets had been intended for anyone, they'd been meant for her, lay like a lead weight in the pit of her stomach. She wished she could believe she was the victim of an incredible number of coincidences.

Incredible is the right word.

There was no point in thinking about that. What she had to do was get started on a painting to send to Denver. Doris had emailed that only two of the canvases Cadie had completed before she left were still hanging in the shop. The idea of losing herself in her painting was appealing. For one thing, she was in control of her environment on canvas, if nowhere else.

She made a face at herself in the full-length mirror. She was wearing a pair of disreputable denim cutoffs and an old paint-splattered plaid shirt of her father's whose original pattern was discernible only on the back. Dad always said he was amazed that any paint got on the canvas. She certainly wasn't in any danger of attracting male attention in this get-up. I don't want any, she told herself sternly.

She gathered up her equipment, and avoiding the clearing where the rifleman had stood at the top of the beach path, made her way to the south side of the house. Setting up her easel at the top of the cliff where she had a good view of the waves crashing on the rocks of the point, she did not consciously choose a location visible from the study where Marc was working.

* * *

The man she had finally managed put out of her mind had been staring at the blank screen of his monitor for quite a few minutes when he caught a glimpse of her slender figure silhouetted against the sky. For the hundredth time, he wished he were sharing the house with a dumpy nonentity who would cower in a corner. Having Cadie, spirited and tempting as she was, where he could constantly see her was driving him crazy.

Embarking on an affair with Cadie would be a mistake, but every hour that passed made him more disposed to obey the old navy cry, "Damn the torpedo. Full speed ahead."

The only thing holding him back was that, if he were fool enough to give in to the temptation, his wouldn't be the only life demolished by the torpedo. He allowed himself one last look at her, intent on her work, with bright strands of her hair catching sunbeams as they were lifted gently by the south wind off the water.

Then he dragged his attention away and forced himself to concentrate on the unholy workings of an imaginary murderer's mind. By the time he turned off the machine, he had become so completely immersed in the struggles of his fictional hero that he was surprised to find the sun was off the cliff, and Cadie and her easel were no longer there. He looked at his watch. Soon he would have to thaw something for dinner. He blessed Vi for her frozen casseroles.

He was digging in the freezer when he heard the phone ringing. He looked at the packages teetering precariously on the corner where he had stacked them, and let the phone ring a few more times. Finally, it became evident Cadie was not going to answer it. He swept the frozen food back into the chest and ran for the phone.

"Banachek," he said into the receiver.

"Marc. I was beginning to think no one was home," Wilf said. "I'm trying to get in touch with Cadie. Is she around?"

"I'm not sure. I've been holed up in the study. If you hold on, I can go look for her."

"No," he said quickly. "I'm involved with a difficult case. While they're prepping my patient for surgery, I dashed out to tell Cadie that I won't be able to get away for our dinner date tonight. Will you tell her for me?"

"Of course," Marc managed to get in before Wilf hung up.

He should be sorry Cadie's date with Wilf had been canceled. He wanted her to find a man who was worthy of her, didn't he? He could not help the silly grin that spread over his face as he took off in search of her.

He knocked at the closed door of her bedroom a couple of times but heard not a sound from inside. *Where is she?* He was standing there wondering where she could have gone when the phone rang again. He knocked once more, then opened the door to get to the bedroom extension. Just as he did, he saw Cadie coming out of her bathroom, in the process of wrapping a large pink towel around herself. She whirled abruptly at the sight of him and dashed back into the bathroom.

He was left saying weakly, "The phone…"

The sight of one pink-tipped breast, her long, bare legs, and a glimpse of her gleaming buttocks as she spun away from him had him almost in a state of shock.

Hell and damnation, he might as well answer the telephone that refused to stop ringing.

"Hello, could I speak to Cadie Haywood?" a hesitant female voice responded to his gruff greeting.

"I think she's in the shower," he replied. *Oh, yeah!* He could testify to that. "Could I have her call you back?"

"Oh, is that you, Marc? You'll do just as well. This is Betty Tibbs. You know, from the flower shop? I called to invite you and Cadie to come to the Casino Night and Dance at the arena next Saturday. It's a combined fundraiser for the Art Guild and the Seniors' Club. Cadie could meet the other members of the guild and I think you'd both have a good time. Luke Wheelwright and I are going and we wondered if you'd like to share a table with us."

"Thanks, Betty. Cadie and I would be glad to join you. Eight-thirty all right?"

"We'll meet you there," she said and rang off.

He was acting as the woman's social secretary.

"We'd be glad to join Betty where?"

Cadie's voice was admirably controlled and cool for a woman who had to be a little off-balance because of her impromptu half-nude appearance a few minutes earlier.

"Betty invited us to join her and Luke Wheelwright at the Casino Night and Dance next Saturday," he told her and waited for her indignant reaction.

It came right on cue.

"And you took it upon yourself to accept for me? How do you know I haven't made other plans?" A definite edge was creeping into her voice.

"If you have, you'll have to change them. I told you that, in the interests of your safety, I plan to stick close to you. I want people to get the idea we're inseparable. I'm afraid you're going to have to put your social life on hold until we find out who is putting bullets through your windows."

The triumphant smile Cadie flashed at him could have powered every home and cottage on the lake.

"You'll have to think again," she crowed. "I have a dinner date with Wilf Raeburn tonight. He should be here within the hour."

"Not tonight, Cadie," he said quietly. "He's not coming."

"That does it! You didn't have the gall to break my date!"

Her fists were clenched and she was almost nose to nose with him. He could smell the lilac scent of her shampoo. Even in an ankle-length, thick terry cloth robe, with her hair wrapped in a towel and her face scrubbed clean of even the little make-up she usually wore, she was the sexiest-looking woman he had ever seen.

"I didn't have to," he said. "You obviously didn't hear the telephone ringing off the wall while you were showering. Wilf called to say he had to do some emergency surgery and asked me to apologize for him and tell you that he wouldn't be able to make it tonight."

Her crestfallen, yet still belligerent, expression was so appealing he could not resist pulling her into his arms and kissing her. She stood rigid for a moment under the teasing of his lips. Then, just as her lips began to soften and cooperate, he pulled away abruptly.

"I'm sorry," he bit out, lifting his hands from her waist. "I said I wouldn't do this. Dinner's in an hour-and-a-half. See you then."

* * *

He left her totally confused. *Damn his irresistible hide anyway.* Even when she was seething with rage at his high-handed treatment, he could make her want him. The novelty of the situation was almost amusing. She certainly was not reacting like the "cold fish" Jerry had told his girlfriend she was.

Her ex-fiancé had the open charm and wholesome good looks of the freckle-faced, redheaded boy next door. One look and you trusted him. In retrospect, that was probably the only reason she had agreed to marry him. She was alone and he had seemed so reliable.

She could see now that he was a man of limited imagination. He liked money, clothes and cars. He paid lip service to her passion for art and reading, but she knew his tastes ran to men's magazines and hard rock music. And he had never come remotely near to firing her blood the way Marc did.

She had met Jerry when he began working for the real estate broker who had offices two doors down from Pastimes. However, it was only after she found out her father's illness was terminal that Jerry became a constant factor in her life. He had made her believe she mattered to him. When she was depressed and exhausted from caring for her dying father, he was always there, making sure she ate and trying to take her mind off her troubles.

Three months after Peter Haywood's funeral, she agreed to marry Jerry. It was not the romantic match she had dreamed of, but she thought they could build a pleasant life together.

They had scheduled a small wedding with only a few close friends as witnesses for the twenty-third of December. One night, about two weeks before that, it all ended.

Jerry had been working a lot of evenings in order to tie up as many loose ends as possible so they could take a two-week honeymoon in Hawaii. The evening in question, he was at the real estate office catching up on paperwork. After Cadie closed Passtimes for the night, she decided to brighten up his evening. She made some of the thickly iced brownies he liked and filled a thermos with fresh coffee.

Arriving at the real estate office, she had waved gaily at an old friend who was talking to some clients at his desk in the reception area and had breezed on past to Jerry's office. When she realized Jerry was in the midst of a telephone conversation, she waited outside the door so she wouldn't interrupt him.

Unfortunately for Jerry, she was able to hear every word he said.

"It's going great, honey," were the first surprising words she heard. "I finally got her to promise to sign the agreement. I should be out of here with the money in a couple of months. We just have to be patient."

In the silence during which "honey" was speaking, Cadie digested the significance of what he had said.

"That's crazy, baby. This is the price we both have to pay. You have nothing to be jealous about. I'm not having any better time than you are. The woman is a cold fish. I don't even want to try to warm her up. No one makes me hot like you do."

There was another pause. "Oh, yeah," he had growled in a voice Cadie did not even recognize. "Waiting is hell. I'm going nuts without you, honey."

Jerry's eyes widened and his jaw dropped when Cadie pushed open the door. She coolly placed the plate of brownies on his desk and removed the plastic wrap. Then she took off her engagement ring and buried it in the icing.

As she slowly licked the icing off her fingers, she fixed him with an icy stare and said, "You don't have to wait to be with honey any longer, Jerry. You're all hers."

The most painful part of the broken engagement had been living with the knowledge of how gullible she had been. She had even let the worm convince her that they should share all their worldly goods. For "their" read "her" worldly goods. If she had not accidentally overheard that telephone conversation, he would have had half of everything she owned, except the bookstore. After all, he had argued, his voice resonant with affection, he was planning to share all his love and all his possessions with her for the rest of his life. How romantic! She had been the perfect mark!

Well, never again. Not that anyone was pursuing her at the moment.

Cadie arrived in the bright, pine-paneled kitchen exactly ninety minutes later. Her feelings were under control and her perspective on Marc's actions much more rational. She was determined to be grateful for his concern rather than miffed at his bossiness and the ease with which he was able to resist her rather questionable charms. He did not want her. Surely she had enough willpower to resist his unintentional sexual appeal and stop embarrassing the both of them.

She hesitated in the archway between the living-dining area and the kitchen and sniffed.

"Not lasagna?" she guessed with real enthusiasm.

"With hot garlic bread and Caesar salad," the chef assured her. "The latter two items provided by me. A sip of chianti?" he asked, pouring two glasses of the deep red wine.

"Of course," she replied as she sat down, relieved they were not going to continue hostilities.

MINE

* * *

For the next few days, although Cadie felt she was walking on eggshells, they managed to maintain the amicable distance that had begun that night. Marc moved into the spare bedroom in her wing. That, apparently, was the arrangement he preferred. She warned him that he'd have to contend with the smell of turpentine and linseed oil because she stored her painting supplies in the closet of that room.

"I don't mind moving them into Pop's study," he had said with a grin. He obviously wasn't going to be discouraged that easily.

They had fallen into a routine where he checked the grounds and the locks on the doors and windows every night while she got ready for bed. He always made sure she was asleep before he came back inside, and, no matter how early she awoke in the morning, he had left the spare room before she passed its open door.

One of the aspects of life at Nighthawk Lake she'd looked forward to before leaving Colorado was escaping the constantly ringing telephone and the continuous stream of friends who kept dropping in for a few minutes to see how she was feeling. But now she was spending most of her waking hours alone, she found herself wishing that at least Vi were around to share a mid-morning cup of coffee and some of her insights into the townspeople she'd encountered.

She'd bet Vi would have a pithy comment or two about Vic Tyler. His certainty she was familiar with the man who wanted to buy her house bothered her. What was his name? Something like Santa. It was Sandor Green. Marc said Green had tried unsuccessfully to get him to sell him his one-eighth interest in the claims. The offer Green had made through Vic Tyler had made no mention of the mineral rights. It had been only for the house and property. Add another small mystery to her life.

When Cadie had called the hospital a couple of days earlier to check on Vi, she was told Luke had taken her home that morning. On impulse, she decided to walk over to the Wheelwright farm via the beach and visit with Vi for a few minutes. She desperately needed some uncomplicated companionship.

Because she knew Marc was struggling to meet a deadline, she slipped away without disturbing him. If she told him where she was going, he would insist on accompanying her and he couldn't afford the time. Knowing he would be annoyed with her for not discussing it with him, she compromised by leaving him a note. Anyway, she would be back long before he surfaced from his novel late this afternoon.

Because the day was warm and sunny, she took the shortcut along the beach. The sensation of the hot sand on the soles of her feet reminded her of the hours she and her father had spent walking on this beach. Dad had never been much for making conversation, but they'd had some important talks on that beach.

Dad had been bewildered and hurt by her decision to switch from geology to fine arts, but she'd been able to make him understand it was something she had to do. That two-week holiday had made their relationship even closer. She missed him terribly; but today, for the first time, she was able to conjure up his square, tanned face with its quiet smile without being reduced to tears.

The quiet beauty of the place was working its magic. She was healing. The incident with the bats and Vi's wounding had not been able to ruin her enjoyment of her new home. And it was her home. It was as if she had waited all her life to take possession of the rambling house on the point of land that jutted out into Nighthawk Lake. This was where she belonged.

She put her sandals back on for the short climb up the path and the last stretch along the road to the Wheelwright farm. Unlike many farms of its vintage, its barn was tight and stained, the lawn was trim and the intricately carved gingerbread trim on the eaves had been recently and carefully painted. She was curious to see the inside of the old farmhouse.

Luke greeted her at the door and told her, a little self-consciously, that he was going to be acting as his mother's nurse for the next couple of days because his dad was staying on in North Bay. Sam's absence seemed odd to her under the circumstances, but Luke did not elaborate. Vi greeted her with genuine warmth and looked and sounded much like her old self.

"Did they catch the fool that was shooting at the house?" she asked.

"Not yet," Cadie told her, "but they found Pop's old twenty-two at the edge of the clearing outside my window. Chuck Fournier's still trying to find out who used it."

Vi gave her a resigned look. "Well, the boy will do his best. I told Doc that I should go back to work on Monday, but he told me I had to rest at home for a whole week. Will you and Marc be able to manage?"

"Vi, you're the one who was wounded," Cadie said, with an affectionate smile. "Marc and I are just fine. We're wiping out the emergency supply of frozen meals you prepared, though."

Vi looked pleased at that news.

"Don't you fret," she said happily. "I'll get to work stocking the freezer again the minute I get back."

There was something delightfully normal about being in Vi's home. The nameless threats Cadie had been living with seemed less substantial as they talked about everyday things and the continuing renovations Luke was doing on the farmhouse. When she left Vi being fussed over by her son, Cadie's mind was more at ease.

However, the pleasant mood evaporated the moment Cadie saw Marc striding across the beach toward her. When he spotted her, he sped up. He was out of breath and furious by the time he reached her. She had no doubt she had made a major error in judgment when she'd left without speaking to him.

"What do you think you are doing?" he demanded. "Have you forgotten the guy who was taking pot shots at your window? How am I supposed to protect you when you take off like this?"

Cadie was tempted to tell him just as forcefully that he was overreacting, but instead, she answered calmly, "I went to see Vi. I didn't leave town. I simply walked over to visit a neighbor in broad daylight. You'll be glad to hear," she added a little acerbically, "that she's fine and will be back to work a week from Monday."

Impatiently, he waved aside her news. "Don't trivialize your rashness. Anything could've happened to you. Have you realized we're all alone here?" He was almost shouting.

"The point is," he said, speaking slowly, as if she were a person of limited intelligence, "I didn't know how long you'd been gone when I found the note. I was worried something had happened to you on the way to Vi's. No, I was frantic. I don't like this guy's way of sending messages. Who knows what he's going to try next to convince you to get out?"

She knew she should have told him she was leaving, but she couldn't let him run her life. She'd left Colorado because she couldn't stand having her every movement monitored by well-meaning friends. "I'm sorry I worried you, but I can't live in your pocket, Marc. I promise I won't do anything foolish."

She could feel the anger seething inside him, but he followed her back to the house without speaking. He went straight to the study and closed the door firmly behind him, leaving her alone again.

Marc was civil but cool when they shared the cold supper Cadie put on the table. The moment they had cleared the dishes away, she retired to her room with a book. The atmosphere was too emotionally charged for comfort. She did make sure, however, to tell him that she intended to spend the morning out in the old log house.

The sun had barely risen over the hills behind the house when Cadie set out to tackle the monumental chore of clearing out the old building to make space for her new studio. The cabin had been closed up for more than six months. When she opened the heavy wooden front door, she was met by a wave of cool air heavy with dust and the smell of long dead ashes from last winter's fires. She threw open the windows and left the door wide open to let in the warm sunshine and clear the stuffiness from the front room.

She tied a dishtowel around her head and began to pack the dusty trophies of her father's youth into the boxes Vi had left for her. She was standing on a chair, reaching for a heavy and particularly gruesome relic, when she sensed Marc's presence in the doorway.

"That's quite a job you're tackling, little one," he said. "I was supposed to help you with that, remember?"

Marc's voice was low and friendly. Apparently she had been forgiven for yesterday afternoon. When she caught sight of his large, muscular frame silhouetted against the morning light, her pulse did a foolish little dance. He brought life into the dusty room. He hurried toward her, rolling up his shirtsleeves. The silky blond hairs on his tanned forearms caught the sunlight.

"Here, let me," he said, as he relieved her of the huge hardwood plank with a long-defunct prize-winning muskellunge attached to it.

"He's a thing of beauty. You planning to keep him?" His expression was deadly serious.

"No. I thought I might give him to you. Or, I've been told there is a section of the township dump that's become a year-round yard sale. I'd considered donating him and his furry friends"—she pointed to a couple of antlered heads—"to help whatever charity the sale supports."

The corner of his mouth twitched.

"I can relinquish that treasure for a good cause," he said. He placed it carefully on top of one of the boxes.

They worked side by side for the next few hours without finding any trace of the core logging journal. Although the only live creatures they found were a few spiders, there was plenty of evidence the building had a good-sized mouse population.

"You'd wonder what they found to eat in here," she commented.

"At least, there is no question about how they got in," Marc replied, pointing to a hole gnawed in the baseboard near the front door. "Luke has his work cut out for him to make this place livable again."

They piled the donations for the dump sale and the bags and boxes of trash in the center of the room and moved on to the drill core shack.

The shack was really a twenty-foot-long lean-to shed that was appended to the main building. One of its doors led to the small kitchen of the house and the other opened on the bush road that had been used for the transportation of the diamond drill core. The only pieces of furniture in the shed were Pop's old maple rolltop desk and his beat-up matching chair. The room was filled with long rows of slotted shelving that still held the drill cores.

The cores—long cylinders of rock almost an inch in diameter—had been bored out of the bedrock by sharp tubular steel bits that had industrial diamonds embedded in their cutting edges. In those long pieces of core, lying there like so many fat pencil leads, lay the secrets of the rock formations far beneath their feet. Cadie only wished she could read those secrets. Pop had read them and had written his findings in the lost log book.

"Do you want to give the desk a thorough going over?" Marc was on the same wave length. "When I did a quick check of it a few months ago, I didn't find anything."

They removed every shred of paper and every sticky old mint and wooden match from the desk, but found no trace of the log book. Cadie let out a deep sigh. She had been counting on finding the log book out here.

"I wish I could think of any place else to look, little one," Marc said, sympathy softening the hard lines of his face. "Come on," he said, taking her hand. "Let's go and get cleaned up. Then, if you're very good, I'll make you a toasted Western sandwich for lunch."

"I'll make the fries and the soup to go with it," Cadie agreed, brightening perceptibly at the thought he was not going back to his word processor immediately.

She tried to tell herself that anybody's company would be welcome and that the large hand holding hers was no warmer than anybody else's.

They managed to spend the rest of the day in each other's company without any flare-up of the banked coals of passion so close to the surface when they were together.

They had timed the cleanup perfectly because Monday morning, bright and early, Luke arrived, eager to measure the log house and discuss the renovations Cadie had in mind.

MINE

"Sure. I can replace the old pine door with sliding glass doors. And there's plenty of support in that north wall to put in a big window."

"Look at the size of those logs," he pointed out to Marc, who had tagged along. Just out of curiosity, he'd said.

"They're heavy devils. Makes you wonder how your grandfather ever got them in place," Luke went on. "Some of the packing in between them looks a little loose. I'll replace that and put some fresh caulking around all the logs on the outside of the building."

"Will that keep the mice out?" Cadie asked with a slight shiver of distaste. "I hate to put out mouse traps. I'd never be able to concentrate on my work if I were listening for a sharp snap that meant I'd just broken some poor little mouse's spine."

"Don't you worry, Cadie," Luke assured her earnestly. "I can mouse-proof the place. I don't like to see them killed, even if they don't do the good that bats do. You may not realize it, but one bat eats hundreds of mosquitoes a day."

His dark eyes held the same enthusiast's gleam Cadie had seen in the eyes of some of her friends who were determined to save the whale population of the world.

"But mice are God's creatures, too. I'll make sure you are all snug for the winter—no drafts, no mice."

He agreed to return the following day with the equipment and supplies he needed. The local building supply house had promised him they'd deliver everything in the morning.

When Luke left, Marc went back to his word processor and Cadie took her paints and easel back to her vantage point at the top of the cliff. The days were getting shorter and she wanted to take advantage of every minute of the bright autumn sun and the clear, dry air. With the breeze on her face and the silence broken only by the creaking of one dry branch rubbing on another and the occasional call of a gull, she could forget she had a faceless enemy who lurked somewhere in the shadows. She was even able to put her unsettling infatuation with Marc Banachek on a back burner for a couple of hours.

She had to work quickly before the light faded. She directed every bit of her concentration at the scene in front of her. When she actually managed to translate the sense of movement in the wave patterns that she had been trying to capture for days into strong strokes of vibrant color, she felt as if she'd won the lottery.

*   *   *

MINE

That evening, while she and Marc put together and ate their supper, conversation flowed easily. The physical effort of the cleanup and Cadie's feeling of accomplishment combined to lighten her mood. They had just finished eating when the kitchen air reverberated with the rare sound of the phone ringing.

Marc answered, then handed the receiver to Cadie.

"It's your lawyer," he said.

"Your housemate has the kind of voice that makes me tingle," Elsie said when Cadie answered.

Elsie's own breathy voice had led a lot of people to think she was just a sexy redhead, who was slightly light on brains. Underestimating her had cost some of them dearly.

"Elly, I'm not in the mood for teasing." Cadie hoped her use of the old nickname her friend hated would signal that she was serious.

"All right, but I'm glad you have the incredible hunk close at hand. I've been a bit uneasy about you. Yesterday, I weaseled a little information from Paul Wills. He was one of the Colorado State Police officers who responded to the scene of your accident. I convinced him to let me buy him dinner so we could talk about any impressions he had that might not have gone into the official report on the wreck."

"And?" Cadie prompted.

"No, no, no. Don't thank me for putting myself out for you." Elsie was evidently determined to keep the tone light. "I didn't mind at all. Paul is almost as beautifully put together as your policeman. I played my ditzy redhead routine and he bought it. By the time we had finished a bottle of wine with dinner and a glass or two of brandy afterward, the man wasn't thinking of me as your lawyer."

"Elsie," Cadie said through clenched teeth, "what did he say?"

"He remembered wondering at the time if the steering column had snapped before or after the impact. Nothing definite could be proved because of the damage caused by the explosion and the intense heat, but he noticed the way the metal had broken so neatly and wondered about the unusual angle of the break."

"That's only a suspicion, Elsie," Cadie objected.

"True," her friend replied. "But it gives you a good excuse to keep the resident hunk close at hand, doesn't it?" Elsie's laugh was intended to be reassuring. "I'd be envious if I weren't going to sacrifice myself again later this evening in the interests of your safety. Who knows? Paul Wills could possibly remember something else about your accident."

"You're such a martyr, Elsie." Cadie forced herself to sound amused.

When Elsie spoke again, all the humor had gone out of her voice. "Be careful, Cadie. I don't have a good feeling about this. Oh, by the way, Doris sends her love and says to tell you that business at Passtimes is doing well. She also asked me to put out a discreet feeler about what you'd think about selling out to her. She's not pushing. There's no rush. She's just wondering if you would give it some thought. Consider this a discreet feeler."

Cadie agreed to consider her partner's request. A few months ago she would never have imagined she could even contemplate giving up her share in the bookstore. It had been a dream come true.

After thanking Elsie and promising to keep in touch, she put down the receiver. She took a few calming breaths before she squared her shoulders and went out to the living room where she had seen Marc carrying the tray with their mugs of coffee and the last of Vi's chocolate chip cookies.

One look at the concern on his face told her that she wasn't hiding her reaction to the news very well.

"What did Elsie find out?" he asked.

"Nothing worth mentioning."

*   *   *

She met his eyes with a fixed stare that reminded him of frightened suspects who had tried to convince him they were telling the truth.

She took a tiny bite of one of the cookies. "I'd better get busy and make some cookies tomorrow. These are the last of Vi's, aren't they?"

"What did she tell you?"

"Vi?"

His glare told her he was not amused.

"Oh, you mean Elsie," she continued, her voice fading a little. "She says you have a sexy voice."

He was not about to be diverted. He moved closer and took her hands.

"Something she told you is bothering you, little one," he said softly. Then it struck him just how much that mattered to him. "Tell me."

"It's only one man's impression. He could be wrong."

"Cadie."

The steel in his voice promised he would persist until she told him what he needed to hear.

"One of the state troopers who investigated the accident told Elsie that he had wondered if the steering of my car had been tampered with. He could be wrong," she added quickly. "Because of the explosion, they weren't able to tell for sure."

The news was no more than he'd expected, but he wished this hunch had been wrong. Cadie was in the way of someone who was willing to kill her to get at something he wanted.

She saw his reaction flash in his eyes.

"Don't worry, Marc," she said. "This doesn't change anything."

But it did.

CHAPTER 8

Someone had attempted to kill Cadie.

Marc watched dark shadows dim the gold in her eyes as the awareness and the horror of that thought took hold of her. He ached to comfort her. If he reached for her this minute, she would welcome his touch and melt trustingly into his arms. However, the one quality that had survived the last few years intact was his integrity. Cadie needed someone she could rely on, and he refused to delude her into thinking he would be there for her for the long haul.

However, anyone who wanted to harm Cadie was going to have to go through him first. If it would keep her safe, somehow he'd see that she went back to Denver. But someone in Denver had tried to kill her. He had no choice. He would have to guard her day and night—and keep his hands off her.

He did manage not to touch her, but that night his dreams of her were so vivid he woke several times, surprised his arms were not wrapped securely around her. The dreams were not the erotic kind that had been plaguing his nights. In the fragments of these dreams that he could recall when he awoke, he was shielding her with his body from something horrible that was poised to attack. Each time he awakened, he leapt out of bed to see she was still asleep in the adjoining room. Even the fact Lurch was sleeping restlessly in her doorway did not reassure him the way it should have.

Finally, at five-thirty, he gave up the attempt to get any solid rest. He had disturbed Lurch so often the dog was thoroughly awake, pacing the short hallway and whining at him. Marc pulled on jeans and a sweatshirt and rammed a flashlight in his pocket. As an afterthought, he took his revolver from the drawer of his bedside table and tucked it into his belt. Leaving the dog on guard, he went outside to patrol the fringe of the woods bordering the house on two sides.

He listened intently for any alien sound, but he heard only the usual rustlings of small animals beginning their daily foraging for food and the isolated early morning chirp of a bird. The only dim shapes he spied in the predawn light were the motionless silhouettes of trees in the mist. There was no trace of any intruder, but he could not shake the creeping tension that had disturbed his sleep. Cursing his unreasonable faith in vague "hunches," he began another, wider circuit of the area. This time, when he returned to the path that merged with the rough bush road to the drill site, he saw, lying on the front step of the old log house, a small, dark shape that had not been there ten minutes earlier.

His flashlight beam shone on it for less than a second, but that was long enough to see the freshly-killed rabbit whose blood was still running freely over the stone steps. It gushed from a deep gash in its throat. He swore as he drew the revolver from his belt and swung the beam of his light around the area. He saw no one. Whoever had done this had struck silently and vanished into the wispy morning mist.

If the perpetrator had left the bloody little body in order to terrorize Cadie further, he was going to be disappointed. Marc wasn't going to tell her about this. He was uneasy about the way the warnings had escalated from shooting at windows of a room that should have been empty to taking of the life of an innocent animal. He did not like any part of it.

* * *

Before Cadie arrived in the kitchen for her morning coffee, Marc made a fast phone call to the O.P.P. office requesting that Chuck Fournier pay him a visit that morning. Then he went back out to the log house and bundled the rabbit into a plastic trash bag to show to Chuck. As he scrubbed down the stone steps, he wondered how many people knew Cadie was going to be accompanying Luke out to the log house that morning. The answer was altogether too many. The carpenter was so pleased to be working on an authentic log house that he'd probably rambled on about it to half the population of Chartwell Falls.

Marc had barely made it back to the kitchen and was pouring himself a much-needed cup of coffee when Cadie appeared with Lurch at her heels.

*   *   *

"This rotten dog of yours wouldn't let me sleep," she said, her voice warm with affection for the big beast. "I even invited him to sleep on my new sheepskin rug, but he wouldn't settle down. So I thought I'd take him for a walk."

She could see by the dark shadows under Marc's eyes that he hadn't had any more sleep than she had. He met her eyes for only a second, then quickly looked away. What was he trying to hide from her?

When she put her hand on his arm, his hand quickly covered hers. The speed with which he captured her hand and the tightness of his grip convinced her that she was right.

"What happened?" she whispered.

"What could've happened this early in the morning?" he asked. "Come on. Lurch needs his exercise. I'll go with you."

His bluff manner did not fool her, but she could not get anything out of him because he was on his way out the door.

Lurch did not stay with them as he usually did, but raced directly to the steps of the log house and sniffed around them. Eventually he seemed satisfied there was nothing interesting on the stone steps, and returned to them at a dead run. When Marc laughed at his ungainly and exuberant display, it spurred him on to even more dramatic feats. He zigzagged across the path in front and behind them and careened in erratic circles around them. Cadie could not help but join in the laughter.

They had barely made it to the bush road when they heard Luke's pickup rattling along the drive. They were still holding hands and laughing hard when they caught up with Lurch at the truck. The dog was nuzzling Luke's pockets.

"Nope. No biscuits today. You're going to get fat, fella," Luke said with a laugh. "Got your glass doors with me, Cadie. The rest of the stuff should be delivered before noon."

"Want a coffee before you unload?" Marc asked.

"No, thanks. I'm anxious to get started," he said, his attention already focused on undoing the tailgate of the truck.

They left him to it and returned to the house to have breakfast. Marc consumed his toast and coffee in record time and started for the door.

Before he could leave, Cadie asked him again, "What happened this morning? There was a reason Lurch was so restless, wasn't there?"

Damn those perceptive hazel eyes! Not even his family had ever been able to read him so easily. If he didn't tell her, she was going to imagine something ten times worse than the corpse of a poor little rabbit.

"Your neighborhood prankster left you a nasty gift on the log house steps."

"What was it?"

"A dead rabbit."

His concerned look was almost as good as a hug. She could have that, too, if she took a step toward him, but she must not allow herself to reach for the comfort of his strong arms every time that crazy person tried to frighten her.

"What kind of person would destroy a rabbit?"

She tried not to visualize the little furry body. She bit back a curse. Whoever he was, he knew exactly how to get to her.

"If he thinks I'm going to leave my home because of a few bizarre tricks, there are some things he doesn't know about me. I'm not going to let that sneak intimidate me."

"He didn't see you tackle Lurch with a stick."

The look of approval in Marc's eyes warmed her.

"We'll stop him together, Cadie. But I need your promise that, until we do, you won't leave the house, even for a minute, without telling me."

It would be foolish to fight him on this. He wasn't demanding she give up her independence. He was offering to help her to fight her invisible, malicious enemy. Marc's intense blue eyes locked on hers. *That's how his eyes would look when he's making love!* The sudden insight brought a rush of color to her cheeks.

"I promise," she said quickly. "It's a deal."

"Good. Then, for a little light entertainment, how would you like to watch Luke take a chainsaw to the settlers' cabin?"

However, Luke was not quite ready to cut the hole for the sliding doors. He was still measuring and carefully drawing chalk lines around the existing narrow door and window.

Marc settled himself on the bare ground under a maple tree about fifty feet away from the house and pulled Cadie down beside him.

"We can watch the operation from here," he told her.

"Move over. Your back takes up the whole tree trunk," she said.

"Lean on me," he invited with a grin.

He draped his arm around her shoulder and she leaned her back against his chest.

"That's much better," she said, turning briefly to smile up at him.

* * *

As Marc sat back against the maple trunk, one arm casually around Cadie, he wondered at the subtle difference in her attitude to him. Since that last kiss, they had avoided touching each other as much as possible. But now, the promise to join forces against whoever was trying to drive her from her home seemed to have redefined their relationship. In fact, in the few minutes since she had agreed to stay near him, the whole atmosphere had changed. She was apparently comfortable sitting here in the shelter of his arm, with her head on his shoulder. And, Heaven help him, it seemed natural and right to him to have her there.

He would bring up the subject of having some electronic security installed later this afternoon. There was no point in ruining the mood.

Cadie tilted her head on his shoulder to look at the maple leaves above her head.

"Look," she said. "The leaves are beginning to change."

Some were still green, some had veins of bright yellow, and others had made the change to brilliant crimson. Distracted by the beauty of the day, she appeared to be, for the moment, able to shut out the chilling threats that surrounded her. Holding her like this, Marc was ridiculously content.

Across the clearing, Luke lifted the door off its hinges. Then the strident screech of nails being pulled out of seasoned wood announced that he was beginning to loosen the frame. As he pried the doorframe out with a crowbar, Cadie marveled aloud at how easily it slid out of the hole in the log wall where it had spent the last fifty-odd years.

As he eased it out, some of the insulating packing tucked between the frame and the big log that ran across the top of it fell onto the floor. With the wad of old sphagnum moss came a long, narrow, red leather notebook.

"Hey," Luke called to them, as he staggered back with the weight of the doorframe in his arms, "what's that?"

He pointed with his chin at the book lying in the doorway.

By the time he had laid the heavy frame on the ground beside the door, they had reached the notebook. Marc picked it up and handed it to her.

"This is the book I was telling you about," Marc said.

MINE

* * *

Cadie opened the book and ran her fingers over the columns of letters and numbers painstakingly printed in heavy black ink. When she raised her dark-fringed eyelids to look at him, Marc saw tears beginning to well up in her eyes.

"This is Pop's writing," she whispered.

Then she looked at the white business-sized envelope she'd thought was a bookmark. In the same black ink, in Pop's distinctive printing, was Cadie's name and her address in Golden, Colorado. The envelope was unstamped, but sealed.

They left Luke to his work and took their treasure into the house. At the doorway to the den, Marc said, "You'll want some privacy to read this, Cadie. I'll be in my study when you're ready to tell me about it."

"Stay with me," she said, taking his hand. "Sit at the kitchen table with me. We'll read it together."

She handed him the log book and sliced the envelope neatly with a kitchen knife. After she had unfolded two lined sheets of paper and had placed them flat on the table, she and Marc sat, side by side, to read Pop's words.

"February fourteenth..." She pointed at the date in the upper right hand corner and turned to look up at him. "The day before he died."

Marc put a comforting arm around her shoulders and they both turned their attention back to the letter.

Dear Cadie,

Tonight, I'm wishing a lot of things were different. I wish Pete was still alive. I wish I lived closer to you. You're going to need help, Midget, if anything happens to me. Not that I expect it to for a long time.

The results of the drilling are even better than your dad and I hoped. I've found gold, girl. Lots of it. We're going to be rich, you and I. But we're going to have to be careful. I haven't shared my findings with anyone yet. When there's this much money involved, there's usually folks who'll do anything to get their hands on it.

I've done everything I can to make sure that legally nobody

MINE

can touch it. I own the surface and the mineral rights to the property. When I insisted on staking and registering the claims as soon as we had enough results to convince the mining recorder, Pete told me I was like the guy who wore braces as well as a belt to be sure to keep his pants up. No matter what, the find is ours now.

I was lucky to tie up with young Marc. You and he are my only partners now that your dad is gone. Marc earned his one-eighth interest by taking out a staking license and working with Pete and me. He's going to be surprised as heck when he finds out how much money that could turn out to be. He appears to be carrying a heavy load of hurting, but he's a good man to have in your corner.

I talked to Stephen Travelle a couple of weeks ago. He's a lawyer with Carver and Richelieu, one of the big brokerage houses in Toronto. He's agreed to put out feelers to get a solid mining company to develop the mine. Stephen's had experience putting together this kind of deal and I trust him to do exactly what I asked. I told him that I would get him the final analysis of the drilling by the end of the summer. But the latest drill holes have indicated such a big ore mass that I'm going to take the information down to him next week.

After that, I'm going to fly out to Colorado to share some other good news with my best girl and spend some time with her. That reminds me, it's the fourteenth. Are you still Pop's valentine?

I love you, Midget.

Cadie drew a deep breath that caught on a sob as she read the signature, "Pop." But she was not going to cry. She had done too much of that.

"No wonder Uncle Jack is so keen to get my property. The greedy, two-faced snake," she ground out between clenched teeth. Outrage was easier to handle than sorrow. "All these months he was calling me 'honey' and reminding me that he was the only blood kin I had left, just to get his hands on Dad's and Pop's claims."

Her uncle was as cold and calculating as Jerry. They both pretended to care for her, when what they really cared for was what she owned. *Could Marc be doing the same?* The kind of money Pop was referring to would make her a lot more attractive to most men.

She turned to look at him. He was still staring at the letter, his eyes bright with unshed tears.

"But I wasn't, was I?" he said. "I wasn't in Pop's corner when he needed me."

"Pop's death was an accident, Marc," she said. "You can't blame yourself for that."

She knew he wasn't interested in her romantically, but, right now, the man needed a friend. She leaned over and slipped her arms around his waist. He held her close, resting his cheek on the top of her head. For long minutes, they sat that way. Finally, he raised his head and loosed his hold on her.

"Well, he wouldn't have wanted us to sit here dwelling on past mistakes. That letter," he said bringing them back to the present, "reads as if he was going to put it in the mail. Why do you think he didn't?"

"Maybe he didn't have a stamp. But why did he hide it? Why did he hide the log book?" she wondered aloud.

"It doesn't make sense." Marc frowned. "According to the letter, the title to the claims was secure."

"If the log book disappeared, getting the mine development started would've been held up for as long as it took to get a geologist in. But who would that help?" Cadie asked. "Anyone who staked any of the property around our claims would probably want the results of Pop's exploration to sell their claims."

"I don't know, but maybe Pop suspected someone wanted the book," Marc went on, frowning. "I just remembered something. One day, a couple of weeks before he died, he asked me if I'd been out to the log house that morning. When I told him I hadn't, he asked me to keep my eyes open. He didn't say what for. I wish I'd asked him, but I didn't."

Cadie knew nothing she could say would comfort him or relieve him of the guilt he was feeling. She let her eyes drift back to the letter.

"I wonder what the 'other good news' was that he was going to tell me. Can you think of anything else going on in his life?"

"No, but I'll bet Vi knows what it is, if anyone does. He spent a lot of time sitting in the kitchen, drinking tea and talking and laughing with Vi the last few months."

Outside, Lurch began to bark furiously at the lumber truck that had just arrived.

"That barking is music to my ears," Marc said. "After the way that dog welcomed Luke, I was afraid he'd given up being any kind of a watch dog. I'll be right back." He headed outside to call off the dog so the delivery man could get out of the truck.

Lurch had not made a peep when Luke arrived this morning. He had not barked at the shadow that had disappeared around the corner of the house the other night. Marc shook his head. He still could not imagine Luke Wheelwright slitting a rabbit's throat. The man got upset at the idea of setting out mouse traps.

When Marc finally rejoined Cadie in the kitchen, where she was trying to make some sense of Pop's log book, he had Chuck Fournier with him.

"I showed Chuck where I found the rabbit this morning," he told her. "We figure that, from the way the guy used the knife, he's probably left-handed."

"That fact could help identify the person harassing you, Cadie," Chuck said. "I understand you came into possession of some important information this morning."

She swung around to face Marc.

"I thought you knew enough not to spread that around, Marc."

"If Chuck is going to help us, he's going to have to understand the situation. We don't know what effect your having the log book will have on the man who left you the ugly gift this morning; it could put you in a lot more danger."

She had not thought beyond the fact that Pop's dream had come true. There really was gold under their feet. But it was a whole new ball game. When Uncle Jack and whoever he was working with discovered she was aware of how much the claims were worth, there would no longer be any point in trying to frighten her into disposing of them at a bargain price. They were going to have to negotiate with Stephen Travelle who, according to Pop's letter, was used to dealing with business of this magnitude.

However, Uncle Jack would still inherit if anything happened to her. She shivered. It didn't take much imagination to see what their next logical step might be.

Marc was right. She was going to have to trust Chuck.

"Yes," she said, handing him the red leather book and the letter. "Pop had hidden this above the doorframe in the old settler's cabin. This letter was in the log book. It explains a lot."

After Chuck read the letter, he asked, "Are you convinced George Haywood's conclusions are valid?"

"He wouldn't have made a mistake about that," Cadie told him. "Pop wasn't a graduate geologist, but as far as reading core was concerned, he might as well have been. He made a good living out of spotting indicators in core samples and outcroppings all his life.

"I'm going to ask Stephen Travelle to handle the business end of this. He'll probably hire an expert to verify the findings, but I expect his geologist will agree with Pop's assessment."

She was a slight figure in her jeans and cotton sweater, but there was nothing fragile about her spirit as she made her position clear to Chuck.

"I don't believe my Uncle Jack would do me any harm, but I can't ignore he's the only person who would benefit if anything happened to me. You'd think, though, if he were tempted to get rid of me, he'd realize he wouldn't get away with it. As my heir, he'd be the obvious suspect."

"You can't count on that being a deterrent, Cadie," Chuck said. "Marc and I know too well that, no matter how thorough the investigation is, sometimes evidence is impossible to find. You'll continue to act as Cadie's bodyguard, Marc? And I'll see what I can do about getting a line on what Jack Haywood is up to."

"I'm not going anywhere," Marc said. "Certainly not before Cadie has done something about writing a will and we've spread the word that she's done it. But it's the guy Haywood's probably hired that we have to find, Chuck. Jack Haywood hasn't been shooting at windows and killing rabbits."

Cadie couldn't help wondering how much of the tentative closeness between her and Marc depended on his need to protect her. The thought it could disappear as soon as she put her affairs in order was even more chilling than Chuck's suspicion that her uncle wouldn't hesitate to have her killed. She had to get control of her life again. She couldn't remain passive, timidly getting more frightened with every word that was said.

"If you don't need me any more, I'm going to call to make an appointment with Stephen Travelle. I'll have him draw up a will for me as soon as he can see me. And the sooner he gets the negotiations for the claims in motion the better."

When she returned to the kitchen a few minutes later, Marc was alone.

"Did you talk to Travelle?" Marc asked.

"Just his secretary. He is out of town the rest of this week, but I have an appointment with him first thing Monday morning. I'm not thrilled with the idea of keeping the log book here that long though."

"Why don't you put it with the books on the shelves in my study? Out in the open like that is probably the best place to hide it."

"Good thought," she said, handing him the slim red ledger. "I think I'll go down to Toronto Sunday afternoon and stay at a hotel near his office."

"We'll both go," Marc said.

She did not argue with him. In fact, the prospect of spending a day or two with him away from the menace that seemed to hover around the house did a lot to lighten her spirits.

* * *

Wilf dropped by that evening, just as they were washing up after dinner.

Marc answered the door.

"Hi, Doc," he greeted him. "Drumming up business?"

"Nope," Wilf replied, adding with a grin when he saw Cadie coming toward him drying her hands on a dishtowel, "I came to see the prettiest woman in the Almaguin Highlands."

"Come into the living room," she said, flushing slightly at the compliment. "Marc was just about to light a fire."

Seemingly oblivious to Marc's glare, Wilf sank into one of the down-filled easy chairs grouped around the fireplace.

"This is much too comfortable," he said, with a sigh. "However, I'm afraid I can't stay long. I have a couple of calls to make, but I wanted to ask you in person. Have you made any plans for Saturday night, Cadie? There's a Casino Night and Dance at the arena."

Before she could answer, Marc swung around, a lighted match still in his hand.

"She's going with me," he said, perhaps a trifle vehemently. "Damn!" He shook the match to put out the flame licking at his fingers.

"Serves you right." Wilf chortled, raising his eyebrows with a so-that's-how-it-is look in his eyes. "It's not nice to gloat."

"I'm sorry, Wilf," Cadie said, smiling.

"Well, then, my dear," he said rising from the chair, "I'll have to get busy to find the second prettiest girl in the Almaguin Highlands. Save me a dance?"

"I'll look forward to it," she said, as he leaned over and kissed her lightly on the cheek.

"See you there, Marc," he said with a grin and a knowing wink. "I'm glad to see you developing some community spirit."

* * *

Marc spent the rest of the week at her side. While she painted, he sat a few feet away from her, jotting long-hand notes on a printout of the latest draft of his novel. They did the laundry together one day, and on another, spent a hilarious few hours at the local dump, recycling center and flea market. The manager of the property was delighted with the trophies they donated and insisted they browse through the acre or so of discarded bicycles, lawn chairs, playpens and furniture.

The day was sunny, and luckily the wind was blowing away from the yard sale area toward the actual dump. Only the occasional pungent whiff wafted in their direction.

"I can't get over the treasures in this place." Marc was wearing the kind of broad grin children do on Christmas morning. "Why would anyone discard that beautifully grotesque ceramic gnome? He's only chipped on one side. Wouldn't he look marvelous peering out of the foliage on the beach path?"

"He'd be lonely," Cadie said. "Maybe we could put those plastic flamingos across the path from him."

That got them started on a competition to find the most bizarre piece of statuary to lurk in the undergrowth to surprise the unwary. By the time Marc proposed that they remove the lampshade from a voluptuous black nude balancing a globe on her head and place her by the kitchen door where she could peek seductively out of Vi's rhubarb patch, Cadie was almost in hysterics.

However, a particularly disgusting blast of wind off the decaying garbage hit them at that point and, laughing, they made a quick dash for the Jeep. The manager/salesman, not ready to let them get away without buying at least one item, was still doing his hardsell at top volume as they drove away.

"How about a ladder? Everyone can use an extra ladder." His reedy voice echoed in their ears as they pulled back out onto the highway.

* * *

Except for the occasional hour Cadie was on the patio painting, in the next room reading or in the kitchen preparing a meal while he sat in front of his computer monitor, Marc didn't let Cadie out of his sight. Of course, during the long, long nights they slept in adjacent rooms.

On Saturday, the sun was still high in the sky as Cadie put the final touch of mascara on her lashes. Marc had invited her to have an early dinner at a golf course not far from Chartwell Falls before they went to the much touted Casino Night and Dance. It felt strange to be going out with Marc. In all but the most important way, they were living together, however, they'd never been on a date.

Cadie had agonized over what a person wore to a social event at an arena and decided the safest thing was her go-anywhere forest green silk dress. Its simple lines suited her. The scooped neckline was not too low, but it did reveal a bit of the upper swells of her breasts; the waist was snug and the skirt flared to just above her knees. She wore her pearls and matching earrings. Elsie teased her every time she wore her "tasteful" pearls, but Cadie felt good in them and wore them often.

She smiled at the image reflected in the mirrored closet doors and tossed her head so the weight of her brightly streaked hair swung across her shoulders. She thought she looked pretty good. Her cheeks were a little flushed and her eyes were bright. Like a woman who was rushing to meet her lover, she thought wryly.

When she stepped into the living room, Marc was waiting for her by the windows that overlooked the lake. The everyday Marc, when he wore jeans and faded knit shirts, was an attractive man, but Cadie was not prepared for the impact of a tanned and blond Marcus Banachek wearing a white shirt and tie, navy blazer and gray slacks. Moving toward her with his hands outstretched, his smile drew her like a magnet. His warm gaze caressed her as it skimmed down her body and came back up to rest on her lips.

"You're beautiful," he breathed as he placed her unresisting hands on his shoulders and slowly lowered his head to kiss her for the first time in more than a week.

* * *

There was nothing tentative about this kiss. His tongue moistened and tasted her lips. Then, for the duration of a heartbeat, he gently sucked her lower lip into his mouth. He did not deepen the kiss. Instead, he paused and held his mouth still against hers for a moment as he memorized the feel and the taste of her before he drew his head back and looked deeply into her eyes.

There was something new in the way she met his gaze, a gleam of excitement, something reckless in the set of her head. He wanted her. He was tempted to meet her challenge and show her what joy they could bring to each other. Only the thought of being the cause of sadness returning to her eyes when she realized how little more than physical pleasure he could give her held him back. Cadie still believed in happily ever after. The struggle between his determination not to hurt her and his driving need for her was a fierce one.

The air between them quivered with sexual energy.

"Oh, Cadie," he said. His face was grim and his voice harsh with the strain of his internal battle. "I don't know how much longer I can fight this."

* * *

A rush of joy filled her. Marc, too, recognized that the fierce magnetism was drawing them inexorably together. She ran a fingertip over his lips.

"Maybe we weren't meant to," she said.

CHAPTER 9

His eyes searched hers for another moment. There was nothing coy about the frank desire that shone in their green and golden depths. His whole body snapped to a blood-pounding, mind-blurring alert.

"Maybe we weren't," he replied. It slowly dawned on him that perhaps he and Cadie were meant, in some cosmic plan, to come to this moment together.

The heat in Cadie's glance made his noble intentions melt away. His body was suggesting quite strongly that maybe what they were meant to do was get rid of their clothes and make love right here on the living room carpet before she could change her mind. His reason told him to move more slowly. When they finally came together, he was determined it would be a beautiful experience they would both remember forever. Praying it would happen soon, he forced his hands to relax their hold on the tempting roundness of her hips. Moving away from her was like fighting the pull of a powerful magnet.

"If we're going to leave at all, little one," he said, the gruffness of his voice revealing how hard it was to make the sensible decision, "we'd better do it now. Our reservations are for six o'clock."

* * *

"Yes." Her eyes glowed with anticipation of the evening ahead. And the night. However and wherever it concluded.

"Hold on a minute," she said and dashed back to her bedroom.

She reached to the very back of her lingerie drawer and pulled out the box of condoms Elsie had given her as a bon voyage present.

Cadie had never once gone on a date with condoms in her purse. But tonight, she told herself, "It's time."

She placed one at the very bottom of her velvet drawstring bag. Then she laughed and added a handful more.

"You never know," she said in a throaty voice she hardly recognized.

When she rejoined Marc and placed her hand in his, he grasped it firmly, and they walked out to the Jeep. When he opened the driver's door for her, she waved her keys at him.

He accepted them with a grin.

"You are a continual surprise," he said as he walked her around to the passenger's seat. "I'd have thought you'd defend to the death your right to drive your own car. You don't feel I'm threatening your independence?"

"Not by driving my car," she said.

The terrifying joy that filled her at the prospect of making love with Marc had changed everything. She had decided before leaving Colorado that she was no longer going to live life with one foot on the gas and one foot hovering over the brake. This was the moment. Ironically, giving Marc her car keys seemed to symbolize grasping the steering wheel of her own life and stepping hard on the accelerator. She had no idea where their relationship was going, but she was going to give it everything she had.

They had been driving for about fifteen minutes when Marc flashed her an unsettling smile and reached over to take her hand. He gently pressed its palm down on his knee. Heat coursed from her palm along every tingling nerve in her body.

"For starters," he said.

For the rest of the ride to the golf club, his warm hand covered hers. Then, when he turned off the ignition, he lifted her fingers to his lips.

"I've stopped fighting," he said.

It was that simple. So had she. He didn't love her and she knew he would leave her eventually, but she was strong enough to deal with that. For now, it was enough that her dreams were about to become a reality.

The evening had none of the awkwardness of a first date, but all of its curiosity and excitement.

* * *

The restaurant at the golf course had a surprisingly elaborate menu and they chose dishes Marc had not tasted since he had dined in more sophisticated city establishments. It was rather fun on a warm evening to eat lightly garlicked escargots, while sitting out on an open deck overlooking the lush green fairways of a hilly country golf course. One of the advantages of dining this early was the privacy it afforded. Theirs was the only table occupied in their corner of the patio. It was over their entrées of rare prime rib and veal scallopini that Marc began to satisfy his curiosity about Cadie's past.

"All I knew about you before you came here was you'd done that terrific painting in the living room of the two galloping horses against the mountain background. Pop told me you left the mining school to study art. Now you own a bookstore," he said. "Why the book business?"

"My partner, Doris, and I were enrolled in some of the same courses at the School for Fine Arts in Banff. You'd like Doris. She's exactly what people think of when you mention a female artist. She's flamboyant and dramatic and aggressive. Even though I'm just the opposite, we got along from the moment we met. She does portraits and miniatures, and I like to do big canvasses of rugged scenery.

"We always said we'd open a small gallery in Denver when we could scrape together the money. When we were ready, the shop we found was a tiny bookstore that specialized in mysteries and romance novels. The idea of having a small steady income was appealing and at the beginning we sold books and hung our paintings wherever we could find wall space. Gradually the market for our paintings expanded and so did the shop."

Cadie placed a small piece of veal in her mouth and made appreciative noises as she chewed. "You have to try a bit of this." She held out a forkful of meat covered in spicy tomato sauce. "It's wonderful."

He didn't have any choice but to accept the bite. "Yep," he said, as soon as he could speak. "Almost as good as my roast beef."

Cadie's smile told him she was enjoying every moment of their evening out as much as he was.

"Doris," she continued, "is more of a salesperson than I am and now she's had Pastimes all to herself since my accident in May, I've been thinking of letting her buy out my interest in it. I could paint here and ship some of the paintings out to her."

"I like the sound of that," he said.

But he wasn't sure he did. The thought of Cadie staying on at Nighthawk Lake inspired intense joy and dread in equal quantities.

* * *

"And I've wondered about you," she said, looking at the odd expression on his face. Perhaps this was not the right time to satisfy her curiosity about Marc's background.

"All I knew from Pop," she forged ahead, "was that you were a retired policeman. I was expecting to meet someone my father's age."

"Sometimes I think I am. Police work ages you. When I was a police cadet, it was all fresh and exciting. For a while, I spent a lot of time in schools talking to kids about trusting policemen and our being there to protect them. However, after a few years out on the streets, I found out no matter how hard you try, you can't protect everyone. I should've quit earlier."

Cadie nodded her sympathy, but said nothing. After a few minutes, Marc began to tell her the whole story about the child murderer's mistrial. He even told her about his unnatural lack of reaction when he discovered how Val had betrayed him with his friend, Willy.

"I guess I hadn't invested enough emotion in either relationship for them to hurt me," he concluded. "Meeting Pop was the best thing that ever happened to me. He was so completely down-to-earth and the most uncompromisingly honest man I'd ever met. The hard physical work we did together helped me to work out some of my frustrations and to start getting my life back in focus."

He gave a self-deprecating laugh. "I just wanted to be sure you knew that you were getting damaged goods."

That sounded as if he was contemplating more than a night or two of lovemaking. What kind of man was he? He seemed to want her to believe he had no emotional depth, that he was a loner, an uninvolved chronicler of the ugliness and violence in the world. At the same time, she could feel the pain in his dispassionate recital of his reasons for leaving the city.

Cadie didn't want to analyze his complicated character tonight. She didn't want anything to make her question the wisdom of the step she was taking.

"Pop was relieved when you called off your wedding," Marc said.

"I guess he was a pretty good judge of character. He never liked Jerry."

Without any further prompting, Cadie told him how Jerry had

fooled her into thinking he cared about her in order to rob her of her inheritance from her father. She did not spare herself in telling the story.

"I can't believe I was so gullible! But what I feel the worst about is that I was so willing to settle for second best. I knew I didn't love Jerry. But I was prepared to spend the rest of my life with a man simply because I was lonely and he showed a little affection for me."

*   *   *

Marc raised his wine glass to her. "To forgetting the mistakes of the past. Tonight, you and I are new and different people."

His deep blue eyes held hers over the rims of their glasses. "Tonight," he toasted.

Tonight he was going to explore the latent sensuality that had been driving him crazy and that Cadie was completely unaware she exuded.

"Tonight," she echoed.

*   *   *

Judging by the number of cars in the arena parking lot when they pulled into it at eight-thirty, Casino Night was a big event in Chartwell Falls. Marc wheeled the Jeep into almost the last parking space at the far end of the lot. When they could not see Betty and Luke in the crowd at the entrance, they went inside.

About three-quarters of the arena was set up with colorful crown and anchor and roulette wheels, and felt-covered tables where black-uniformed men and women wearing incongruous straw boaters were dealing blackjack. The gambling was relaxed and the conversation cheerful and loud. Betty and Luke did not appear to be among the gamblers.

Holding Cadie firmly by the hand, Marc shouldered his way through the crowds and drew her along in his wake. When they reached an open area where the band was setting up on a spotlit platform, Cadie saw Luke waving at them from across the room. He was standing beside one of the large tables covered with red-and-white-checkered tablecloths that circled the section of the arena floor where the dancing was going to take place.

"Over here," he called.

One of Luke's hands was resting possessively on the tanned shoulder of a smiling Betty Tibbs. Her deep rose backless dress suited her spare frame, and her large brown eyes were bright.

MINE

"It was filling up so fast we figured we'd be smart to snag a table right by the dance floor instead of waiting for you outside," Betty explained.

"This is Luke's sister, Mary Tibbs," she said, indicating the small, blonde woman on the other side of the circular table. "She's married to my brother, Rob."

"You missed Mom," Mary told them. "Dad just left to drive her home."

"Vi is still supposed to be resting at home, but she was determined to play her yearly game of blackjack," Betty explained. "So we gave in and brought her along with us for an hour or so."

"The whole family was here then," Cadie commented. "Is Sam coming back?"

There was an awkward silence. Then Mary said, with a bitter smile, "Oh, Dad wouldn't waste a whole Saturday night with his family. He'll probably spend the rest of the weekend with his little friend in North Bay."

A flurry of conversation covered Cadie's embarrassment. So Sam had a woman in the Bay. That explained Vi's cool attitude to her husband.

"I don't want to be a pest, Cadie." Betty changed the subject abruptly. "But I wanted to be sure and mention the monthly meeting of the Art Guild is Monday night."

"You're being anything but a pest," Cadie reassured her. "I wish I could go, but I have to be in Toronto for a meeting on Monday. Maybe I can join next month."

"I'll send you a copy of the newsletter."

Marc's left arm was resting across the back of Cadie's chair, while his long fingers glided in small circles across the green silk covering her shoulder down to the smooth skin of her upper arm and back again. She felt the electric tingle of his touch to the roots of her hair. She leaned back against his hand and turned to meet his gaze. His cobalt blue eyes held a warmth she had never seen in them before. This wasn't the standoffish man she had been sharing the house with for the past few weeks. Was this the real Marc?

"Would you like to try your hand at gambling? Or would you like to do a little dancing first? The band is playing a nice slow piece."

"I'm not much of a gambler." Then she laughed. "I've never been much of a dancer either. But if you want to risk it, I'd like to dance."

When they stepped onto the dance floor, Marc placed his hands on her waist and gathered her close. Draping both hands on his shoulders, she relaxed against him and pressed her cheek to his chest.

"I'm glad you decided to dance, little one," he whispered into her hair. "I've been so desperate to hold you that, if you'd decided to play cards, I'd probably have insisted you do it with my arms around you."

He made her feel attractive and desired. She wished she could spend the rest of her life encircled by his strong arms, moving to the music, and breathing the intoxicating mix of Marc and a hint of spicy aftershave. The band's choice of middle-of-the-road sixties rock and nostalgic big bands tunes encouraged closeness.

* * *

All Marc could think of was how soon he could take Cadie back home to the lake. After spending weeks alone together, chaperoned only by their own reluctance to get involved, it was ironic they had chosen this night of all nights to surround themselves with company. Under his hands, the thin silk shifted sensuously over the smooth skin of her back. He lowered his hands slightly to the base of her spine, so he could feel the firm muscles of her buttocks moving against his fingers.

By the end of the second set, Marc was in such a state of arousal he didn't dare suggest returning to the table. The first few sharp, strident notes from the accordion told him he was being given the chance to avoid embarrassment. They threw themselves wholeheartedly into the lively polka. Afterward, breathless and laughing like happy children, they returned to the table.

They found Wilf and his date had joined the group, and, contrary to his daughter's prediction, Sam Wheelwright had returned to the party. Surprisingly, the center of attention was Luke. A couple of bottles of beer had made him quite forceful about expressing his opinions. He was explaining in great detail the dire consequences of man's casual disregard of the normal ecological balance of the northern woods. When Luke stopped to take a swig of his beer, Wilf managed to interrupt long enough to introduce his date, Wanda, and Marc went in search of two long, cold drinks.

"And so much of the lakefront is being built up"—Luke took up his lecture where he had left off—"that bats, for instance, don't have the undisturbed shelters they need for nesting. So I wrote away for the plans and built some bat boxes."

At Cadie's quizzical look, he explained. "I put a bunch of these wooden boxes up in a large grove of trees and the bats flock to them. They're sociable little beasts. Like to have a community."

Betty was patting his hand, trying to get his attention.

"What, honey?" He flushed at something in her smile. "Oh, you'd like to dance, wouldn't you? Excuse me, folks."

Wilf's date shivered as she watched them walk away.

"Bats make my skin crawl," she said.

Wilf grinned at her. "Luke tells me they eat hundreds of mosquitoes a night."

"I'd rather slather myself with foul-smelling bug repellent, thank you."

Marc returned with their drinks. "That sounds a little kinky, Wanda. Rather than what?"

Cadie answered for her. "Luke is raising bats to get rid of mosquitoes. He thinks we should all do the same, but I'm with Wanda. It's not for me."

"He's really raising bats?"

Marc frowned as his eyes sought out Luke and Betty. They were laughing as they moved around the dance floor with not much skill but a lot of enthusiasm. Luke's boxes could have been the source of the bats in Cadie's room. But the picture of Luke taking time out from building a bat nursery to slash the throat of a rabbit was ludicrous.

* * *

Cadie saw the whole evening through a kind of sensual haze. She and Marc spent a brief time in the casino, but the thrill of gambling paled into insignificance beside Marc's hot gaze, the little touches of his hand and his thigh brushing against hers. They exchanged obligatory dances with the other couples at their table, but even across the floor, she felt the heated thread that connected them.

That thread drew her back into his arms as the band began a set of romantic ballads. They didn't speak, but Marc's eyes held hers. Cadie was lost in their bottomless blue depths. Her arms were looped around his shoulders and her body melted against him, as their feet bore them around the floor in a semblance of dancing. Marc held her close with one hand, while the fingers of the other hand slid under her shoulder length hair to cup the back of her head. The desire that thrummed through her made the rest of the world disappear when their lips met in a long, soul-meshing kiss.

By the time Marc realized where they were, the music had stopped and the other dancers were leaving the floor.

As they walked slowly back to the table, arms about each other's waists, he whispered, "Look at those grins. We seem to have made some kind of a public statement, love."

They braved Wilf's overt amusement and the Wheelwrights' quiet curiosity for a few minutes, but, as soon as they could, Marc mumbled something about the long drive to the lake and they said their goodnights.

* * *

The walk to the Jeep parked under the trees at the end of the parking lot seemed interminable. Marc reluctantly released his hold on her waist to open the door for her, then went around to let himself in the driver's side. He used the few moments when he was not touching her to try to regain some self-control. If he was going to be able to concentrate on his driving and then—oh Lord, then—be able to make the kind of love with Cadie that would prove to her what a desirable woman she was, he had to cool down. He took several deep breaths, then slipped quickly into his seat. However, one look at Cadie's eyes, darkened with desire, and his good intentions vaporized like steam over boiling water.

Cocooned in the dark privacy of the vehicle, he took her flushed cheeks in his hands and lowered his open mouth to kiss her. He tasted her sweet parted lips with sucking, nibbling kisses. Cadie plunged her fingers into his hair and made a sobbing sound deep in her throat. His answering moan seemed to rise all the way from the stiffening heat of his groin. His tongue plunged deep into the sweet, dark depths of her mouth and he drank from her with a thirst that had been growing since he had first seen her dancing in the sunlight at the top of the cliff.

* * *

The roughness of his kiss sparked a fierce greed in her. The coals that had been smoldering deep inside her all evening burst into flame. She had to touch him. After a struggle with the stubborn buttons of his shirt, her hands glided over the smooth, hot skin of his chest. Under her fingers, she felt his heart pounding like her own.

When he attempted to lift her from her seat to hold her against him, the gear shift interfered. Sanity returned with a jolt. They were in the middle of a crowded parking lot.

"We can't, Cadie," he whispered hoarsely. "Not here. People are going to start leaving any moment. We have to go home. To bed. Oh, yes, love. I want you naked in my own bed in my cabin when we make love tonight."

The thought of Marc's unclothed body against hers was almost too much for her. So this was what a full-blown attack of lust was like. She ignored the niggling voice that told her what she was feeling was not as simple as that.

"Yes," she whispered.

Marc threw the car into gear and moved it quickly out of the parking lot onto the highway. They had been cruising along for a few minutes before Marc looked over at her. She was deliberately sitting as far from him as she could, leaning against the door on the passenger side.

"This is a nice vehicle, sweetheart, but I wish we'd taken Pop's Lincoln," he complained. "I can't even put my arm around you."

He halfheartedly cursed the man who invented bucket seats and reached for her hand.

Cadie looked at his rugged profile in the dim illumination of the dashboard lights. Her hungry gaze caressed every feature. His thick, blond hair was longer than he probably had worn it in his days on the police force. The bones of his face were strong—his forehead high, his nose long and straight, and his cheekbones prominent. His firm lips were softened into a sensuous half smile. He was every woman's dream man. And tonight he would be hers.

He drove with the total concentration that he seemed to apply to everything he did. *Would he make love the same way?* Her pulse sped up at the thought. His thumb on her wrist must have picked it up. He looked over at her with a smile that held a world of promise.

A chilling thought struck her. What if he was put off by her lack of experience, if she failed to please him? She'd be devastated, but she wasn't going to change her mind now. She wanted him too much to spend the rest of her life wondering what making love with Marc Banachek would have been like. He squeezed her fingers as if he sensed that she needed reassurance.

Lurch's enthusiastic welcome distracted them only momentarily. They took a moment to pat him, but left him outside to patrol the grounds for the night.

In the warm confines of the Jeep that had been bursting with sexual tension, Cadie had been certain Marc wanted her as much as she wanted him. But once she stepped out into the cool night air, she suddenly felt unaccountably awkward and shy. By the time the front door of his cabin closed behind them, her qualms about disappointing him had returned in force.

The roomy cabin reflected Marc's way of life. The main room was cozy, yet big enough to hold his large desk and a chocolate brown leather sofa and easy chair. Two walls were lined with bookshelves and a glass-fronted airtight stove dominated the wall between this room and the tiny kitchen. The two bedroom doors were open. Through the first she could see about half of an intimidatingly huge navy blue bed. She could feel her confidence shrinking.

* * *

Marc was reaching for the knot of his tie when he caught a glimpse of hesitation in her eyes. *No. She couldn't have changed her mind, could she?* He knew it would only take a few kisses to change it back. But he wouldn't do that to her. He remembered what she had told him about her fiancé's description of her. Her ego had taken a real beating from that poor excuse for a man. He mustn't rush her. He continued removing his tie and his blazer and laid them on the back of one of the chairs.

"Would you like a nightcap? Maybe a glass of wine or a cognac?" he asked, unbuttoning the top button of his shirt.

* * *

She leapt at the suggestion. Anything to delay telling him that she'd lost her nerve.

"Cognac, please," she told him. Perhaps the liquor would give her the courage to take what she wanted so badly.

He splashed cognac into two snifters, and placed them on the coffee table before joining her on the sofa.

He slid one arm around her shoulders and tenderly brushed the hair back off her forehead. Lightly, he smoothed the tiny, fading scars, then ran the tips of his fingers down her cheek and slowly across her lips.

He reached for his glass and raised it to her.

"To the most exciting woman I've ever known," he said before taking a long sip.

She raised her own glass and took a big swallow of the amber liquid. It burned a fiery path all the way down her throat and brought tears to her eyes. She gasped, then laughed self-consciously. "I guess this is where I admit I've never tasted this before."

"Cadie, love," he said, his fingers tightening just a little on her shoulder, "you know I want you. I'm pretty sure you want me, too. But if you feel it's too soon, tell me."

She placed her hand on his cheek as she looked up at him with large eyes now almost as dark as the deep green of her dress.

"I do want to make love with you, Marc, but I'm afraid I'm not very good at it."

He covered her hand and held it against the light stubble already beginning to roughen his cheek.

"Do you think I don't have any doubts about how I'm going to perform? It's been more than two years since I have been to bed with a woman, and never in my life was it as important to me as this is. What if I want this so much I lose my control and ruin it for you? Sweetheart, let's just hold each other the way we want to and see what happens."

That was the moment she knew she had fallen in love with him.

"Yes," she said.

She put her slender arms around his neck as he bent his head to accept the surrender of her mouth. This time there was not the desperation of their earlier kiss in the parking lot. It was a kiss of sensuous exploration, the first of a nighttime of kisses. Marc stroked the smooth inner surface of her lower lip with his tongue and led her to do the same. His taste was familiar and addictive. The parry and thrust of their tongues increased the hunger that had been growing all evening.

He undid the back zipper of her dress and slipped it down off her shoulders. He tested the throbbing pulse below her ear with his lips, then gradually, nibbled and tasted his way down the creamy slope of her breast to the lacy top of her bra.

Cadie undid the buttons of his shirt and pulled it out of his pants. Her hands moved, tentatively at first, up and down his naked back as she savored the smoothness of his warm skin and the bands of hard muscle under it. Gaining confidence, she drew her fingers around to his chest. More surely, they circled the tiny buds of his nipples. When she pinched one gently, he jumped.

"I'm sorry," she gasped. "Did I hurt you?"

He took both of her hands in one of his. "The very opposite, love. I'd better take you to my bed while I still can."

He swung her up into his arms, took one step, then stopped.

"I just realized the only protection I have for you is more than two years old. I guess we'll have to be creative."

"Not to worry." Pleased at her foresight, yet a little embarrassed about having condoms in her purse, Cadie smiled up into his face. "Put me down, Rhett Butler. I have something in my purse on the other side of the room that'll solve our problem."

"I don't want you that far away from me, Scarlett." He kissed her lightly on the lips, then ran his hand over his chin. "Damn! I shaved but my chin is like sandpaper already. Why don't you get the protection and I'll run a razor over my stubble."

"I don't mind a little roughness."

"Your skin is perfect. I'd hate to mark it."

He lowered her slowly and groaned with a delightful mixture of pleasure and pain when her soft mound encountered, then slid over the hard bulge straining at his zipper.

"I'll hurry," he whispered. He set her on her feet and headed for the bathroom.

Cadie picked up her purse. She gave a long, shuddering sigh, straightened her shoulders, then moved swiftly into Marc's moonlit bedroom. Apparently, as he'd dashed by the bed, he'd snatched back the bedspread, revealing a truly huge expanse of white sheet. She could hear the buzzing of his razor in the next room. He was probably wondering if he should have given her this time to change her mind. To her surprise, she realized she had no hesitation at all about what she was going to do.

She quickly took off her shoes and stockings, then skinned off her panties, shedding any traces of apprehension with them. Her unzipped silk dress barely covered her nakedness. She wished she had a sexy negligée to put on for Marc, but thought, with a happy smile, that she wouldn't be wearing it long anyway.

The sound of the razor stopped. When she turned toward the door, he stepped into the room, pulled the door closed behind him, and walked slowly toward her. The moonlight, streaming through the window, outlined his body with silver light. He had stripped down to white bikini briefs, which barely stretched to cover his arousal. He was magnificent.

She couldn't speak. She simply opened her hand to show him the condoms, then slipped them under the pillow.

Marc opened his arms and Cadie moved toward him, shrugging out of her dress as she went. She stepped over it as it slipped to the floor. His palms caressed her waist, then her back and, finally, savored the satiny texture of her rounded hips. He unfastened her lacy wisp of a bra and slid the straps off her shoulders. Cadie let it fall to the floor.

Marc stared at the beauty of her breasts, creamy-white below the tan line of her bathing suit, the nipples dusty-pink and slightly swollen. He cupped one breast, almost reverently, then bent to touch its tip with his tongue.

Cadie's whole body started as if she had been given a jolt of electricity. He began to suck gently, bringing the nipple to a rigid peak. She could hardly bear the intense pleasure it gave her. When Marc focused his attention on making the nipple of the other breast as diamond hard as the first, her breath began to come in shuddering moans and her lower body to sway rhythmically against his thigh.

"Cadie," he whispered, "I wish I could tell you how beautiful you are this minute. I want to kiss every lovely inch of you. And I want to lose myself deep, deep inside you."

"Please," she whispered back. "I want you."

* * *

With their mouths joined, and her arms wrapped around his neck, he lifted her off the floor and carried her to his bed. He laid her down and broke the kiss for a moment so he could drink in the sight of her, her silky hair spread on his pillow and her eyes unfocused with passion.

"You don't need those," she murmured, as her hands drifted down from his shoulders to the elastic of his briefs. "Let me."

He stood, trembling, by the side of the bed. The light touch of her fingers as she eased the cotton material over his erection intensified the pressure that was building all too quickly. When he had kicked off the last scrap of clothing, he lay on his side beside her.

"Oh, yes," Cadie sighed. At last she felt the hot length of his naked body against her.

Cadie rubbed her damp, sensitive breasts slowly back and forth across the light line of smooth hair where it began its course from between his nipples to the heavy thatch of hair that surrounded his aroused manhood.

"That feels so good," she said.

Marc could feel his control slipping. He slid his hand between her legs and found her swollen petals hot and wet. He ached to slide into her moist heat, but he was determined to make this a loving she would never forget. He pulled back a little and stroked her gently. Then his thumb found the tiny nub and began to massage it.

"Please," she moaned, clenching his buttocks and pulling his body back against her.

"This is for you, love," he said through his clenched teeth.

"Please, Marc. No. I want us to feel it together."

He did not need any more convincing. He groped under the pillow until he found one of the little foil packets, ripped it open with his teeth and sat back on his heels. His fingers were unbearably clumsy, but eventually he managed to unroll it onto himself. Time had never gone more slowly.

"Open your eyes, Cadie. I want to see your eyes."

He rose over her and slid the tip of his engorged member into her waiting softness. He watched the pupils of her eyes dilate as he eased into her heat. Instinctively, she wrapped her legs around his waist to welcome his full length. They lay perfectly still, wrapped in the wonder of the moment. He sensed they had been waiting all their lives for this mating.

Marc's body had quivered with driving need for physical release before. But the towering emotions that overwhelmed him were totally unfamiliar. Cadie's warmth and light filled the emptiness that had always been at the core of his being.

And you are mine, Arcadie. He wasn't ready to say the words aloud, but that did not make them any less true.

* * *

He began to move, slowly at first, then, as the fever rose, his movement accelerated. Cadie's hips swiveled against his thrusts, the incredible tension inside her twisting and tearing at her until at last it broke.

"Marc," she cried as the world shattered into tiny shards of brilliant light.

The first of her internal spasms triggered his release. His triumphant shout as he spilled his seed almost blended with hers. His body, when he collapsed on top of her, was a burden she had waited all her life to hold. He tried to roll off her, mumbling he didn't want to crush her, but she held him where he was, imprisoned by her arms and her legs.

"Not yet," she pleaded. "Stay."

He did not reply but kissed her tenderly.

Then he said, "Hold on tight," and turned over onto his back holding her snug against him. "There we are, love," he grinned up at her. "Nothing lost, and you can breathe."

"I love your weight crushing me," she told him, kissing his damp chest.

He chuckled drowsily. "Don't worry. I plan to crush you again soon."

An exquisite lassitude filled her mind and body. So this is what it was like to make love. Marc was such a sensitive and generous lover. He seemed to take as much satisfaction in giving her pleasure as in taking his own. She wondered if she had made him as happy as he had made her.

She was pretty sure she was being silly, but she had to ask.

"Marc," she murmured against his chest, "was I all right?"

"All right?" Her question had jolted him wide awake. "Sweetheart, you must know…you were magic. You were fire and lightning. I haven't been with all that many women, but I've never experienced anything like making love with you. You make me feel like the sexiest man alive."

Marc took her lips in a tender kiss that grew slowly in intensity. His hands moved over her lower back and her thighs in slow circles.

After a few minutes, Marc rolled her over onto her back and lay beside her, lazily stroking her as if memorizing the tempting curves of her body before he kissed her again. His tongue caressed the sweet, sensitive lining of her mouth.

When Cadie tentatively met his tongue, she was astounded to feel an immediate response in that part of Marc's body that lay against her thigh. She was doing that to him! Cadie became bold enough to do some exploration of her own into the dark recesses of his mouth.

The embers deep within her that she thought had burned out in that last spectacular blast of flame began to spark and crackle again.

*   *   *

Making love with Cadie had opened the floodgates of emotion Marc had kept pent up for years. He felt a burst of pure joy so intense he laughed aloud. Still laughing, he rolled off the bed away from her and pulled her to her feet.

"Let's take your sexy, little body into the shower," he said. "Maybe the water will keep us from spontaneous combustion."

Their lovemaking this time was slow and thorough. Marc caressed every inch of her body as he soaped and rinsed and kissed her. Then, Cadie stroked and massaged him until there were suds on every part of him. Before she could rinse them off, he slipped into her and they made wild love balancing against the slippery tile wall.

When they tottered back to his bed, they were weak from lovemaking and laughter. Cadie dropped off to sleep immediately, snuggled in his arms. Drowsy and completely satisfied, Marc watched her sleeping. Her generous mouth was relaxed in a smile, strands of her damp hair trailed across his chest. *What a woman!* She was so responsive and giving in her lovemaking that she had made him feel stronger and more virile than he had ever felt in his life. Over and above that, a powerful tenderness that was unfamiliar and unnerving permeated everything.

He felt a stab of conscience. He didn't know how long he could keep her happy. He had long ago accepted that Cadie would want more from him than he was capable of giving. God knew, he had tried to keep away from her.

Perhaps she would tire of him before she discovered she had been cheated. Maybe by the time the menace was gone from her life, she would no longer need him. After all, she was going to be so wealthy that she could go anywhere in the world, have any man she wanted. Maybe she'd never learn what an empty shell of a man he was.

However, having tasted her sweetness and experienced the most wholehearted and earth-shattering lovemaking of his life, he couldn't give her up. He was being as selfish as the despicable Jerry, but he was going to grab every moment of happiness that she offered him.

* * *

Cadie usually took a long time to wake up, but this morning, her eyes snapped open,. A muscular leg lay across her thighs and warm fingers loosely cupped her left breast. Memories of the long hours of wild and tender lovemaking she had shared with Marc came flooding back to her. She didn't want to move. She couldn't bear it if he retreated into himself again this morning. She snuggled her bottom a little closer to his warmth.

"Be careful, love," Marc's deep voice cautioned her softly. "You don't know what that wiggle could lead to."

She turned and was relieved to see his tender smile.

"Good morning, love," she said as she reached up to kiss him. Well, if he could call her "love," she was entitled to do the same. The difference was, she acknowledged to herself, that she did love him.

"I've never woken up in a man's bed before. What's the proper etiquette? Do I get up and make breakfast now?"

"You let me return your kiss before we discuss insignificant matters like food."

The long, cozy kiss inevitably became more passionate and it was no longer early morning when Cadie went off to the house to dress for the day.

She was wondering what Pop would think if he could see her padding home from Marc's cabin in her bare feet, with her hair wild and dressed only in his dressing gown. She had crossed the living room and was about halfway to the closed door to the bedroom wing, when she caught a strong whiff of it. For a moment, she couldn't place the unpleasant smell.

Then, appalled, she recognized the distinctive smell of propane gas.

CHAPTER 10

"Marc!"

When he heard the urgency in her voice, he ran to meet her, still dripping from the shower and pulling on his jeans. Cadie met him halfway to the house.

"Gas," she said.

The minute he stepped inside, he smelled it. The heavy, cloying smell caught at the back of his throat. *Propane! How could that be?* The gas hadn't been turned on since last April, when a tree had come down on the power line in a thunderstorm.

Grabbing Cadie's hand, he pulled her back outside.

"Go back to the cabin," he told her. "I'll go around outside and turn the propane off at the tank."

Cadie had never seen the emergency gas fixtures in use. Pop had installed a gas light at the far end of the hallway in the bedroom wing and a light and a two-burner gas hot plate in the kitchen. The five-hundred-pound storage tank was just a few steps away outside the kitchen door on the edge of the patio.

Pop had made sure she understood what could happen if there was a gas leak. Of course, the obvious danger was breathing the poisonous gas, but, equally as serious was the possibility of explosion. If the fumes built up in an enclosed space, the smallest spark, even of static electricity, could set off a major blast.

They had to make sure the gas was dissipated quickly.

She followed Marc around the corner of the building and went in the side door that led through the mudroom to the kitchen. By the time Marc had turned off the valve on the propane tank, she had the mudroom door and window wide open and was struggling with the kitchen window over the sink.

"That should deal with any gas that seeped in here." He reached around her to raise the heavy window. "The handle on the propane tank had been cranked as wide open as it could go."

"I'm pretty sure the leak isn't in the kitchen burners," she told him. "I didn't smell the gas until I got near my door. And this light hasn't been turned on," she said, checking the knob on the gas light in the kitchen. "There must be a malfunction in the emergency light in the hall outside my room."

Knowing someone had deliberately opened the gas valve, Marc was sure there was no malfunction. At least, an activated gas lamp would be easier to deal with than a break somewhere in the yards of copper tubing that carried the gas to the fixtures.

Cadie did not appear to be frightened. But Marc shuddered at the thought of what could have happened. If Cadie had slept in her own bed last night and he had been in her guest room with the doors open to the hallway outside their rooms as usual, they both could have died in their sleep. His fists clenched. The enemy meant business.

"There's no propane feeding in from the tank now," he said. "But even with the door to your wing closed, the gas will continue seeping under it into the open area."

"Right. It's heavier than air," she agreed.

Cadie's speech was noticably slow. He looked at her sharply. She wasn't flushed, but she looked a little dazed. Of course, it was hard to concentrate with that sickening smell lingering in your nostrils.

"Go back outside, Cadie. I'll meet you on the other side of the patio after I get this window and the front door open. There's a good crossdraft. After the breeze off the lake has blown most of the propane out the front door, we'll tackle the windows in your wing."

* * *

"You deal with that one and the dining room windows." Cadie shook her head to clear it. The more quickly they got the gas out of here the better. She dodged past him to the living room.

"I'll get the front," she said over her shoulder.

It took no effort to slide the front window open and all she had to do was release catch on the front door.

The concentration of invisible gas fumes hovering over the living room floor didn't seem too heavy at first, but by the time she had waded through them and opened the front door, Cadie was dizzy and a bit nauseated. She stepped out front and took a fast breath before opening the window. Then, she plunged back toward the open kitchen doors to the patio about thirty feet away through the waves of pungent gas billowing at about knee level.

She had almost reached the door when she began to weave. Her head was pounding and her feet did not want to behave properly.

The next thing she knew, Marc was scooping her up in his arms and carrying her out across the patio. Then, gasping for his own breath, he set her back on her feet and, with Marc half-dragging her, they staggered into the breeze off the lake that was pushing the gas in toward the house. At the edge of the cliff, they threw themselves on the coarse grass and took great gulps of the clean, fresh air.

After a few minutes, the world stopped spinning. Cadie raised her head slowly and met Marc's concerned gaze.

"Wading through propane gas is another thing that short people shouldn't do," Cadie said, with a weak attempt at humor. "It's a good thing Lurch wasn't inside last night."

"Lurch!" Marc scrambled to his feet. "Where is he? I haven't seen him this morning."

"I didn't hear him bark at whoever turned on the propane," Cadie said, anxiously. "Lurch!" she shouted. She couldn't stand it if something had happened to that oafish mutt.

Marc was already halfway back to the house. She followed him along the outside of the bedroom wing where the closed windows still kept most of the gas inside.

"Lurch!" she called again at the top of the beach path. "We'll cover the ground faster if we separate," she suggested. "I'll go down to the beach. You take the driveway and the path to the log cabin."

"We'll search together," Marc stated.

*   *   *

He was not letting her out of his sight until he'd caught the bastard who had tried to kill her. Under his rage was a core of icy fear. He was familiar with every potential danger of the city, but out here he was out of his depth. A local man might have been prepared for something like this, but the silent gas attack had been outside his experience. Because he had not forseen the possibility, it had come too close to killing them

MINE

both.

He only hoped the attacker had not been more successful in dealing with Lurch.

Taking turns calling the dog, they moved through the undergrowth along the edges of the paths and the driveway. Marc could see by the strained look on her face that his optimistic Cadie was steeling herself against the discovery of Lurch's bloody body in the shrubbery.

Cadie saw him first.

"Over there," she whispered, pointing at the dark shape lying at the foot of the steps of the core shed.

The unconscious dog was sprawled on the path, with two large steak bones near his front paws. Marc bent over him and felt for the pulse at his throat.

"He's alive."

Lurch's eyelids quivered slightly and the end of his tail twitched at the touch of his master's hand on his head.

"He seems to be regaining consciousness. Looks as if he was doped, not poisoned. We'd better get him to the vet. Stay with him. I'll get the pickup."

"He's coming out of it," Cadie said, when Marc got out of the truck. She helped him hoist the big dog up into the back of the pickup.

"I have to get dressed," she said, when he leaned over to open the passenger door. "I can't go into town like this."

*   *   *

He grinned for the first time since Cadie had discovered the propane. How could he have forgotten she was naked under his cotton robe?

"I left some shorts and a sweatshirt in the mud room dryer yesterday. There shouldn't be any gas in there."

"Hurry. As soon as you're back in the truck, I'll rush in and open the door to your apartment, Cadie. We'll leave everything wide open to air out while we're gone."

He left Cadie by the open door to the scrub room at the far end of the L-shaped house from her bedroom.

A long couple of minutes later, he saw her heading back to the pickup and started toward the front door. The sharp aroma of the gas was still strong. It was a good thing neither of them smoked and that he had not lit the fireplace when they got home last night. The smallest live coal could have sent the place up like a bomb. He took a deep breath, crossed the living room in half a dozen strides, opened the door leading to the hall outside Cadie's study, and propped it open with a chair. Then, leaving the front door wide open, he raced back to the truck to rejoin Cadie.

"Dr. Mott is the closest vet I know of," Marc said as he rammed the pickup into gear and sped down the driveway spraying the freshly spread, loose gravel as they went. "He's just this side of Sundridge. Shouldn't take more than fifteen minutes."

Cadie looked as if she were going to argue with him, then closed her eyes.

"That's it. Relax," he said. "The traffic's light this early on a Sunday morning. I wish I had a siren," he muttered.

Not even fifteen minutes later, the pickup screeched to a stop outside the front door of the veterinarian's house. The brusque, gray-haired man who emerged took their arrival in stride.

"We are not officially open on Sunday," Dr. Mott told them even as he unlocked the office attached to the small boarding kennel beside his house.

He and Marc lugged the half-conscious young dog inside. After a quick examination, Dr. Mott confirmed their suspicions.

"He's been given some kind of narcotic. I'm afraid you'll have to leave him with me while we flush out his stomach."

Cadie winced at the unfairness of the situation. She was the target and Lurch was suffering for it.

"He's a strong, healthy dog, but as we have no idea how big a dose he has ingested, I'd like him to stay where I can keep an eye on him for a good twenty-four hours after he's cleaned out."

After a short discussion, they decided to leave Lurch with Dr. Mott until they returned on Monday or Tuesday from their meeting with Stephen Travelle in Toronto.

By the time they got back to the lake, the gas had pretty well dissipated, although its odor was still heavy in the air. Cadie rushed around opening the windows they had missed in the central portion of the house, while Marc dealt with those in Cadie's wing.

"Someone turned the gas jet full on without lighting the mantle, Cadie," Marc told her when he rejoined her. "With no flame to burn it off, the moment the valve on the tank end was opened, the gas just poured in."

"He must've turned on the light while we were out and then switched on the tank outside after we were asleep," she said slowly.

The horror was beginning to dawn on her. Lurch had not made a sound. Had the drugged meat been left for him to consume before her enemy approached the house, or was the enemy someone the dog knew well? Even more repugnant was the knowledge that, while she and Marc were making love, the silent figure had been moving purposefully outside the house. They had been too intent on each other to hear him doping Lurch and turning on the gas intended to kill her.

Cadie had thought she wasn't capable of hating anyone, but she could almost taste the bitter hatred for this shadowy person who was determined to kill her. He had even marred, by his presence, the memory of the most beautiful experience of her life.

However, the emotions that had been awakened last night had not been tainted. She looked at the golden man she would always love. Only Marc's existence kept the horror at bay.

"Thank God, you were with me," she whispered.

* * *

Marc wrapped his arms about her. His mind was working furiously. Jack Haywood was the one with the glaring financial motive. But he wasn't the one tormenting her. Someone else was pussyfooting around here in the middle of the night. Marc could sense malice, as well as greed in these attacks. This cowardly enemy who attacked from the shadows had shown he was no longer content with his campaign of fear. They had to find him and soon.

Marc didn't mention to Cadie that he'd been able to find no evidence of a break-in. As they had been careful not to leave the door unlocked for a minute, the intruder must have used a key to enter the house. They must get the locks changed right away and he knew exactly the kind of electronic security system they needed. If Cadie was still resistant to the idea, he'd damn well have it installed himself.

* * *

Marc was holding her so tightly she could hardly breathe, but the inner quaking she'd been trying to ignore was fading away.

"We'd better call Chuck," he said. "And I think we'd be wise to have an electronic surveillance system installed while we're in Toronto."

"You're right." Reluctance was heavy in her voice. "I hate the thought I can't throw open a window whenever I feel like it. I'm going to feel caged. But safer, I guess." She grimaced. "I don't know anything about them, Marc."

"I do. We don't have any choice, Cadie. The guy seems to be able to walk in and out of here at will. Shall I call the company in North Bay after I've talked to Chuck?"

"Yes," she capitulated.

"We can turn the system off when all this is over."

He was reaching for the telephone when it rang.

"Luke tells me," Vi began without preamble, "that you and Cadie are headed down below tomorrow. Do you still want me to come in?"

"Please. I'd be upset if you didn't. We're out of cookies," Marc said, surprised that, after the stress of the past few hours, his voice sounded so normal. "You don't mind being here alone, do you?"

Vi could reasonably feel vulnerable in this isolated location where she'd been shot a little more than two weeks ago.

"Gracious no," she said with a laugh. "That was a freak accident. The person who used the window for target practice was likely a kid who had snuck out his father's rifle. He's probably terrified at what he did. Anyway, Luke will be there working on Cadie's studio. I'll be fine."

"I'm having Wilde Brothers from the Bay come down to set up an alarm system tomorrow or the next day. I thought I should warn you." Before he rang off, Marc added, "Don't worry if you smell propane, Vi. We had a bit of a leak in the line, but it's been fixed and the place is just about aired out now."

"I'll bring some of my homemade potpourri," she said. "I'd been meaning to anyway. You won't smell a trace of the gas when you get back from the city."

Before the phone could ring again, he called Chuck. The O.P.P.'s wife was not too happy to be disturbed on a Sunday morning.

"He's just getting dressed for church," she told him, not trying to hide the exasperation in her voice.

When Chuck heard Marc's story, he agreed to leave for the lake right away.

"He should be here in less than half an hour," Marc said.

"Then, while we're waiting for him to get here," Cadie suggested, "I think we'd better get changed for our trip to the city. And we still have to pack."

"At least we can get you out of here for a couple of days," Marc said grimly.

Cadie was putting the first piece of lingerie into her suitcase when the phone rang again. This time the caller was totally unexpected.

"Katie?" Uncle Jack sounded anxious. "It's good to hear your voice, honey."

Could even her insensitive uncle have tried to have her killed and then brazenly call to see if she was still alive?

"What do you want, Uncle Jack?"

Cadie was past pretending that they were a loving uncle and niece. A welcome click on the line indicated Marc had picked up a receiver.

"Why, I wanted to ask if I could come up to see you." Jack seemed taken aback by her tone of voice. "There's something important we need to discuss."

"Important for you or for me?" Cadie asked.

"Believe me, honey, for both of us."

"I'm not going to be home, Uncle Jack," she told him with some relief. "But I would like to talk to you. I'll be in Toronto later today. We could meet there tomorrow afternoon."

"Fine. I'm in the city now. Where will you be staying?"

"It'll be easier if I call you. Where can I reach you at noon tomorrow?"

He sounded a little put off by her brusque tone, but told her he was staying at the Royal York Hotel. After she broke off the connection, she leaned against the dresser and took a couple of deep breaths. She was still standing there when Marc joined her. He slipped his arm around her shoulder.

"You handled that well, Cadie," he said. "I'm glad you didn't tell him where we're staying. Now we can meet him on our own terms and make it clear to him there's no way he can win."

* * *

He left her then and sped through finished his own packing. He stared at the open suitcase for a long, hard minute, then took his old .38 caliber Smith and Wesson pistol out of his dresser drawer. He weighed it in his hand and, with a resigned sigh, tucked it into the bottom of the bag. Then he did something he had been steeling himself to do for a few days. He picked up the phone and dialed a number he had not used for over two years.

A clipped male voice answered, "Yes?"

"Willy?"

"Marc! It's been a long time."

Yeah, Marc thought, since the afternoon I caught you with Val in my bed.

"I've run into a problem up here that I could use some help with," he said, as if they had parted on the best of terms.

"I'll do anything I can."

Marc recognized an unspoken apology in the short response. Maybe some part of the friendship could be salvaged. He told Willy what he needed to find out.

It was not quite two o'clock when Marc slammed down the lid on the trunk of the gleaming seven-year-old Lincoln. Chuck had been and gone, having examined the propane installation and promising to check on the house while they were away.

"If we've forgotten anything, we'll buy it in the city," Marc said, looking at Cadie's furrowed brow. Her mobile face was so easy to read. He could see she was relieved that they were finally on their way, but he could sense she was concerned about something. He suspected she was uneasy about their new relationship. After what they'd had together last night, he was determined not to let her distance herself from him again.

"I called Dr. Mott a few minutes ago. Lurch is coming along fine," he told her, misreading the reason for her silence on purpose. "We'll call him again the minute we get to our hotel room."

* * *

She raised her eyebrows. She did not regret one minute of their night of lovemaking, but she hadn't given him control over her life. She had the right to decide whether or not she was going to spend tonight with him.

"Room?" she asked, with a touch of asperity.

"Room," he pronounced. "We can get two beds if you prefer, but we're going to be in the same room."

Her knee-jerk reaction to his autocratic statement was to argue, but, to be honest, she didn't object to Marc hovering over her. She wanted him close by. Very close by. It would be idiotic to spoil the time they were going to be together in a vain attempt not to lose her heart to him. It was already too late for that. The day brightened perceptibly at the thought. They were alive, Lurch was on the mend, no one knew where they were staying, and tomorrow's meetings would look after themselves.

Some of her thoughts must have shown in her face because, when she looked up at Marc, he was already smiling at her.

"One room it is," she said.

"Well, scoot over here." He patted the seat beside him with a suggestive laugh. "Love a car with a bench seat."

He gave her an innocent kiss on the tip of her nose. "I need you close, but no fooling around while I'm driving," he warned her with a sexy chuckle. "Buckle up."

He took her lips in a second kiss that was not the slightest bit innocent. "That'll have to hold us until we reach the King Eddy. Can you behave yourself that long?"

His eyes were filled with laughter. She met his challenge. First, she dutifully did up her seat belt, then she placed one hand high on his thigh. She felt the muscles tighten under his gray flannel trousers.

"I'll try, love," she said, trying to look serious, "but I do have a problem with what I'm going to do with my hands on that long a drive."

He picked up the offending hand and kissed every tempting finger.

"Do what you like with your hands, little one," he told her, "but, if you want the car to stay on the road, don't do that."

"Maybe I should drive. That would keep me occupied."

"I've been itching to drive this car for a long time. If you behave yourself, maybe I'll give you a turn later."

"Give me a turn? It's my car!" she protested in feigned indignation.

As it turned out, Marc got to drive the Lincoln the whole way. By the time they reached the four-lane highway at Huntsville, Cadie had fallen asleep. She did not awaken until they were caught in the stop-and-go traffic of the Don Valley Parkway, the busy highway that cut a tree-lined swath through the center of Toronto. When they left the parkway, she declined his offer to allow her to negotiate the maze of busy one-way streets to their hotel.

Massive, sky-scraping office towers and impersonal, marble-faced financial institutions shaded the streets. Even the theaters and restaurants of the downtown area were substantial and a bit smug looking. Marc moved the Lincoln with confidence through familiar territory for a few minutes before wheeling sharply into a short, circular drive. He stopped in front of the glass doors of the refurbished famous, old hotel.

An immaculately gloved doorman in a long, beige topcoat and top hat handed Cadie out of the car, gave a gray-haired bellman charge of their bags, and accepted Marc's car keys in order to have their car parked in the underground garage. Having never been past the airport

MINE

in Toronto, Cadie had no idea what to expect of one of its downtown hotels. Now that Marc was taking her elbow and guiding her inside, she was glad she'd decided to wear her white wool pant suit with her best flowered silk blouse.

Entering the lobby was like walking into the Victorian era. Enormous oriental rugs carpeted the floor and little conversation clusters of blue and gray velvet wing chairs and love seats broke up the area. Against the walls, huge urns of fresh flowers stood on long tables of black marble. They were reflected in heroic gilt-framed mirrors hung behind them. The high ceiling met the marble walls in an ornate frieze of plaster flowers, fruit, and plump cherubs.

Cadie felt as if she should be draped in yards of velvet and wearing a bustle and an elegant hat with an ostrich plume.

After they registered, they were whisked up the elevators to a one-bedroom suite on the eighth floor. As soon as the bellman unlocked the door, Marc exchanged the key for a folded bill and sent him on his way.

Cadie stood in the middle of the large sitting room, which was decorated in much the same style as the lobby. She turned around slowly, taking in the velvet couch and easy chairs, Degas prints in ornate frames, huge mirrors and royal blue brocade draperies at the picture window that offered a glimpse of Lake Ontario between the tall buildings across the street.

"It's another era," she said softly. "A woman in this room should either be a sheltered young spinster traveling with a chaperone or a woman of easy virtue waiting for her lover to join her for an illicit assignation."

"I vote for the lady of easy virtue," Marc said, reaching for her, "provided that her virtue is easy only with me."

Laughing, she ducked under his arm.

"Sit down," she said, waving toward a brocaded love seat. "Take off your jacket. I'll see what I can do to loosen up this Victorian atmosphere."

Marc raised a quizzical eyebrow, then, with a broad grin, followed her instructions.

Cadie took off her suit jacket and tossed it onto one of the chairs. She slipped off her shoes, then placed herself primly and carefully on his lap. She looked seriously into his eyes, her expression a mix of sensuality and innocence, then wriggled her bottom experimentally. She placed her hands on either side of his face, and whispered, "Don't move a muscle. I want to see if I can do this."

Marc let her lead the way. She licked her lips, then lightly touched her damp mouth to his eyelids, his temples, the clenched muscle at the point of his jaw. The tremor that she felt under her lips was most gratifying. She ran the tip of her tongue around the outside of his lips and gently prodded at the corner of his mouth. When he opened his mouth for her, she thrust her tongue inside the way he had done the night before. At her bold move, she could feel his body's immediate response pressing urgently against the backs of her thighs through the fine woolen fabric of her pants.

* * *

The rhythmic movements of her stroking tongue and her fingers massaging his scalp were sending jets of fire coursing through Marc's veins. His tongue met hers in a mighty thrust as he undid the buttons of her blouse. Just as speedily, she pulled the shirt out of his pants and ran the palms of her hands hungrily over his bare back.

Marc gasped, "I'd say you can do it fine, sweetheart."

They left a trail of garments all the way to the king-sized bed. Then, they stood beside it, still kissing, with their naked bodies clasped together, their hands touching and stroking almost desperately. At last, on the big bed, they came together as if they had been waiting for this moment for months instead of only hours. There was something elemental about their coupling. Perhaps it was a reaction to the escalating nature of the attacks on Cadie, or perhaps it was the increasing certainty there was more to their lovemaking than merely consuming passion.

Afterward, when she collapsed against his chest, Cadie was weeping. "Please hold me," she murmured. "I don't want it to end yet." He wiped her tears with his fingers. "I'll hold you as long as you want me to."

For the moment, he didn't care whether she was asking him to continue making love to her or wanting more from him than that. Whatever she wanted, whatever it cost, and, he suspected, for however long she wanted it, he'd try to do it for her.

* * *

The next morning, when Marc reached for the telephone to answer the wake-up call, he had to lean over a soft, warm woman whose bottom was snuggled against his lower abdomen and whose tangled mass of golden hair was spread across his pillow. He hung up the receiver and hovered over her for a few moments until she stirred and smiled sleepily at him. The feeling that squeezed his heart and made him swallow hard was new and achingly beautiful. He kissed her warm lips and forced himself to keep the kiss brief.

"No time to wake up slowly this morning, little one," he said, as he slid out of bed. "We have two hours to shower, get dressed, eat a massive breakfast, and get to Stephen Travelle's office."

* * *

As she sat up, clutching the sheet to her bare breasts, her stomach growled loudly.

"Right," she said, wishing that she did not feel so gauche about their nakedness and the rude noises her stomach was making. "My stomach is complaining we haven't eaten since we had that cheese sandwich before we left the lake."

"I'd love to start the day by sharing the shower, love," Marc said, "but it'll be much faster if we do it separately."

She remembered their long, soapy lovemaking in his shower at Nighthawk Lake.

"Go," she said with a wistful sigh, and he headed quickly for the bathroom.

They made it to the dining room in record time. Although it was early, the room was crowded. Cadie, in her green paisley shirtwaist dress, and, Marc, in a well-tailored gray suit, fit in perfectly with the restaurant's morning clientele of business people. Both hungry, they tackled their hearty breakfasts with gusto.

After a few minutes of concentrating on his food, Marc broke the silence.

"Sorry to be so rude, sweetheart," he said. "But something seems to have given me an appetite this morning."

She returned his reminiscent grin.

"Not rude," she replied in a low voice. "Preoccupied sometimes, but never rude."

She could think of other words to describe him, starting with handsome, sexy, much too easy to fall in love with, but she merely smiled. "We do need to keep up our strength."

The tantalizing gleam in his eyes made it hard to focus her attention on the serious matters that had brought them to the city. However, when they went back up to the suite to get the log book, Marc brought reality back in a hurry. He took a small revolver out of his bag, loaded it and, with the ease of familiarity, tucked it in the waistband at the small of his back.

"Marc," Cadie gasped. "You don't have to take that. We're only going a few blocks in broad daylight to a lawyer's office."

"That gas attack yesterday changed the rules, Cadie. What if Pop was wrong about Travelle? He could be one of the bad guys for all we know. If he is, he won't expect us to come armed. We'll have that advantage."

She deferred to his experience, and a few minutes later, they were being ushered into Stephen Travelle's office by a tall, pencil-thin brunette whose smile looked as if it had been painted on and then shellacked. The middle-aged man who rose from his desk, wearing a wide smile and exuding welcome, was fit-looking, easily as big as Marc, and only about ten or fifteen years older. He shook hands firmly, first with Cadie, then Marc.

"Arcadie Haywood and Marcus Banachek. What a pleasure to meet you."

"Call me Cadie, please," she told him.

"And Marc."

"Stephen, then. I was sorry to hear about your grandfather, Cadie," Stephen told her. "I'd known George since I was a boy. He was a good man. I didn't get to the funeral because I didn't hear about the accident until a month or so after he died."

"It was a very small service," she said. "I only learned that he had consulted you when Marc and I found this letter mentioning your name a few days ago."

Although Travelle's hearty voice and overly sincere manner could lead a person to dismiss him as a superficial, high-powered promoter, something in his shrewd eyes convinced Cadie that he should be taken seriously. Whichever side of the fence he turned out to be on, Stephen Travelle was a force to contend with. She handed the letter to Marc, who passed it to the lawyer.

He skimmed it.

"Yes," he said. "George was in to see me last year, in mid-April. I hadn't seen him in years. My father, when he was alive, was the one who acted for him.

"George told me the kind of deal he wanted and asked me to put out some feelers for a mining company that could put up the capital to develop a really big gold mine on his terms. He explained he had only two partners in this: Cadie had inherited Peter's quarter of the shares and you, Marc, owned an eighth. He said he'd get back to me by the end of the summer with the final analysis of the drilling results.

"But, to tell you the truth, I was surprised to see the notation on my appointment pad that George Haywood's heir wanted to see me. Your letter indicated you had decided to make other arrangements about the claims."

"My letter?"

"Yes." Stephen looked at her strangely, opened the manila folder on his desk, and handed her a brief, typed letter from it. "When I heard about George, I sent you my condolences and indicated I'd like to talk to you at your convenience. This is the reply."

The message on the sheet of paper was exactly as he had stated and the signature was simply, "Haywood."

Cadie couldn't conceal her confusion. "I did not send this letter."

Both men waited silently. Marc looked angry.

"Uncle Jack!" she exploded. "I was right out of it most of the time those first few weeks in hospital after my accident, and he took it upon himself to pay my bills for me." She shook her head in disbelief at her uncle's duplicity. "I thought he was being thoughtful. I should've known he had his own agenda."

Marc leaned forward. "You haven't changed your mind about having Stephen continue with Pop's instructions, have you, Cadie?"

"I certainly haven't."

Stephen did not pursue the topic of the unauthorized letter but cut straight to the chase.

"I've talked to some people who are very interested and waiting to hear more," he said. "According to his letter to you, George was happy with the results of the drilling. We'll have to get a geologist up there to do an official logging of the core and do a work-up."

When Marc looked at her quizzically and tapped his breast pocket, Cadie nodded.

"We have George Haywood's own log book," Marc told him. "It was with the letter."

"That will speed things up," Stephen told them.

He went on to identify the two reputable and well-established mining companies he had approached about possible development. In Stephen's opinion, either one of them was capable of handling a major find.

"I received an offer a couple of weeks ago from a company called

NorthAm Mining Corporation," Cadie told him.

"That's to be expected." Stephen completely abandoned his genial affability at the name. "You knew Jack Haywood and Sandor Green are the major shareholders, didn't you? Green runs the day-to-day business."

"I didn't." But, that piece of information answered a number of questions.

"What did you tell them?"

"I told them I wasn't interested." "That's a relief," Stephen said. "NorthAm is absolutely the last company George would have any dealings with."

"Do you know the reason my grandfather was so against Uncle Jack?" Cadie was eager to satisfy her curiosity about that little mystery.

"I got the impression Jack had been involved in quite a few minor scrapes with the law as a young man. But the final straw came for your grandfather when you must have been just a baby," Stephen told her.

"I was a kid myself. I heard George and Dad talk about it at the time. It seems Jack and Sandor ran some kind of scam where they used George's reputation to get his friends and business associates to invest in some worthless claims. When the facts came to light, George paid off the investors and kept Jack out of jail, but, as far as I know, he never spoke to his son again.

"Jack and Sandor have been associated with a number of questionable deals since then. In mining circles, they have a reputation for being pretty unscrupulous. You don't want them to get their hands on your mine."

A man is as good as his word. How many times had she heard Pop say that? Jack could not have chosen to do anything that would hurt or anger his father more than cheating people who trusted the Haywood name. *He deliberately smeared Pop's reputation!* She could feel the heat rising in her cheeks as she fought to keep her anger to herself.

Marc appeared to be having much the same problem. In spite of the non-committal expression on his face, she could read the fury in his steely eyes and in the tension of his clenched jaw. Their meeting with Jack this afternoon promised to be interesting.

After Travelle gave them some background on the mining companies he recommended they deal with, Cadie and Marc authorized him to act for them in the negotiations. He agreed that most of their future discussions could be conducted from the lake using the telephone and Marc's fax machine.

Before they left, Travelle made one suggestion. "I know it's not my business to give you personal advice, Cadie, but you're on the verge of becoming a very wealthy woman. If, by any chance, you don't have a will and Jack Haywood is your next of kin, I'd suggest that you do something about one circumstance or the other as soon as possible."

"I intended to ask you to draw up a simple will for me," Cadie agreed. "Can I give you the terms now and come in to sign it first thing tomorrow?"

"Of course," he replied.

*   *   *

On the long walk to their hotel, Cadie and Marc were both very quiet.

"Do you think that we can depend on him?" she asked.

"First impression? I think so. He comes across more like a promoter than a lawyer, but I think he's being straight with us."

"Pop trusted him."

That seemed to say it all. Hand in hand, they walked slowly along King Street, barely conscious of the traffic and streetcars that inched down the canyons between the skyscrapers. They hardly noticed the crowds of unsmiling pedestrians rushing around and past them. There was the kind of electricity in the air that you only find in the busiest part of a big city. Cadie had felt it holidaying with her father in New York and London. But this time, there was the additional emotional charge of being with Marc. It would be easy to let herself forget why they were here and play tourist with him. *Lovers should have the chance to have fun.* She caught her breath at the wonder of it. They were lovers!

They entered the hotel by way of a little side street.

"This is definitely coffee time for me. Where would you prefer, little one. Here?" Marc waved at the restaurant they were walking past. "Or room service?"

"Up in the suite, please," she said. "I want to take off my shoes." She indicated her navy blue high-heeled pumps. "I love the way they make me feel tall, but they sure aren't made for walkin'."

"I'll carry you," he said, grinning fiendishly and making a feint at her.

She dodged and scooted ahead of him into the elevator. "You'd do it, wouldn't you?"

"Any chance I get."

MINE

She flushed, but her smile was that of a woman who would not mind a repeat performance of the last time he had swept her up into his arms.

However, when they reached the room, they turned their attention to the upcoming confrontation with Jack Haywood. By the time their carafe of coffee arrived, Cadie had spoken to her uncle and the meeting was set up for three o'clock in the large bar off the lobby of the Royal York Hotel.

Cadie couldn't believe her ears when Marc picked up the receiver the moment she hung up to call the Royal York reservations desk to reserve a room for the night.

"What on earth did you do that for?" she cried. "I have no intention of changing hotels. We're meeting Uncle Jack there because we don't want him to know where we're staying."

* * *

"I should've talked it over with you before I called." Anyone with two wits to rub together who had ever spent any time with Cadie would know that. "I'm sorry. But I'm so used to making decisions on my own and acting on them…" He shrugged apologetically.

"It crossed my mind while you were talking to him that we should give him the idea he knows exactly where we are. If we check into the RoyalYork and call your uncle to say that, in the interests of privacy, you'd like to meet him in our room, he won't look for us anywhere else. We won't stay the night."

Cadie looked unconvinced but not hostile.

"This way," he continued, "has another advantage. Jack Haywood can't prepare any surprises for us."

"He wouldn't," Cadie stated flatly. "Uncle Jack might be eager to cheat me, but he'd never cause me any physical harm. If NorthAm is behind the attacks, I'm sure Uncle Jack doesn't know about them."

"He's the one with the obvious motive, Cadie. I know he's your only living relative, but I'm afraid I don't have the faith in his scruples that you do."

They glared at one another.

"You have a point," she said grudgingly. "It can't hurt to change the location. I'll call him when we get to the Royal York."

Cadie exhaled a deep sigh and leaned her head on the back of the couch. She stretched out her legs on the glossy finish of the walnut coffee table and wriggled her stockinged toes. She stared at them, dreading the distasteful meeting ahead. "We know where we're going to be. I just wish I knew exactly what I'm going to say."

"Personally, I'd like to let my fists do the talking." Marc sat down beside her. "But that would solve nothing."

He took her shoulders gently in his hands and turned her to face him. "Stephen Travelle suggested there are two things that you should do immediately. One is write a will."

"Yes," she said. "I was waiting for you to say, 'I told you so' when he suggested that. Stephen is drawing one up that leaves everything to the Cancer Society."

"There is something else you might consider, Cadie," he said slowly.

There was something in his voice that made her nervous. He did not move his hands from her shoulders, but he avoided meeting her eyes.

"Of course, it's your choice," he went on in that same tight voice.

Marc was finding this difficult. He felt like a fraud making the suggestion, even as a temporary measure. The next time Cadie contemplated marriage, it should be for all the right reasons. But announcing they were married was the only course of action he could see that would take her out of the line of fire. If it were a done deed, her husband would be her next of kin. Her uncle would no longer have any reason to try to eliminate her. At the very least, it would make it necessary to get rid of both of them. And Marc would make damned sure that would be impossible.

*   *   *

"My choice?" Cadie asked, her voice trailing off as she began to suspect where this was heading.

Stephen had said the other thing she could change was her next of kin. *Was Marc going to propose some kind of marriage of convenience?*

"If we convinced Jack that we're man and wife, there would no longer be any point in creating another 'accident' for you. We could make double sure by telling him we've drawn up a prenup guaranteeing me half your shares in any deal you made about mining the gold, even if we split up. And, of course, you'd make your husband your heir."

The word "prenup" hit her with a sickening thud. It was happening again.

Calm down, she told herself.

This was different. The whole thing was to be a pretense. And she trusted Marc. Besides, he had never seemed to be overly interested in the money he would make from his own share of the claims. Her experience with Jerry, however, had made her leery about prenuptial agreements.

* * *

He could see her shrinking away from the idea. His business was words, but he knew he had explained his plan very awkwardly.

"We wouldn't have to go through with it, love," he assured her. "We could play the newlyweds without getting the agreement drawn up. You could still get a will drawn right away and leave everything to the Cancer Society to be doubly safe. But don't reject the idea without thinking about it. Short of taking the offensive ourselves and designing a fatal accident for your Uncle Jack, it's the best weapon we have right now."

"I don't need to think about it. I won't play at being your wife."

* * *

Her knee-jerk reaction was to reject the whole idea. It would demean what she felt for Marc if she took part in this pretense of being married to him. She couldn't do it. But what he said did make sense.

She saw his shoulders sag. *Oh, Lord!* This whole topic was too sensitive. Now she'd hurt his feelings by blurting out her rejection of his plan.

"But I will go part way," she mumbled reluctantly.

"What did you say?"

"I will play at being your fiancée."

The flash of joy she saw in his eyes couldn't have been more intense if his proposal had been a real one.

It wasn't. But why not enjoy the pretense she was loved and Marc wanted to be with her forever? She put her arms around his neck and pulled his head down for a long, tender kiss that could have been interpreted as a promise of enduring love.

"It might even be fun." She sighed. "We can have the fantasy without the obligation."

* * *

The almost painful surge of emotion that filled Marc's chest to bursting when he kissed her was beginning to feel familiar. But, even as he tasted her lips and deepened the kiss, he wondered why he wasn't happier about how easily she accepted the fact that he was not promising forever.

He wasn't too thrilled about her obvious relief she didn't have to make any commitment to him either.

CHAPTER 11

Pretending to gaze out at a panoramic view of Lake Ontario and the Toronto islands through the window of their second hotel room in as many days, Cadie sat across a round, glass-topped table from Marc. The Royal York Hotel was as at least as elegant as the King Edward, but modern in style. However, she cared as little about the decor as she did about the view.

It was almost two-thirty. They had only moments to wait for an audience of one to arrive for their little charade.

Fresh from the bittersweet experience of buying a bogus diamond ring to proclaim a bogus engagement, Cadie was afraid to air her private thoughts. She sensed Marc was as unreasonably excited and acutely conscious of the sparkling half-carat zircon solitaire on her finger as she was.

"It looks real enough to convince me that we're engaged," she said with an embarrassed laugh.

Marc stared at her left hand for a minute, then took it and raised it to his lips. He kissed each finger and let his lips linger on the symbol of the promise that they had not made.

"You said it earlier, little one. Why not enjoy this fantasy?"

A crooked smile softened his hard features. When he looked at her like this, with his blue eyes warm and clear as a summer sky, it was hard to discern the cynical loner he had proclaimed himself to be.

"We've never talked about personal dreams. I would guess they include children," was his amazing next statement.

Before she could think, much less respond, the expected knock came at the door.

"Show time," Marc said, placing a quick, hard kiss on her lips. "For luck."

When she opened the door, he was standing at her side, his arm firmly about her waist. If Jack Haywood was surprised to see Marc with her, his affable smile hid it well.

"Katie, honey," he said, his broad grin fading a little when he took in the grim look on her face. "You look wonderful. The northern air—or something," he drawled with an exaggerated, knowing look at Marc, "has done wonders for you. Put roses in your cheeks."

Unsmiling, she waved him to sit in one of the armchairs facing the window. She and Marc sat on the love seat with their backs to the view.

"I can understand why you're surprised to see Cadie at all, much less looking so healthy," Marc said. His voice was tight with suppressed anger. "She was supposed to have spent Saturday night in the room your buddy filled with propane gas."

"Propane?" Jack Haywood's face blanched.

Cadie would have sworn that the news of the latest attempt on her life was a surprise to the older man. Jack's eyes shifted to her. With the color draining from his ruddy cheeks, he looked ill and frightened.

"Did you have an accident with the gas, honey?" he croaked, making a visible attempt to regain his composure.

"Not exactly an accident," Cadie replied. "But I'm sure you're aware of that."

The apparently bewildered man in front of her was not reacting at all the way she had expected.

"I found out about the gold Pop discovered on the property, Uncle Jack. We found the notebook he used to log the core."

"My partner told me about the results. Aren't they amazing?" Jack was managing a pale imitation of his usual vigorous manner. "Who would have believed Dad was right all the time? I want you to know that the offer on the claims I spoke to you about on the telephone still stands. And in my considered opinion, you'd be smart to take it." He beamed as if he had never lied to her about the worth of the claims.

"But tell me about the accident," he said, a thread of worry perceptible in the hearty timbre of his voice. "What caused the gas leak?"

"It was no accident." Marc's voice held the authority of a decade and a half in law enforcement. "Someone opened up the valve on the propane tank as wide as it could go and then turned on the wall light by Cadie's bedroom without lighting it. By morning, all the rooms in the bedroom wing were filled with gas. It's a good thing we didn't sleep there as we usually do, or we wouldn't be alive today. Even at that, we were lucky nothing sparked an explosion."

Jack Haywood was visibly shaken, but years of reacting quickly to confrontation helped him now.

"Just who is this man, Katie?" he blustered. "Should I know him?"

"I'm Marc Banachek. Your father was my landlord and my friend. And, yes, you should know me because, as of today, I'm also Cadie's fiancé. And I'm going to see to it that nobody gets another chance to hurt her."

Cadie extended the third finger of her left hand, with its sparkling ring, toward her only living relative. She hated this travesty of what should have been a happy scene. But she was well aware that there was very little warmth and no real love in this room.

"Well," Jack said. "Well."

For a moment, he didn't seem to be able to even muster a smile. Then he bared his teeth in the best one he apparently could manage, and reached over to shake Marc's hand.

"Congratulations," he said. Then, after a perceptible pause, he muttered, almost to himself, "Yes. That's probably best. Yes."

"I think you should know we're having a prenuptial agreement drawn up, Uncle Jack," Cadie told him crisply, ignoring his congratulations. "Marc already owns a one-eighth interest in the claims. Once we sign the agreement, he would get half if we separate and, of course, inherit the rest of it, if anything were to happen to me."

Jack Haywood's reaction to this news was difficult to read. He nodded his head in acceptance.

"You're putting a lot of trust in this young man," he said with a long look at Marc. "But it's your decision. Anyway, you're too young to be talking about dying and what you're leaving to your heirs, honey. Speaking of the claims…"

When he mentioned the claims, a real note of urgency sounded in his voice. "I hope you'll reconsider the offer I put to you. I might even be able to convince my principals to go higher."

"No, thank you," she said. "This morning, Marc and I gave Stephen Travelle our authorization to negotiate with the companies he and Pop had agreed to approach a few months ago."

"My God, child!" Jack whispered. "You didn't!"

He took her hand and gripped her fingers so hard her pseudo-engagement ring bit into the flesh.

"Don't tell Sandor you did that," he said.

"Sandor? Why would I be speaking to him? I don't know the man."

"Sandor Green has been my business associate for a good many years." Jack paused as if he was deciding what he was going to tell her.

Then, he drew a deep breath and spoke quickly. "The two of us have worked together on a variety of enterprises. Sandor has always been an extremely cool-headed businessman but, recently, the desire to control the Nighthawk Lake claims is becoming an obsession with him. I tried to convince him that, because I'm family, I was the one who could get you to accept our offer, but he insisted on being present at this meeting.

"Because I wanted to have a chance to speak to you first, I misled him a little by telling him that you were coming to the NorthAm suite at three-thirty. He'll be waiting there now. I must call him about the change of locale."

His voice was uncharacteristically subdued. "Trust me on this, Katie. It will be in your own best interests to lead Sandor to believe you're still considering his offer."

As far as Cadie was concerned this unpleasant conversation was over. They had given him their message and she was in no mood to prolong the meeting.

"Uncle Jack, I can see no point in our talking to your partner."

Marc caught her eye. She could see that, for some reason, he did not want her to refuse to meet the man.

"It can't hurt us to hear what Mr. Green has to say, sweetheart," he said.

* * *

From what Jack had all but stated flatly, Marc gathered that Sandor Green was the man behind the attacks on Cadie. Meeting the CEO of NorthAm Mining Corp. face-to-face would give him a chance to size up their opponent.

Jack went to the telephone at the far side of the room. From his end of the telephone conversation, it was clear his partner was less than thrilled with the change in plans. They couldn't make out the words, but they could hear his angry voice across the carpeted expanse.

"That's fine then, Sandor," Jack said with a hearty stage laugh that covered his partner's reply. "They're looking forward to meeting you in a few minutes."

To cover the awkward tension while they waited for Green to arrive, Jack enquired about their imaginary wedding plans.

"Have you decided on a date?" he asked Cadie. "Your Aunt Rose will want to hear all the details."

"As soon as possible," Marc replied for her. "We don't see any reason to wait. Do we, sweetheart?"

The affection in his smile and the eagerness in his voice were convincing enough that Cadie smiled back and returned the warm pressure of his hand.

"We applied for the license this morning," he went on, warming to his role.

"It has all happened so quickly." Cadie jumped in before he could invent any more details.

Jack Haywood's shrewd glance did not miss her blush. Up to that point, he hadn't been inclined to believe in his niece's impetuous love affair. Marc Banachek was certainly a different kettle of fish from that greedy, little operator Cadie had been engaged to last year. Jerry had been easy to deal with, but Jack knew instinctively that there would be no point in ever trying to strike a deal with this fiancé. Although it was totally out of character for Cadie to fall so suddenly, apparently she had done just that. Jack looked at her sparkling eyes. She was completely infatuated with the man, and, from the way he looked at her, Marc was just as nuts about her. The way things had been going lately, perhaps it was just as well.

* * *

When Sandor Green arrived, Cadie was relieved to see he had cooled down and seemed to be prepared to be civil.

From what Stephen Travelle had told them about Sandor Green, Cadie had expected him to be a tougher and slightly rougher version of her uncle. She was dead wrong. Her uncle's partner was a dapper, silver-haired man in his early sixties. His well-modulated voice and crisp mannerisms would be at home in any of the financial boardrooms of the city. He wore an air of authority that was as palpable as the pungent lime aftershave, which struck the only false note in his cultured façade.

"Arcadie Haywood." Inclining his head toward Cadie, he acknowledged Jack's introduction. "I've been looking forward to meeting you. And Marcus Banachek. It's a pleasure."

"The youngsters were telling me, Sandor, that they've just become engaged," Jack warned him.

For a split second, Sandor's heavy-lidded eyes widened and fixed on his partner's bland face.

Then he said smoothly, "My congratulations. I hope you'll allow Jack and me to share in your celebration. I'd be honored if you would be my guests for dinner this evening in the Epic Room."

"That's very generous of you," Marc said, just as smoothly. "But Cadie and I have made other plans for the evening."

Any further conversation was delayed by the arrival of a waiter bearing the coffee service and French pastries Cadie had ordered.

Finally, Sandor came to the point of his visit.

"Jack has informed you, I believe, that I'm interested in being involved in the development of your mining operation at Nighthawk Lake."

His attempt to make the observation sound casual was a failure. Although he kept his eyes focused on the action of his own manicured fingers as they added cream and sugar to his coffee and stirred slowly, his grip on the spoon was tight enough to whiten the tips of his index finger and thumb. He paused while he waited for Cadie's reaction to his opening gambit.

"Yes, he has—" Cadie began.

"Your offer is one of several that we're considering," Marc added.

"But," Cadie hurried on, ignoring Marc's attempt to avoid telling Green the facts, "you should know we met with Stephen Travelle this morning. My grandfather had such trust in him that we've retained him to look after our interests."

Even though Uncle Jack, probably for his own reasons, had advised them to jolly Sandor along, she was determined to get everything out in the open. When Sandor knew she had made other arrangements for the development of the claims and that Uncle Jack was no longer her heir, there would be no point in his attempting to coerce her into dealing with him.

"Why don't you have your legal people get in touch with Stephen?" Marc cut her off again.

Above his fixed, genial smile, Sandor's shuttered eyes gave away nothing.

"I'll do that," he said, setting aside his coffee, untouched. "I'm sorry we will not have the opportunity to celebrate together this evening. However, quite possibly, there will be other celebrations."

He stood and took Cadie's hand. He bared his gleaming teeth at her, then bent to kiss the air above her fingers.

"You're a lovely and charming young woman," he said. "We could have a very enjoyable association."

He turned to Marc and extended his hand. "Take great care of your beautiful fiancée, Marc. The city is dangerous and full of unscrupulous people."

When he left, taking a silent Jack with him, and his cold smile hung in the air like the empty grin of the Cheshire Cat.

An involuntary shudder moved up Cadie's spine and across her shoulders as she stared at the door that had just closed behind her uncle and Sandor Green. Jack Haywood might be a brash four-flusher, but beside his cold-blooded partner, he was almost an appealing figure.

CHAPTER 12

Marc stood beside her with his arm firmly around her waist. His shoulder and arm muscles were still tense with the effort it had taken not to wipe the plastic smile off Sandor's face. Cadie's enemy now had an identity. He wasn't convinced of Jack's innocence, but after seeing him with his partner, Marc had no doubts about which man was orchestrating the attacks against her.

"Don't let them frighten you, love," he said. If he could help it, they would not get near her again. "Come and sit down."

He sat down on the love seat and drew her down onto his lap. Cadie burrowed herself into the warmth of his embrace. "What a horrible man!" she whispered into his shirt front as Marc stroked her back. "I think Uncle Jack's afraid of him."

"It's easy to see why," Marc said. "Cadie..."

A tentative note in his voice made her sit up and look at him.

"You're not going to like this. I should have mentioned it earlier," he began. "I did something else without consulting you. While you were packing yesterday at the lake, I made a phone call to my friend Willy. He's still on the force here and he agreed to have your Uncle Jack and Sandor Green run through the computers for me. Something tells me that our elegant friend Sandor's name will turn up in the files. Maybe we'll get lucky and Willy will get a line on who might be doing NorthAm's dirty work these days.

"Willy's day off is tomorrow so I'm meeting him at his apartment at ten o'clock to see what he's come up with. That means, at best, we won't be able to leave the city before noon."

"Willy?" Cadie could not help asking.

"Willy and I were good friends for almost ten years before the fiasco with Val. He seems to be more than willing to help us out."

With the warm silk under his hands sliding back and forth over the smooth skin of Cadie's back, Marc wasn't wasting another thought on a meaningless affair in the distant past.

"But that's tomorrow morning. Let's concentrate on this evening. What would be the best way to entertain my new fiancée?"

Cadie was relaxing against his chest. She seemed unaware of how her firm thighs were pressing against his eagerly awakening flesh. He nuzzled her neck until his lips and tongue found the sensitive spot just under her jaw where he could feel her pulse beginning to race.

"Should I take her dining and dancing?"

He took her earlobe into his mouth and sucked on it gently. Cadie's moan and the involuntary tensing of her buttocks as she arched against him snapped his semi-arousal to rigid attention.

"Or do I take her to bed and make love to her until neither of us has the strength to move?" he growled as he felt her breast respond against the sensitive palm of his hand. "I know which plan has my vote."

"I guess it's unanimous," she said, with the sensuous half-smile to which he was rapidly becoming addicted.

She had unbuttoned his shirt and was beginning to explore the depression at the base of his throat with little dabbing touches of her tongue when the telephone on the table beside them rang.

"It's probably a wrong number." She sighed. "They'll hang up."

The phone rang twice more. Grudgingly, Marc gave in and yanked the receiver off the hook.

"Banachek," he snapped.

"You're in danger." The person behind the sexless whisper could not get the words out fast enough. "Get out of the hotel before you're both killed."

The whisperer severed the connection. The dial tone droned in his ear as Marc turned back to her. Cadie was looking up at him, the flush of passion draining from her face as she read his reaction to the call.

"Who was it?" she asked.

"I'm not sure. But we have to get out of here right away."

While he quoted the caller's short message to her, he was dialing the front desk. The clerk who responded treated his request to find the source of the phone call as an everyday occurrence and was able to discover with amazing efficiency that the call had originated from a house phone somewhere in the hotel.

"Uncle Jack and Sandor are the only ones who know we're here," Cadie thought aloud, as she straightened her clothing. "Did you tell your friend Willy where we were?"

"I told him we'd be at the King Eddy," Marc replied, quickly buttoning his shirt. "When I was talking to Willy, I didn't know we were going to be here."

Cadie's face was pale but did not show any other trace of fear at this newest threat. He felt a surge of affection and pride. She probably would face all of life's crises with the same spirit. He cautioned himself that he wouldn't be the man at her side when she faced them. This mock engagement was simply a cover they were using until she no longer needed him. In three months, he thought bleakly, his lease would be up.

"We won't check out of this room," he said, drawing himself back to the urgencies of the present. "When we get back to our own hotel, I'll call Willy to get someone to keep an eye on it tonight."

Luckily, when he called the precinct, Willy happened to be there to take the call. Their brief conversation when Marc had called from Nighthawk Lake had been stiff and awkward. This time, he had the feeling they had both come to terms with the incident that caused the two-and-a-half year gap in their friendship.

"No problem," Willy said. "My partner and I have a couple of days off. We'll get down there right away and stake out the room. Leave the key for us at the desk. If the guy who called to warn you knew what he was talking about, we should have a good shot at getting whoever is after your lady."

When Marc tried to thank him for his help, Willy broke in forcefully, "No. No, for Christ's sake, Marc, we both know that I owe you. I'll give you a full report when I see you in the morning."

* * *

That evening, Cadie did her best to make conversation around a room-service dinner and a light romantic comedy on the hotel's movie channel, but the talk was flat and disjointed.

There was too much on her mind that she didn't want to talk about. Wondering what was happening in the hotel room a few blocks away was, of course, predominant. Then there was the question of why Jack—if it was Jack—had warned them. And why he had disguised his voice to do it. Cadie tried to stifle her curiosity about the current state of Marc's relationship with Willy—and with Val.

And she found her eyes coming back to that sparkling fake engagement ring.

* * *

The insipid romance on the television screen wasn't doing anything to divert Marc either. His attention remained focused on the unsettling woman sitting so quietly at his side. He was afraid the announcement of their pseudo-engagement and the disclosure of the terms of a prenuptial agreement had been a poor idea. The whispered warning that had probably come from Jack Haywood suggested it had been an extremely bad one. The plan would have been much more effective if they could have presented their marriage as a *fait accompli.*

When Cadie made up her mind about something, there was no budging her. He could understand her reluctance. He didn't take the idea of playing man and wife lightly either.

He tested the words again in his mind. *Man and wife.* They didn't throw him into the tailspin that they always had in the past.

Had living with a woman who always looked for the best side of everyone and everything clouded his perception of reality? In his experience, most of the time "man and wife" equaled domestic violence or some kind of emotional abuse; fidelity was a locker room joke; and "forever" usually could be translated as "until I get bored."

On the other hand, even though his parents' marriage had always seemed to him to be one of prolonged boredom, it had been solid. And his sister, Eva and her husband, Karl, were deeply in love. He found himself wanting to find examples of marriages that worked—of strong, lasting love that was every bit as real as the other side of the coin.

Good Lord! Maybe being around Cadie had already twisted his realistic perspective.

He jerked his thoughts back to the current problem. Their phony engagement had boomeranged on them by putting pressure on Sandor to get rid of them before they had a chance to sign the agreement or get married.

Impulsively, he reached for Cadie. His need to hold her was almost painful. Her vibrant nearness filled the emptiness he had been living with for so long.

"Marry me, Cadie."

Her marvelous cat's eyes widened.

MINE

The words were as much of a surprise to him as they were to her. Then came the stunning truth that he meant them. She had come to mean so much to him in the past few weeks that he could not imagine a life without her.

* * *

Cadie saw the strange look flash across his face. *Damn him!* Why was he doing this to her? He was regretting his proposal even as the words came out of his mouth.

She would die of embarrassment if he was doing this because he had guessed she was in love with him. Or maybe he had fooled her about his lack of interest in the potential gold mine. Whatever his motives were for this unexpected proposal, her pride would not let her marry a man who did not—who would never—love her. She forced herself to hide her turmoil behind a fond smile.

"You don't really want to marry me," she said, draping her arms around his neck. "You're a good friend, Marc. And you are a fantastic lover. But we mustn't let ourselves forget the ring is only a zircon pretending to be a diamond. This engagement charade is exciting and fun, but it was designed to fool Uncle Jack and Sandor—not us."

* * *

He did not blame her for doubting he was serious. He had made it abundantly clear to her that he would never promise forever to any woman. But, as he looked into the revealing, green-gold depths of her eyes, he saw her lighthearted words were a lie. Cadie would never have made love with him at all if her feelings for him had not run deep. And her untutored and wholehearted lovemaking was driven by something more compelling than a need for physical fulfillment. Cadie might not be aware of it yet but she loved him. And he cared for her…deeply. For now, he would play it her way.

"I'm not withdrawing the offer, little one. I was serious. I want you more than I've ever wanted anything in my life. But"—he grinned when he saw her eyes begin to glow—"until I can convince you to make this a real engagement, I'm willing to do my best to make your charade exciting."

His lips met hers in a playful, nibbling kiss that quickly lost its playfulness. When his tongue found the hidden places he had discovered drove her wild, her fingers plunged into his thick hair.

Marc's lovemaking held a touch of desperation that night. He was not quite ready to admit in words how much he felt for her, but he tried to show it to her without speaking.

In the dim light of morning, he watched Cadie begin to stir in his arms. Her face in repose was serene; her lips relaxed into a half-smile. Her silky dark blonde hair with its brilliant streaks of platinum trailed in thick strands across his chest. She lay half on top of him with her left hand curled over his heart. He smiled wryly. She didn't know that, such as it was, it now belonged to her. If she decided to go back to her life in Colorado, she would take it with her.

* * *

Her eyes opened slowly and her smile deepened as she met his tender gaze.

"Hi," she breathed, wishing she could freeze this moment and keep it fresh in her mind forever.

He leaned down and kissed her forehead. "Good morning, sweetheart," he said.

"I love you, Marc."

The calm statement of absolute fact came from nowhere.

He held her for a long moment. He had hoped she loved him, had even begun to believe she did, but hearing her say the words made him even more uncertain if what he felt for her was enough to make her happy. She apparently knew what she meant by the word "love." He didn't. Was "love" feeling alive only when she was near, being willing to lay his life on the line to keep her safe, being willing even to give her up so she could be happy? What if he could not be the kind of man she needed him to be? Lord knew he wanted to try!

"Cadie—" he began. But she put her fingers over his mouth.

"You don't have to say anything. This doesn't change our agreement. I shouldn't have said anything, but I feel better now you know."

Marc's expression was unreadable. His eyes searched her face, then he pulled her into his arms and held her there.

She should have controlled her tongue, but, even at the risk of losing whatever it was they shared by her admission, she wanted him to know. Had her selfish need to express her love had made him sorry he couldn't love her back?

"I wish we didn't have to get moving again this morning," he said. "But we have business that has to be done before we leave. Someday…"

Cadie was afraid her confession had probably ruined the chance of their having any "somedays."

She slid out of his arms. The sight of her poised naked by the side of the bed made him reach for her again. However, she eluded his grasp and said with a forced grin, "Right. Business. But this morning, I get the first shower."

* * *

While he had the room to himself, Marc called Willy's apartment to find out the results of the stakeout. After half a dozen rings, however, he got only the answering machine. He wondered if that meant they had captured whoever Jack Haywood thought was going to attack them and were at the station going through the formalities of booking them. Unfortunately, it was just as possible something had gone very wrong and, for some reason, Willy had been unable to reach Marc to tell him about it.

He would try to call Willy again later. In the meantime, Marc could only hope his ex-buddy was at the precinct involved in paperwork. In order to save time, he phoned room service and ordered croissants and a large carafe of coffee for their breakfast.

Cadie, clad only in a short terry cloth robe, emerged barefooted from the bathroom vigorously brushing out her damp hair. Marc forced himself to keep his eyes off her and told her about the calls he had made.

"I hope you're right about why Willy isn't home yet," was her only comment.

By the time Marc had finished his own quick shower, breakfast had arrived.

"Now that I'm almost awake," Cadie said, after her first swallow of coffee, "what is the business we have to take care of this morning before you see Willy?"

"I've been thinking about the act we put on for your Uncle Jack and Sandor, Cadie. All we've done to back it up is buy that ring. I don't know how carefully the NorthAm pair might check up on our activities, but if I were in their shoes, I wouldn't simply take us at our word. I'd find some way to check if we'd taken out a marriage license."

"What are you suggesting?"

"It would be simple enough to take care of. After you see Travelle and sign the will, we take a few minutes to go over to city hall and get one."

Cadie's stiff expression was not encouraging.

"Humor me," he coaxed. "There aren't any medical or citizenship requirements. For a few bucks and about an hour of our time, we'd have an official piece of paper to back up our statement. And there's only a three-day waiting period before we could be married."

Cadie's lips tightened into a straight line. He couldn't tell if she found his suggestion ridiculous or painful.

"Are we trying to put pressure on Sandor to make a move?" she asked.

"Good Lord, no. We're going to remain invisible. Then, as far as they're concerned, we're going to be married."

"Do you think all this intrigue is necessary?"

"I do. Of course, if that's not enough"—he picked up her hand and pressing his lips to its palm—"we could actually get married on Friday."

* * *

"Don't joke about it," Cadie snapped, getting to her feet. She did not even try to hide her reluctance to make a mockery of these real steps toward marriage. How could he treat the idea lightly when he knew how she felt?

"Let's get the show on the road." She made her voice as brisk and unemotional as she could. "If you're meeting Willy at ten o'clock, we'll want to be first in line at the license bureau."

Two hours later, they left city hall with the marriage license in Cadie's purse. It was only a flimsy piece of paper, but it seemed to weigh a ton. They had actually filed their intention to be married within the next three months! She felt as guilty as if she had committed perjury.

When they returned to the suite, the message indicator on the phone was flashing red light. Marc called down to the desk immediately and had the operator connect him to the caller's number.

"Willy?" he responded when his friend answered. "How did it go?" There was a short silence. "Thank goodness for that. You and your partner are okay? Yeah. Did you find out who they are?"

He blew out a long whistle. "Patel, you say. Nope. I've no idea."

From Marc's laconic utterances, Cadie gathered neither Willy nor his partner had been injured. She waited impatiently for him to get off the line and tell her what had happened.

"All right," Marc signed off. "I'll be there in about half an hour.

Thanks, buddy."

"The warning was right on, Cadie. Willy and his partner got to our hotel room at the Royal York at about seven o'clock and got themselves set up. They rolled up two blankets and put them in the bed. Then they hid in the closet. And, sure enough, at two in the morning, two armed guys broke in. Willy and his partner surprised them, but not before one of the gunmen put bullets into both rolled blankets."

Cadie gasped. "Your friend and his partner weren't hurt?"

"Not a scratch. The perps dropped their weapons without any attempt to fire them again. They won't wriggle out of this charge. They were caught in the act. Willy says they kept at them all night at the station, but couldn't get them to reveal who'd sent them. At least, not yet."

"I got the impression from your side of the conversation that the police know who they are," Cadie prompted.

"They're a couple of pros. Both of them have a long list of arrests. One of them, Sal Boni, is known to work for Franco Patel. Patel's lawyer is acting for them."

"I never heard of Franco Patel."

"He's considered a comer in the ranks of organized crime in this area. He stays out of the news and out of prison, but he's connected. I wonder what he has to do with our problems."

He looked worried when he took her chin between his thumb and forefinger and raised it so he could look into her eyes. "We're not out of the woods yet, love, but we've made a start.

"I wish I didn't have to leave you, but Willy has some information on Sandor and a list of his past connections that he wants me to look at. I'm pretty sure Willy will be more willing to share confidential material with me if I'm alone." "I shouldn't be gone long. You'll be fine if you don't leave the suite. No one knows you're here. Just read the weekend papers and try to relax. Don't answer the door. As soon as I get back, we'll check out and head back up north."

Without even waiting for her to agree to go along with his orders, he pressed a hard kiss on her lips and was gone.

To her surprise, Cadie didn't resent Marc's series of abrupt commands. This, obviously, was the way he dealt with a crisis. Besides, he'd called the situation "our problems."

The room was not just empty without him. He left a vacuum in his wake. She raised a finger to touch her still- tingling lips and stared unseeingly at the intricate pattern of the carpet. Her brain seemed stuck in one groove. If they had stayed in the room at the Royal York, they would have been shot! Hired gunmen would have killed them.

She shook her head. It was all too melodramatic to be happening to her. She hadn't really allowed herself to believe how serious the propane incident had been. However, there was nothing ambiguous about this latest attack. Someone wanted her dead.

By announcing that they were engaged, Marc had made himself a target along with her. Oh Lord, why hadn't she seen that? She had even gone along with putting a semi-official stamp on the lie this morning. She had been too eager to live the fantasy to think about the consequences. The sensuous haze created by their lovemaking had blinded her to the fact that the pretended engagement put Marc in danger.

There must be something she could do. She thought of her uncle's pale, perspiring face as she had seen it yesterday afternoon. He must be afraid he was next in line if his partner got rid of her before her supposed marriage. Was he too terrified to testify against Sandor? If she talked to him alone, maybe she could get him to open up to her about Sandor's activities. They could go to the police together. He had, after all, warned them about last night's attack. His statement could convince the police to arrest Sandor for attempted murder.

Marc would be furious if he knew what she was about to do, but she hadn't ever believed she was in physical danger from Jack Haywood. If she could convince her uncle to go to the police with her, this whole nightmare would be over.

He might be easier to convince if she caught him by surprise. She would not call him until she got to the Royal York.

* * *

"I'm downstairs in the lobby," Cadie repeated into the house phone a very few minutes later.

"Have you lost your mind?" Her uncle's frightened whisper sent chills down her spine.

"That's great, Walter!" he said loudly. "I'll pick up the papers later this morning. I knew we could count on you."

She heard a muffled voice in the background, then what could have been a door closing.

"Get out of the hotel before someone sees you," Uncle Jack said urgently. "There's a tunnel from the lobby that leads to Union Station across the street. Look for the sign. You can't miss it. I'll meet you in the Union Station coffee shop as soon as I can."

She stood holding the receiver for a few moments after he hung up, while she looked around to see if anyone appeared to be paying any special attention to her. In her Italian leather boots, trim beige pants, and hand-knit fisherman's sweater, she blended in quite well with the upscale clientele of the hotel.

With the exception of the fast-talking salesman on the phone next to her who was giving her a thorough once-over as he made his pitch, no one seemed to notice that she was there. She scanned the lobby unsuccessfully for a moment before she spotted the discreet sign for the entrance to the tunnel that led to Union Station. She hung up the receiver with relief and walked quickly toward it.

Some of Uncle Jack's tension seems to have rubbed off on me, she thought as she hurried down the brightly lit, tile-lined walkway under Front Street. It seemed odd to find herself alone in such a busy city, listening to the solitary, sharp echo of her own rapid footsteps. Then the echo was joined with another, then one more. Whoever was in the tunnel behind her was gaining on her. She lengthened her stride.

She emerged, breathless, into the cavernous heart of the old train station where crowds of people were going about their reassuringly normal business. Only then did she turn to see who had been following her. She had a brief moment of panic when she recognized the heavy-set salesman who had been using the next house phone in the hotel. To her relief, he paid no attention to her and joined the stream of people hurrying toward the train concourse.

Inordinately relieved, Cadie told herself to calm down. No one had followed her. She spotted the coffee shop and quickly stepped inside. It was not crowded. She ordered a cup of coffee, and took it to an empty table at the very back, where she settled herself to wait for Jack. She wished she had bought a magazine to look at as she fought the temptation to check her watch every few seconds. Not many interminable minutes later, Jack Haywood arrived. When he sat down across from her, she could see he had regained some of his bluff manner.

"Well, Katie, honey, I didn't expect to see you again so soon."

His smile was broad, but his eyes looked strained.

"Sandor was just leaving when you called. He didn't catch up with you in the lobby, did he?"

"I didn't see him. There's no time to waste, Uncle Jack. You're going to have to help me," she said. "I know about the men who were sent to our room last night."

"What men?" he said with obviously feigned surprise.

"You called Marc to warn us."

* * *

He clamped his jaw shut and frowned at her. Only the uncertain shifting of his eyes revealed the state of his nerves.

Jack Haywood swallowed. For the first time in his life, he was having trouble finding words. The shocking realizations he had come to yesterday afternoon after he and Sandor left Cadie and Marc's room seemed to be short circuiting the workings of his brain. Until then, he hadn't realized that his partner's interest in the Haywood claims had become a full-blown obsession. When the door to the company suite closed behind them, Sandor had given vent to his frustration in a long string of vulgar epithets.

"I thought he was imagining things," Sandor had muttered, sitting down at the little table and rummaging in the briefcase that he had left in the room. "He told me the other night that she and Banachek were shacked up together, but I didn't think that was important. I was more concerned that they'd found the log book."

"Who was it that told you?"

Jack had begun to realize how little he knew about Sandor's recent activities.

Sandor ignored his question. "That little bimbo has more lives than a cat. I'm not going to let her cheat me out of what you Haywoods owe me. Your Daddy George kept you out of jail for the Bachelor Lake thing, but paying my lawyer's fees didn't balance out the five years of my life I lost. It's payback time, Jack. There's no other way. She has to die before she can sell the claims out from under me or get married."

"What good would killing her do?" Jack had tried to reason with him. The dreadful reality of his position hit him. "Even the stupidest cop will realize I'm the one who profits from her death. We'd never get those claims."

Sandor found the phone number that he had been looking for and was reaching for the telephone.

"Why would anyone connect you with her death when she and her fiancé are killed by a thief they surprise in their hotel room?" he said disdainfully. "I warned them about the dangers of the city. You heard me do it."

His bark of a laugh had been empty of humor. When Jack had seen the cold implacability in his partner's eyes, he'd realized there was no point in trying to talk him out of making his call. His partner's greed had taken him beyond reason. He intended to eliminate Cadie and Marc. And, the killing might not stop there.

"He ran his handkerchief over his damp forehead. His partner had him in a vice. With the damning evidence that Sandor had locked away in that safety deposit box, Jack knew he'd have no choice but to transfer the title of the claims to NorthAm. And once he'd done that, he had to admit that quite possibly, his days would be numbered.

NorthAm had had financial problems before, but this time Sandor had apparently lost his grip. Yesterday in the kids' hotel room, his usually cool, controlled partner had begun making threats like the villain in an old melodrama.

Jack had thought he knew what was going on in NorthAm's quest to get the claims he should have inherited from his father. He'd been taken completely by surprise when Marc and his niece had all but accused him of hiring someone to engineer a propane leak in her bedroom. The memory of Sandor chewing somebody out on the phone Sunday afternoon for "screwing up again" had passed through his mind; however, until he overheard Sandor actually arranging to have them killed last night, he would never have believed he would go so far to get control of a prospective gold mine.

* * *

"Katie, I don't have any way to prove it to you, but I didn't have anything to do with the attempts on your life."

How was it he could always sound sincere when he was putting over a shaky deal, yet sound this phony when he was trying to convince Cadie of the absolute truth?

"Sandor and I have shaved some laws to swing the odd deal in the past, but we've never come close to murder. I don't even know him any more."

His voice became more urgent. "You don't know the kind of connections he has. Go away. Leave the country with your fiancé until your business arrangements about Nighthawk Lake are sewed up tight. You won't be safe until then."

"There's no guarantee that he won't have us harmed anyway. You have to help me to turn him over to the police. You were there when he hired the men to kill us. Your testimony could get him put away."

"I can't, Katie." His drumming fingers showed his agitation. "I tried to dissolve our partnership a few years ago, but he has some papers with my signature on them that would ruin me. Your Aunt Rose has stuck by me through some hard times, but if this came out, she couldn't handle it. I can't do that to her."

Cadie's hopes for a quick end to their troubles faded. She saw her uncle for the weak man he had always been. She should have known he wouldn't do the right thing simply to get her out of danger.

"Marc is convinced you're the one trying to kill me. I told him you were capable of stealing from me, but I didn't think you would hurt me," she said bluntly.

Anger flashed in his tired eyes. "Getting Dad's property from you wouldn't be stealing. Damn it, I was his son."

He grasped her hand and looked straight into her eyes. "You're right in a way. I did go after Peter's claims. I made an agreement with that ass, Jerry, to get you to sell them to me, but I have never done anything to put you in danger."

She told him what she had learned from Elsie about the possibility the car crash that had nearly killed her in Colorado had not been an accident. She described the attempts to frighten her into selling out and leaving Nighthawk Lake—the bats, the rabbit, the shooting, and finally the propane incident.

"I swear, Katie, I knew nothing about any of that. But I don't know Sandor any more. I think he's losing his mind. He has twisted something that happened years ago around so he believes he has a right to the Nighthawk claims. I don't know who he has working for him up in Chartwell Falls, but Sandor and I have been together a couple of times when he has received phone calls from up there. My old partner plays his cards close to his vest a lot of the time. But until yesterday, I thought he was abiding by our agreement that I was to be in charge of convincing you to sell to us."

"We need you to testify against him, Uncle Jack," she pleaded. She had to make one last attempt. "The men who tried to kill Marc and me won't say a word about who hired them. You're the only other one who knows Sandor is guilty."

"I can't do it, honey."

There was real regret and a touch of shame on his florid face.

"I wish to hell I could, but I can't face prison at this stage of my life, and the disgrace would kill your Aunt Rose. I just can't.

"Leave," he said, standing up. "Marry your young man. Leave and don't come back until you've made sure there's no way that NorthAm can get your mine."

He gave her a half-hearted wave before he turned to leave the coffee shop. Cadie stared after him. His rotund figure had lost its brash jauntiness. She had failed. She pushed aside the half-cup of cold coffee, placed some coins beside it and looked at her watch. She had plenty of time to walk to the King Edward and still get back to the suite before Marc did. Maybe the exercise and the fresh air—or what passed for fresh air in the heart of downtown Toronto—would raise her spirits a little.

She emerged from the station right at noon as hordes of office workers were pouring out of the concrete towers for their midday escape. When she reached the corner of King and Yonge streets, she had to wait for the light with an impatient crowd who did not want to waste a minute of their lunch hour. The heavy traffic passing by seemed to be made up of drivers who had the same turn of mind. Every driver seemed to be looking for a chance to change lanes to save a few seconds. A turquoise-and-pink taxi was in the act of cutting off a dawdling van to swoop into the curb lane in front of her when Cadie felt two strong hands push hard into the small of her back.

The last thing she was conscious of as she stumbled forward into the path of the taxi was a whiff of lime-scented cologne.

CHAPTER 13

Cadie opened her eyes to find herself staring at the polished metal interior of an ambulance. She was lying on a stretcher with an itchy red blanket tucked tightly around her. A wiry, middle-aged man in a dark blue uniform was taking her blood pressure. He nodded pleasantly at her and smiled. Outside the open back doors of the ambulance, she could hear a man protesting loudly to a policeman that he was not guilty of careless driving.

It hurt to turn her head. When she did, she could see the rear end of a taxicab. By its flamboyant paint job, she recognized it as the one into whose path she'd been pushed.

"I swear," the driver was insisting, "she jumped out in front of me. I did my best to miss her. If I hadn't done a one-eighty, I'd a run right over her."

"She's awake," the paramedic called out as he removed the pressure cuff.

"I didn't jump," she told the police officer. It was a struggle to articulate her words. "I felt someone's hands on my back. He pushed me right into the path of that cab."

"Did you see the person who did it?" The policeman's voice was noncommittal, and she wasn't able to tell from his impassive, square face whether he believed her or not.

When she shook her head in reply, the resulting jolt of pain blurred her vision.

"You're lucky that cabbie had such good reflexes. If he hadn't swerved when he did, you'd be history. And, believe it or not, some honest citizen picked up your purse off the pavement," he said, tucking it in beside her on the stretcher. "I'm going to see if I can find some witnesses to the incident. Then I'll come to the hospital shortly to get a detailed statement from you."

By the time the ambulance reached the hospital, the paramedics had treated the cut on her forehead and the scrapes on her cheek and her chin and put a temporary splint on her left wrist. It had apparently twisted under her when the broadside of the taxi had swung around and knocked her to the ground. Her ribs, which had taken most of the impact, were painful when she breathed.

She'd had the distinct impression it had been Sandor Green who had given her that vicious push into the oncoming traffic, but she couldn't be sure. She was basing her suspicion on one second's awareness of a strong scent of lime cologne. Green was only one of thousands of men who had the bad taste to wear it. Besides, the scent didn't necessarily have to have anything to do with the person who had pushed her. Whoever that was must have followed her from Union Station. Her impulsive decision to trust Jack Haywood and ask for his help was looking extremely foolish at this point.

She wished she'd taken Marc's advice and waited for him in the suite. *Marc!* He had no idea where she was. As soon as she could get to a phone, she had to call him. He should be back at the hotel any time now.

During the next two hours, while she was waiting for various medical personnel to see her, Cadie managed only once to talk a nurse into allowing her to go as far as the pay phones. She reached the hotel but there was no answer at the suite. Where was he? Frustrated and on the verge of tears, she called the front desk on the off chance Marc had left a message for her. He had. Actually, he had called three times and, each time, had left a number where he could be reached. He must be beside himself with worry.

Before she could dial that number, a determined orderly arrived to wheel her down to Radiology. After another long, frustrating wait in a hospital corridor, the x-rays were taken and read. Back in the emergency ward, the frazzled-looking young doctor who had examined her initially informed her that, fortunately, no bones were broken. Her ribs were only bruised and her wrist sprained. At long last, she gave her a prescription for pain medication and Cadie was released.

As soon as she was dressed again in her own clothes, Cadie made her painful way to a telephone to call the latest number Marc had left for her.

After two rings, an answering machine clicked in.

"Hi," a woman's low voice greeted her, "you have reached 555-8124. We can't come to the phone right now, but if you leave your number, we'll get back to you as soon as we can."

She stared at the receiver. The woman had not identified herself, but Cadie had a chilling hunch that the confident voice belonged to Val. She told herself she was letting her imagination run away with her. But it could be that seeing his friend, Willy, had not been Marc's only mission this morning. He'd also gone to visit his former lover.

Cadie reminded herself that he had left the woman's phone number for her. But it appeared they did not want to be interrupted. She told herself her jealous suspicions were ridiculous...but could Val be the reason he'd looked so guilty when Cadie had blurted out that she loved him?

Compared to the excruciating pain that gripped her heart, the aches of her body paled into insignificance. She had done it again. She had believed that a man really cared for her. When she had discovered Jerry's deceit, only her pride had been damaged. But this time, she had been incautious enough to fall in love.

Oh Lord, she did not have the strength to handle this now. She wished she could take Uncle Jack's advice and run away so she did not have to face Marc. But she wasn't in any condition to take off on her own. Dejected and defeated, she depressed the telephone hook to get a dial tone and called a taxi to take her back to the King Edward Hotel.

* * *

In the meantime, in their suite at that hotel, Marc's state of mind had gone beyond worry. He paced the two rooms searching again for the note that should have been there. Where could she have gone? She'd agreed to stay in the suite. The first couple of times he'd called, he thought she might have slipped out for a moment to pick up something at one of the shops in the hotel lobby. But she had been gone for hours. What had happened to take her away from here? Had Sandor found her?

After leaving Cadie here this morning, he had gone directly to Willy's apartment. In their telephone conversation, Willy had let slip that he and Val were still working as partners, but having Val answer the door to Willy's apartment was a surprise.

MINE

"Hello, Marc," she'd said. Val's voice was neutral, but she avoided meeting his eyes.

He gave her a cautious greeting and followed her into the living room. Seeing her again was awkward. Their parting had been swift and unemotional. No more than a few clipped words had passed between them when she had moved her things out of his condo two-and-a-half years ago.

"He's here," she said unnecessarily and moved to stand by Willy.

He grasped Marc's hand and shook it. "It's good to see you again, Marc. I didn't want to explain over the phone," he said, slipping his arm possessively around Val's shoulders. "And I can't tell you how much I wish you'd found out about Val and me some other way two years ago. But it was something we couldn't help. We've been together ever since you left and we're planning to get married at Christmas. It would mean a lot to me if you could wish us well."

Marc looked at the statuesque redhead standing with Willy's arm around her, and could hardly believe he had ever been intimate with her. He certainly couldn't raise the slightest twinge of jealousy about Willy's claim on her. It was more important to him to know Willy hadn't betrayed his trust for an insignificant roll in the hay. Suddenly a great weight shifted from Marc's shoulders. His face relaxed in a sincere smile.

"Congratulations," he said.

That out of the way, they got right down to business. Willy and Val were the police officers who had done the stakeout on the hotel room and captured the two suspects the night before. As of a few minutes ago, the gunmen were still silent about who had hired them and were closeted with Patel's lawyer. Nevertheless, Willy thought they would eventually cooperate.

Val had come up with a short list of Sandor Green's and Jack Haywood's brushes with the law that spanned the last three decades.

"I made a printout for you before we left the precinct." Val handed him a couple of sheets of perforated computer paper.

"I think you're barking up the wrong tree with those two," Willy had said. "They're a couple of slippery con men, just smart enough to stay on the right side of the law. If Sandor had hired those guns who tried to kill you and Cadie last night, it was a far cry from his usual style."

Marc took a few minutes to look it over.

"I see what you mean," he said. "Sandor has bad taste in friends, but he and Jack don't appear to have gone in for violence. They've sailed pretty close to the wind a few times, but Jack's managed to stay out of jail."

In fact, the only time Jack had even had charges laid against him was the fraud case thirty years ago and those charges had been dropped. Sandor had served some jail time over that incident.

"You remember Scully?" Willy had asked.

"I heard he retired."

"Yeah, he's working security at the RoyalYork," Willy told him. "He was able to get me a copy of the record of incoming and outgoing phone calls billed to the NorthAm's suite over the past few days. Interested?"

When they met the ex-policeman at a nearby donut shop after he came off shift, Marc wasted no time running down the list of phone numbers. Immediately, he recognized one that appeared several times. It belonged to the Wheelwright farm. There was also an unfamiliar number with the Chartwell Falls' exchange.

Willy had pointed out another call to the travel agency that served as a front for Franco Patel's less legal businesses. That call had been made at four o'clock the previous afternoon, right after Sandor and Jack had left his and Cadie's room...

Where the hell is Cadie?

There was the sound of unsteady footsteps in the hall. Marc stopped mid-stride when he heard them stop outside the sitting room door. He rushed to open it.

A pale and battered Cadie stood there, tottering a bit as the door jerked open just as she was reaching to put the electronic key in the lock. Dark bruises and scrapes marked her cheek and her chin. There was a good-sized bandage on her forehead and a splint strapped to her left wrist. Her hair was disheveled and her jacket was streaked with dark oily stains and had a jagged tear on the front. She looked as if she'd been mugged.

"My God, sweetheart! What happened to you?" Marc drew her into the room and closed the door behind her. He attempted to embrace her, but she crossed her arms in front of her body like a protective cage to avoid his hug.

"No. Don't. My ribs hurt," she said, moving slowly and painfully to the couch.

He squatted down in front of her, obviously deeply concerned.

"Tell me. What happened?" he repeated.

"I was hit by a car," she told him.
"Where?"
"Not far from the hotel."

* * *

She bit her lip. He didn't love her, but he did care about her safety. She had to tell him what she'd done, but she was at the end of her emotional tether. She didn't want to talk about it now. She would either scream at him or break down and cry if she had to deal with the anger she could see building in him.

"Sweetheart," he said through clenched teeth, "don't make me drag it out of you. What were you doing on the street? You knew it was dangerous to leave here."

"I went to see Uncle Jack."

"You went to... For the love of God, woman, don't you have any sense at all?"

* * *

Marc wanted to throttle her. He wanted to kiss her. Didn't she know what it would do to him if anything happened to her? She was glaring back at him, her pointed chin in the air, obviously in pain, but feisty as ever.

"He as much as admitted he knew about Sandor hiring the men to kill us. I tried to get him to go to the police. But he can't. Sandor is holding something over his head."

When he saw a sheen of tears forming in her eyes, he stifled his automatic response. The last thing she needed was a lecture. He moved to sit beside her on the couch and took her hand. He had to touch her to reassure himself that she was really here.

"All right," he began, making himself speak calmly. "First, tell me about the accident."

"I was on my way back here after talking with Uncle Jack. I was standing at the curb with a crowd of people waiting for the light to change, when somebody gave me a hard push. I didn't see who did it."

Looking at him with wide eyes that still held terror in them, she poured out every detail of what she had been through since she had stumbled into the path of a taxi, with the strong scent of lime cologne in her nostrils.

"Oh, Marc, I was so frightened and bewildered. When the doctor finally told me I could leave the hospital, I called the hotel again. You weren't here so I called the desk and got the number you left. But when I dialed it, all I got was a taped message on the answering machine."

"I should never have left you," Marc said. "Your call must have just missed me at Willy's apartment. Willy and I went to see a friend who works at the RoyalYork. He gave us the list of phone calls made from the NorthAm suite. Val should have still been at the apartment though."

He caught the flash of pain in her eyes. Cadie couldn't believe that he still cared about Val, could she?

"Willy and Val are still partners. They were the ones who captured the men in our hotel room last night," he told her, irrationally pleased that she might be jealous. "The apartment where I went today belongs to them. Actually, they're planning to be married at Christmas."

* * *

Marc's expression told Cadie what she wanted to know. His relationship with Val and its painful ending had been laid to rest. The only emotion in his eyes was concern for her.

He leaned over and touched the dark bruise beside the gauze bandage on her forehead with a gentle caress.

"Did the doctor tell you to stay put for a day or two or do you think you're up to the drive back to the lake in the morning?"

"All she told me was that time and rest would heal the bruises and the sprained wrist. She didn't forbid me to travel."

She tilted her head back, inviting the reassuring warmth of his lips. The intensity of his kiss showed her how unwarranted her jealousy had been. Maybe he could learn to love her. Cradled in his arms, she felt safe for the first time since he had left her this morning. But they weren't safe.

"Uncle Jack suggested we leave the country until we have an ironclad agreement on the mining claims," she told him.

"Jack Haywood is the last person I'd rely on for advice," he muttered, "but maybe I should take you some place where he won't be able to find you."

"It's not Uncle Jack. It's his partner who is trying to kill us, Marc," she insisted. "But please, let's go back to the lake right away. Why can't we go home tonight?"

* * *

Cadie looked as if she needed to be tucked into the nearest bed for a week's rest, but he shared her urgent need to get out of the city quickly.

Sandor seemed to be able to find her too easily here. At least, strangers were easily noticed in Chartwell Falls.

He made the decision.

"I'll call Wilde's," he said, striding to the telephone, "and tell them we want the new alarm system activated first thing in the morning. We won't check out. We'll just get ourselves out of here immediately and head up home. We can do the checking out by phone in the morning."

Cadie closed her eyes and sighed. He could see the deep breath was painful for her. "I'm looking forward to sleeping in my own bed."

Marc hung up the receiver. "The senior Wilde brother is going to meet us at Nighthawk Lake at nine o'clock tomorrow morning," he said.

"Good!" she said and opened her eyes. Marc was looking at her thoughtfully. "What is it?"

"I'm having second thoughts about spending the night at the lake before the security system is working, love. You can still get a good rest if we book a room at a lodge near the lake. You can stretch out in the back seat on the way up. We'll still be home when Joe Wilde shows up in the morning."

"Marcus Banchek! No one who saw the accident, and the man who pushed me, would ever believe I'd be in any shape to spend four hours in a car tonight. Or crazy enough to want to. But I am. I want to go home."

"We'd be there at the crack of dawn, Cadie."

But Cadie was not to be swayed. "Tonight. Please, Marc."

They made only two brief stops on the way up—one at a fast-food drive-through and the other to pick up an extremely happy Lurch at the vet's. With those exceptions, Cadie slept solidly while Marc drove. As a result, when she had to move her sore muscles to give up the back seat to the dog, she had difficulty maneuvering herself into the front seat.

At ten o'clock that night they turned onto the driveway at Nighthawk Lake. The outside lights were on, but the house itself was in darkness when they pulled up in front.

"Stay where you are while Lurch and I check the place out, sweetheart," Marc said.

Cadie rolled down her window and breathed the crisp, clean air. There was no moon and the windless night was eerily silent. She could hear Lurch's energetic inspection of the outdoor perimeter of the property, but the black dog had disappeared from sight almost immediately. It was easy to keep track of Marc's progress through the house by the lights he turned on.

When the whole building was ablaze with light, he emerged.

"Everything looks good," he said.

When Cadie tried to stand, she gasped with pain. Without a word, Marc gently picked her up and carried her inside. He placed her on the sofa in front of the fireplace and tucked the bright crocheted afghan Vi had left folded on the end of the sofa around her. Then he proceeded to touch a match to the ready-laid fire.

"Vi seems to have been hard at work," he said, over his shoulder. "She left a full cookie jar in the middle of the kitchen table. Can I get you something to drink and a couple of her cookies?"

"You're almost too good to be true, Marcus Banachek. There's no reason why I can't walk to the kitchen and back, but I like the way you spoil me. I'd love a cup of decaf and some of Vi's cookies."

Every muscle in her body ached and her wrist throbbed. She stretched her hands out toward the fire. The heat felt good.

"This is bliss," Cadie sighed when Marc returned with two steaming mugs and a plate of chocolate chip cookies on a tray.

"I could've called Vi to ask her to be here when we arrived," he said, placing the tray on the coffee table, "but she'll be here in the morning anyway."

He lifted her legs, draped in their afghan, as he sat down, then lowered them across his lap. Cadie couldn't believehow natural the casual intimacy felt.

"I decided," he went on, "it probably wouldn't be smart to let the Wheelwrights know we're back."

Cadie raised a quizzical eyebrow.

"I told you about the printout of phone calls to and from the NorthAm suite. The number of the Wheelwright farm appeared several times over the last few days. I can't believe the whole family is involved. But one of them sure as hell is."

"But not Vi."

"Probably not Vi," he agreed, "or she;d have stayed out of the bedroom when someone was shooting at your window. But if it's Sam or Luke or both of them, that would explain how they know what's going on in this house."

"But they're not killers!"

"There's a lot of money involved, little one."

*   *   *

Marc was too familiar with the crimes people committed when only a few dollars were involved. He wished he could somehow shelter her from the unpleasant fact that her persecutor was probably someone she knew and liked.

"There was another Chartwell Falls phone number listed on NorthAm's account. I'll get Chuck to find out whose it is."

"That means Sandor's man is not necessarily Sam or Luke." Cadie was grasping at straws, but these were people that Pop had known all his life.

"Maybe." Marc did not sound hopeful. "Val dug up a few facts about the mess that Jack and Sandor were in thirty years ago. It seems Sandor served time for fraud, but Jack came out of the scam without a stain on his record. It was Sandor's testimony that cleared him.

"Something else about Sandor. Apparently, he grew up on the same street as Franco Patel. They're friends, but there's no record of the two of them doing business together. Sandor and Jack have skated pretty close to the edge of illegal activity and their names have come up in the occasional investigation over the years, but the only thing on the official record is the one fraud conviction. One of Willy's business sources told him there've been persistent rumors over the last year or so about NorthAm having serious financial trouble."

"So that's why Sandor is so desperate to get his hands on this property."

Cadie's eyelids kept drifting closed. She had finally run out of steam.

"Come on, little one. Put your arm around my neck," Marc said, picking her up in his arms. He got no argument. "We're going to bed."

After he had helped her into her nightgown and tucked her into bed, he kissed her lightly on the lips and went to do another tour of the house. He brought Lurch in, told him to lie down at the foot of the bed, then, placing his revolver on the floor under the head of the bed where he could reach it quickly, stripped down to his briefs, and crawled in beside Cadie's sleeping form.

* * *

He awoke with the heat of the morning sun streaming through the window onto his face and a dog's cold nose in his ear. Cadie was lying close beside him with one leg across his knees and her right hand on his chest. Some guard he was! He had slept so soundly he had been unaware of her moving. Lurch's tail was beating a tattoo on the hardwood floor. The beast was going to wake her up if he didn't let him out. Marc eased out from her unconscious embrace.

He opened the sliding doors to the patio and Lurch bounded out into the sunlit morning. He was standing in the open doorway, taking deep breaths of the pine-sweet air, when he heard a sharply drawn in breath.

When he swung around, Cadie was sitting, half-awake, on the edge of the bed.

"I'm fine," she reassured him with a little smile. "Sitting up was not great, but my headache is gone."

Pink-cheeked and drowsy, even with the dark bruises and scrapes on her face, she was devastatingly appealing. He wanted her. Ever since they had become lovers, he seemed be in a constant state of semi-arousal. Her sleep-warmed lips drew him like a magnet. He stopped himself. He couldn't kiss her the way he wanted to without hurting her. He loved her too much to cause her any pain.

He loved her!

How could he be so sure? Maybe it was the danger she was in that was heightening his awareness of Cadie's sexy body. He could be confusing his need to protect her with love.

Bull! You're so proud of your ability to face facts, Banachek, he told himself. Face this one. You didn't think you were capable of falling in love. You were wrong. Since the first moment you saw her, your emotions have gone berserk. When you kiss her, you go up in flames. Yesterday when you didn't know what had happened to her, you were in a state of utter panic.

The thought of how bleak his life would be if he lost her was like icy fingers gripping his heart. *Damn it!* Now that she had come into his life, he was going to see that she stayed there. He wondered if she knew he loved her. He wanted to shout it out, but this was hardly the right moment to tell her he wanted to spend the rest of his life with her. He smiled as he told himself there would be a right time. *Soon.*

He had better get some clothes on.

"That's great, love," he said as he dragged on the jeans he had been wearing the night before.

The most comfortable-looking thing he could find in her closet was a pale green, short-sleeved angora sweater and a pair of well-worn jeans. He placed them on the foot of the bed.

"Would you like help with these?" he asked.

"No, thank you," she said. He could see she was bristling a little that he had adopted the distant, care-giving attitude of a middle-aged nanny. "You don't have to dress me."

She stood up and took a couple of slow steps toward the bathroom. When he was sure she was steady enough on her feet, he dropped a quick, hard kiss on her lips and made his escape.

"I'll get the coffee on and see you in the kitchen."

As it turned out, by the time he had stopped by his own room to pick up a fresh shirt, Vi had arrived and put the coffee on. Cadie joined them as he was filling the housekeeper in on the propane incident Saturday night. Vi did not so much as raise an eyebrow when he explained that they were alive only because they had both spent the night in his cabin.

"Thank the Lord, you're both all right."

Vi turned away from the stove, where she was cooking pancakes, and caught sight of Cadie.

"Merciful Heavens!" she exclaimed. "What happened to you, child?"

"I walked into the side of a taxi," Cadie told her with a reassuring grin. "It looks worse than it is. All I got out of the collision were bruises and a sprain. I didn't break anything."

"Is that true?" Vi asked Marc. When he nodded, she turned back to Cadie.

"What's going on, Cadie?" Vi used the no-nonsense voice that could still intimidate two grown children.

"She had some help walking into the taxi," Marc stated. "Someone pushed her into a busy city street."

"Who?"

"We're not sure," Cadie told her. "But it seems to have something to do with my refusing to sell Pop's claims to NorthAm Corporation. Ever since we found the notebook that Pop logged the diamond drill core in, someone has been trying to kill us."

Vi's round face paled. "Luke said you found the book. George told me the week before he died that someone had been going through his things in the core shed. I guess that's why he hid it." She was quiet for a moment. "NorthAm is your Uncle Jack's company, isn't it?"

"He has a partner," Marc said.

"Sandor Green." There was a world of disapproval in Vi's voice. "He got young Jack in trouble years ago. I heard they were still in business together. Was Sandor the one who pushed you, Cadie?"

"I didn't see who did it, Vi," she said wearily.

"Dear Lord, the pancakes." Vi turned and swooped down on the frying pan, which was giving off clouds of black smoke. "No more talking until you get some breakfast into you."

She cleaned up the charred debris and started a new batch. Soon they were sitting down to eat.

"Jack Haywood was a sneaky little kid, but he wasn't ever mean," Vi pronounced, sitting down to join them with her mug of coffee as she usually did. "He lied and he stole, but I never heard of him hurting anybody."

When she was settled across the pine plank table from Cadie, she caught sight of the zircon ring.

"Oh, my," she said, taking hold of Cadie's hand to look at it for a moment. She went around the table, kissed her warmly on the cheek, then hugged Marc. "I'm so happy for you both. George would be pleased. When's the wedding?"

* * *

Cadie began to shake her head.

"We thought maybe a week from Monday," Marc answered catching Cadie's eye. The heated message he was sending made her heart race. "That is, if we can make the arrangements. We don't want to wait. Do we, sweetheart? Besides, I can't think of a better way to celebrate Cadie's birthday."

"How did you know it was...?" Cadie began. Then she remembered the telephone conversation he had overheard. "Elsie. I told Elsie I'd be in Denver next Monday for the closing on the sale of my house."

"I guess she'll have to come here if she's going to be at the wedding," he said with wide grin.

Marc's performance was infuriatingly convincing. Cadie was having to remind herself firmly that it was all pretense.

"I'll call her." Cadie warned him with a look. He was making things unnecessarily complicated.

"Elsie will be surprised at our news." She changed the subject away from a discussion of the fictional ceremony.

"Well, I'm not." Vi beamed at them. "I could see it coming from the day you got here. And when Luke got home from Casino Night, he told us to expect an engagement soon. Betty made him a bet on it."

Cadie could see Marc was thinking the same thing that she was. Luke had seen their kiss on the dance floor. But so had half the town. Then someone had turned on the propane.

"Oh, before I forget, Sam asked me to deliver his bill for the driveway."

Vi delved into her pocket and placed a handwritten invoice on the table. Something about the slant of the script caught Cadie's attention.

"Is Sam left-handed?" she asked.

"Oh, yes." Vi laughed as she cleared away the breakfast things. "He, Luke and I are all lefties. Mary likes to tell people that she's the only normal one in the family."

While Cadie was figuring out how to ask her about who had been using the phone at the farm on Sunday morning, Marc was teasing Vi about playing blackjack on Saturday night. That led naturally to his asking if she had slept in Sunday after her big night out. Cadie congratulated him silently.

"Heavens no," she replied. "Mary and Rob were staying late for the dancing so I told her they could sleep in and I'd take the kids to early church service and stay on to teach her Sunday School class."

That meant Vi would have no idea who had called the Royal York from the farm that morning. So much for eliminating anyone.

"I guess I was a little tired myself, though," Vi went on, "because I forgot the game sheets Mary had given me for her class. We got almost all the way to the church before I remembered and had to ask Luke to turn around and go back for them."

She gave a bitter laugh. "Of course, if I hadn't gone back I'd have missed my daily spat with Sam. He was upset when I interrupted his phone call. I figure he must have a new lady friend because he wouldn't talk while I was in the room. Luke thinks I should send him off with a flea in his ear." She slammed the pile of plates down on the counter. "It's certainly time I did."

More likely, Sam was telling Sandor about the propane incident. At the time Vi and Luke were heading for early service, she and Marc were still sleeping. Sam would not have been aware yet that he had gassed an empty bedroom.

CHAPTER 14

Early that afternoon, Cadie was awakened from a doze on the living room couch by the sound of Lurch barking furiously. She heard Marc calling him off and then shortly, Marc's voice in conversation with someone on the patio. She had given in and agreed to read for an hour after lunch and had fallen asleep with her book on her lap. As she straightened up and rubbed her stiff neck, she thought she recognized Betty Tibbs' light, cheerful voice.

"I didn't know she wasn't well. Don't wake her," Betty was saying. "I just dropped by with some handouts from Monday night's Art Guild meeting."

"I'm awake, Betty," Cadie called to her. "Come on in."

"Wow!" Betty greeted her when she saw the bandages and the bruises and scrapes on her face. "Marc warned me you were a little banged up. Are you in a lot of pain?"

"It's easing off," Cadie assured her, trying to smile as she accepted the photocopied sheets Betty handed her.

"This is the list of local art shows I picked up for you at the meeting on Monday. The shop is closed on Wednesday afternoons and I hadn't made any plans," Betty told her, "so I thought I'd bring it out to you. I should've called first."

She stared at her empty hands as if she didn't know what to do with them. With a self-conscious smile, she settled for ramming them awkwardly into the pockets of her jeans. Cadie's heart went out to her.

"Would you like to come out to the studio to see the kind of stuff

I'm doing?"

"I was hoping you'd offer." Betty's plain face lit up. "But should you be moving around yet? We can save it for another day."

"If I don't walk around a bit, I'll soon be too stiff to move at all." Cadie stood up carefully. "Come on. I'm eager to see Luke's renovations."

"He told me he was almost finished. He was trying so hard to have it ready when you got back he couldn't come over to my place for lunch after church last Sunday like he usually does. He said he had to dash right over here to prime the walls for painting. He's been having a really great time with it."

That meant Sam was the only one who had been at the farm when the phone calls had been made to the NorthAm suite Sunday morning. Of course, if Luke had gone home briefly to change into his work clothes, he could have made the calls.

It was then that Betty noticed the sparkling ring on Cadie's left hand. After that, Cadie was too busy fielding questions about the mythical wedding to have a chance to pump her guest about the Wheelwrights' activities.

Luke was packing up his tools preparatory to leaving the log house when they arrived. He appeared genuinely shocked and concerned at the sight of her injuries.

"I'm fine," she told him. "Just a bit bruised."

After she had explained she had been pushed into the traffic, he nodded sadly.

"There's a lot of violence in the city," he said. "A person is best to stay up here in God's Country."

She didn't tell Luke how much violence she had found right here in God's Country.

"A sprained left wrist would put me right out of business." He shook his head at the thought. "Couldn't work. Wouldn't even be able to play golf. Vic Tyler and I are playing in the Pine Lodge Invitational Tournament this afternoon. Wouldn't neither one of us be able to play with your injury. We find being lefties is an advantage, though, on the local courses.

"All the trouble is on the right hand side of the fairways where a righthander's slice would take his ball. Vic and I play it different. He uses left-handed clubs, and hits a long ball with a mean slice that usually stays on the fairway. I use right-handed clubs and use the strength in my left arm to power my drive. Works for us," he said with a chuckle.

"Speaking of left hands…" Betty's change of subject effectively cut off Luke's monologue and drew his attention to Cadie's engagement ring. Luke's round face beamed at her as he offered his congratulations.

"As soon as you feel up to it, the four of us will have to go down to Huntsville and celebrate," he said.

Then he waved proudly at the new windows and freshly painted walls. "I've pretty well finished here, Cadie. What do you think?"

She looked around the large, bright, airy room. "It's perfect, Luke. I can hardly wait to get my easel set up."

With a pleased smile, he picked up his toolbox. "The fixtures should be here next week for your new washroom. For the rest of the week, though, I'm afraid it's the outhouse. And"—he gestured toward the washstand and rain barrel outside the door—"you can clean up out there.

"I'll be leaving you ladies to your wedding talk. I promised Dad I'd meet the North Bay bus at the depot in Huntsville and drive him out to the farm. His truck is in the shop again. I'd better hustle or I won't make it back for our tee-off time."

"That Sam!" Betty exploded when Luke was out of earshot. "Luke just keeps setting himself up for disappointment. You can't tell him that being at his father's beck and call won't ever be appreciated. Sam's too self-centered and dissatisfied to realize what a great family he has. He always manages to be somewhere else when they need him. But when he's around, the whole world has to revolve around what he wants, when he wants it."

Cadie's original impression that Vi's husband was a simple, settled farmer and handyman had certainly been off target.

"I didn't know he was away a lot," she said.

"He's always taking off somewhere." Betty was warming up to her topic. "Chasing after a woman, or prospecting the latest find. He's supposed to be raising beef on the land he leased from your granddad, but he lets Luke look after that. Sam is always too busy with some important deal that never pans out. Vi's a saint. But I get the feeling even she has run out of patience with him."

The two women talked easily as they unpacked Cadie's canvasses and hung them on the picture hangers Luke had placed at intervals on the walls.

"I really like your work," Betty said reaching for yet another sketch. "You haven't been wasting time either. How long is it since you arrived from down below?"

Cadie laughed. "Down below? The folks in the Mile High City would find that a strange description."

Betty joined her laughter. "Guess it is. Up here, everything south of the forty-ninth parallel, whether it's in a valley or on a mountain top, is down below."

Cadie was counting silently on her fingers. "My goodness. I'll have been here a month in a couple of days."

It seemed like forever. She could hardly believe she hadn't lived here for years. It was certainly incredible she had only known Marc for that long.

* * *

When Marc joined them a few minutes later, he didn't say much beyond a few words of greeting. He was more interested in searching her face for signs of fatigue.

"You're not too tired to be doing this?" he asked.

When Cadie informed him a little impatiently that she was fine, he looked at her intently again and, apparently satisfied that she was up to hanging a few pictures, he set about carrying in the few bits of furniture from the core shed where they had been stored.

"Where do you want this easel set up, love?"

She showed him a spot where the light from the north window would fall on it.

Betty had been staring at a large, almost impressionistic painting of a gnarled pine tree reaching for the first morning beams of light. "This one is powerful," she said. "Dramatic. I know I've seen that exact same twisted pine somewhere around here."

Cadie laughed. "It's at the edge of the garbage dump."

Marc looked at the painting. So it was. Only his Cadie would focus on the one beautiful detail in that offensive gully of decaying garbage and rusting metal. No wonder he loved her.

After Betty left a few minutes later, Cadie told Marc what she had learned about Luke's whereabouts at the times of the Sunday telephone calls.

"And he's gone to the bus station to meet the bus from North Bay to pick up his father. I wonder if Sam's been in the Bay since Sunday," she finished. "Oh, I guess it doesn't matter, does it?"

"I wish I knew. We know Sam was in this area when the propane valve was opened because he was at the farm, probably on the phone with Sandor, Sunday morning. But he wasn't one of the guys who put the bullets in our beds Monday night."

"I can't believe anyone could be such a two-faced sneak!" Cadie fumed. "I thought he was a friend of the family."

Being able to put Sam's weather-beaten face on the unknown enemy had changed Cadie's perception of her situation. There was no omniscient and powerful evil being stalking her. Sam was only a tough, old man with no sense of loyalty or conscience. A recognizable human opponent was much less terrifying.

"Of course, Sam has no problem finding out where we are and what our plans are," she said. "There's always at least one member of his family around here. All he has to do is listen to Vi and Luke chat about how they spent their day."

She remembered a laughing Sam Wheelwright feeding Lurch dog biscuits and putting him through his paces.

"And, if Sam is the creep who's been trying to kill me, that explains why Lurch lets him wander around here without barking to warn us."

Hot flecks of golden fire danced in her eyes. The pain she'd been in since she was injured just yesterday noon could not keep Marc's feisty Cadie subdued.

"There doesn't seem to be much doubt about who is Sandor's man in Chartwell Falls." Marc's voice was like gray steel.

He clenched his fists. "But we don't have any actual evidence he was involved in any of the incidents. The only thing those phone calls prove is that he's been in contact with Sandor."

The steel that tinged his voice had reached his eyes. Their blue-gray was cold. "Now that he's home, I think I'll go and have a chat with Sam."

Cadie covered his fist with her uninjured hand.

"Are you sure we want Sam to know that we suspect him? Maybe we should wait and see what his next move is. It might be a good idea to get Chuck to help us set a trap for him."

* * *

"Get that idea out of your mind." The words exploded from his lips. "There's no way I'm going to let you be used as bait. Sam's never getting another chance to hurt you. We're lucky you're still alive."

He slid his fingers up into the hair at the base of her neck and tilted her head so he could cover her mouth with his. His kiss was direct and rough with need and when she parted her lips, his tongue plunged deeply inside. But even in his desperation for a taste of her, for a reassurance that she was alive and his, he refrained from pulling her bruised body against him. He concentrated on conquering and making love to every inch of her mouth.

"Oh, God, Cadie," he muttered into her hair, when he forced himself to end the kiss. "I can't lose you. It would kill me."

* * *

Cadie rubbed her cheek against the roughness of his late-afternoon stubble, reveling in the almost painful sensation of the bristles on her tender skin. His maleness, his toughness, stirred her body but, at the same time, his neediness touched the depths of her soul. She could hardly contain her love for him.

Marc had all but said he loved her. For the first time, she dared to hope that she was becoming as necessary to his happiness as he was to hers. Maybe, when this nightmare was over, he wouldn't simply feel he had done his duty and move on.

"Fate couldn't do that to me," she said. "I've been waiting for you for too long."

Then she was in his arms. The restlessness she felt in every nerve of her body was soothed a little by pressing her tingling breasts against his chest. However, she could not help flinching when his arm came in contact with her bruised ribs. Marc quickly drew back.

"Oh, love," he said with a shaky laugh, "Vi's right. We have to feed you up so you can heal quickly."

They locked the studio and walked slowly back to the house. Marc's arm circled her so lightly she almost told him that she was only bruised, not ready to shatter into pieces. However, she smiled to herself, this being cherished was not at all unpleasant.

* * *

The next couple of days passed without incident. Marc was watchful and kept Lurch with them day and night. They went back to the sleeping arrangements they had had before the Casino Night changed their lives. Neither of them slept soundly. Even though Marc and Lurch patrolled the area several times during the night hours and Chuck drove by any time he was in the vicinity, Cadie had the uneasy feeling she was being watched from the darkness of the woods at the edge of the clearing.

Vi spent the days filling the house with delectable aromas and the freezer with a good supply of prepared dinners. At the same time, she somehow made sure Cadie was always in sight.

At lunch on Friday, after pointedly comparing Marc's healthy appetite with Cadie's, Vi finished with her familiar refrain, "I keep telling you, Cadie, we have to get more good food into you to speed up the healing. Now eat up those scrambled eggs. I've put sprouts in them for you."

Knowing that arguing would do no good, Cadie attempted to divert her attention by asking about her family. She was astounded with how freely Vi unburdened herself.

"Luke's not very good at taking advice either," she said, making a funny little sound that could be best described as an affectionate snort. "He spends so much time with Betty that I hardly see him anymore. I wish he'd be sensible and marry the girl. I told him that they could have the farm.

"I'd be happy to move into one of those new apartments in town that are within walking distance of Mary and the grandchildren. But I think he's a little leery about marriage after watching me and his father over the years."

She brushed a non-existent lock of hair off her brow and tucked it into the tidy bun at the back of her head. "I'd hoped that before now Sam would've decided on his own to move out without a fuss." She shrugged. "But, ever since I told him at Christmas time that I was filing for divorce, it seems to me he's been around the farm more than he has in years. I had to tell him, when he came back from North Bay on Wednesday, not to bother to unpack."

"I had no idea..." Cadie began.

"It's no big deal, child," Vi assured her. "Sam hasn't thought of himself as a husband for years. I just wish now I'd made sure he signed the papers before he took off for the Bay again. I guess there's no rush, but I'd like it over with."

Cadie wondered if Pop had known about the divorce, and if it had anything to do with the "other good news" he'd mentioned in his letter.

Vi busied herself with rolling out the dough for shortbread cookies as if her mention of divorce had been no more important than a comment on the weather.

"Now you get off to bed for a good long nap," she said. "You need rest as well as good food if you're going to be well enough to get married a week Monday."

After Cadie went off to her room, Vi looked at Marc and raised a quizzical eyebrow at him. "I haven't heard any more about that wedding. Where is it taking place?"

"I'm making the arrangements," he assured her, readying himself to make a quick exit to his study. "I am. Don't you fret, my little dumpling."

Cadie was still sleeping an hour later when Vi came to the door of Marc's study.

"Jack Haywood is on the phone. He wants to talk to you," she told him.

Marc snatched up the receiver. "Yes, Jack?" he said.

"Marc." The older man's voice had lost a lot of its bluster. "How's Cadie?"

"She's alive," Marc stated flatly.

"The hospital said she'd been released the same day. Was she badly injured?"

"Some bruised ribs and a sprained wrist." He wasn't going to waste any words on Jack Haywood.

"Thank God." His words sounded heartfelt.

"Cadie told me you think I'm the one who had somebody try to kill her by gassing her at the lake. I know there's no reason for you to believe me, but I didn't. I'm a selfish coward, but I'm not that low.

"I didn't know anything about it when I was talking to Cadie, but I did hear something Tuesday night. I overheard Sandor raising hell with someone on the telephone for 'messing up the job at Nighthawk Lake.' Sandor told the guy he was fired because he'd done the job himself."

"Sandor admitted pushing her in front of that cab?" Marc asked.

"He was so proud of himself, he couldn't shut up about it. Kept going on about having to do things yourself if you want them done right."

"You realize I'll report what you've told me about Green's involvement." Marc wished he had his hands around Jack's fat throat. "And that I'll hound your worthless hide until you testify to what you know," he snarled, fighting to keep his temper under control.

"I'll tell them myself," Jack retorted. "I can't keep quiet about what I know about Sandor's role in the attempts on your lives any longer."

"Why now? Why didn't you say something earlier?"

"When Sandor came back to the hotel Tuesday afternoon and told me he'd killed Cadie, I believed him. At first, I was in shock and terrified that the police would think I did it. After all, I was the one who was going to inherit. They didn't know Sandor could blackmail the title to the claims out of me.

"But I listened to the news all day Wednesday and there was no report of a fatality in an accident at King and Yonge. I began to wonder if Sandor could've been mistaken. He was in such a wild state when he got back to the hotel he could've jumped to the conclusion she'd been killed.

"When I was alone, I located the ambulance services that took her to the hospital. The hospital that treated her told me her injuries hadn't been serious enough to admit her.

"Is Cadie going to be okay? They couldn't tell me any more than that she'd been released."

"She's going to be all right," Marc granted grudgingly.

"I can't let Sandor try again. I have to talk to the police. You used to work for the Toronto Police Force. Who should I talk to?"

"Officer J.W. Wilcox is the man working on the Royal York case."

Marc told Jack how to get to the right Toronto precinct and said he would contact Willy himself to tell him to expect Jack Haywood to come in. Jack agreed to call back when he knew anything more.

After he replaced the receiver, it was all Marc could do not to cheer at the top of his lungs. They had him! He tried to contain his elation. Haywood could change his mind about testifying, he cautioned himself, but maybe, just maybe, Cadie had nothing more to fear. He would have to tell her that her uncle had called with the news Green had fired his local man, but it might be smart to wait to see if Jack Haywood actually did volunteer to testify against his partner before telling her the rest of the message.

He got Willy right away at the precinct. He said he would eagerly await Jack's visit. Marc had just hung up from that call when Chuck phoned to say he'd checked out the other local number that had been on the list of phone calls charged to the NorthAm suite.

Marc gave up all hope of getting any work done that afternoon and headed into the kitchen where he found Cadie talking to Vi.

"Your rest seems to have put a little color in your cheeks," he told her.

"You mean other than pale green and purple?" she answered with a wry smile. "You can't fool me. I looked in the bathroom mirror."

"You look lovely to me." He meant it. "I just had a call from Chuck. He tells me the local number he was looking into is Vic Tyler's unlisted number."

"That name seems to pop up a lot," Cadie said thoughtfully. "Why don't we drop in to see Mr. Tyler? We could ask him if he's informed his would-be client that this property is not on the market."

"Good idea," Marc agreed. "I promised to email my manuscript to my editor in New York today or tomorrow, but I can do that when we get back."

"That little Tyler fellow has been strutting around almost bursting his buttons lately," Vi told them. "He's telling people he just pulled off the biggest sale of his life. Sold off one whole side of the lake to some outfit in Toronto. Hope they're not going to build a lodge on Nighthawk. The lake's not big enough to support that many more people."

As he and Cadie were walking out to the pickup, Marc broke the news. "Your Uncle Jack phoned while you were asleep. It seems he overheard a conversation between Sandor and the man who's been working for him up here. According to Jack, he fired him for messing up the propane attack."

Cadie stopped stock still, a look of incredulous joy on her face. "Really? Do you think that means it's over?" Her happy expression faded. "Or do you suppose Sandor's hired someone else? Just when we think we know who it is. Do you think that's why he called Vic Tyler?"

"I don't know. But it could be good news. If the thugs he hired decide to talk, Sandor may have enough on his plate without starting anything else. All his plans so far have pretty well fallen through. At least, when we talk to Tyler, we maybe can find out when he had his last conversation with him."

"Yes," she responded thoughtfully. "I wonder what exactly Mr. Tyler was willing to do to get that big sale."

Vic Tyler did not seem the slightest bit surprised or upset to see them when they entered his office about half an hour later.

"Hello there, Ms. Haywood," he called out to her, his big, rich voice filling the room like a chocolate fog. "Change your mind about selling the house?"

"I'm afraid not. I dropped in to ask if you'd had time to inform Mr. Green that I wasn't interested in selling."

Vic Tyler slowly shook his narrow head back and forth morosely. "I surely did. And he wasn't happy about it, I'll tell you. He seemed to feel he needed it to go along with some other holdings."

"Do you remember exactly when you called him?" Marc asked.

"As a matter of fact, I didn't call him at all. Mr. Green called me last Friday. He hadn't been able to get any answer at Sam

Wheelwright's farm. He wanted me to get Sam to call him as soon as possible. I said I'd do that and told him what you'd said while I had him on the line." His smile was full of self-satisfaction.

"Better talk on his nickel than mine." He actually chortled.

When they were back in the pickup, Cadie said, "I don't believe Mr. Tyler has any connection with Sandor other than selling real estate to him, do you?"

"No," Marc said, a little more cheerfully. "He was a long shot. It looks as if Sam is our only real candidate."

Vi had obviously been watching for them because, when the pickup pulled up in front of the house, she ran out onto the drive to meet them.

"The phone has been ringing off the wall," she said, breathless with excitement. "Jack Haywood called again. He said this time he would talk to either of you. And there was an urgent call for you, Marc."

Curiosity fought with concern for control of her round face. "An Officer Wilcox said you were to call him at the precinct the minute you got in. It's a Toronto number. You didn't get into any trouble when you were down below did you?"

"Pick up the phone in the kitchen, Cadie," Marc snapped. "I'll call Willy from the study."

"Officer Wilcox is a friend of Marc's who is looking up some information for us," Cadie explained as she and Vi hurried after him into the house.

Cadie had a number of questions of her own. She wondered what else Uncle Jack had to say. Had Willy called to say that the men who'd been sent to their hotel room to kill them had been convinced to implicate Sandor? Or had he discovered some other threat to their safety?

CHAPTER 15

"That's great!" Marc was saying when she picked up the receiver. "I hear Cadie coming on the line now, Willy. Tell her the good news."

"Hello, Cadie. I hope when we meet in person, it'll be under happier circumstances," a crisp yet friendly baritone voice greeted her. "Right now, I'll just fill you in on the highlights. As of this morning, we have Sandor Green in custody, charged with one count of attempted murder and one of conspiracy to commit murder."

The relief that swept over her was so intense she found it difficult to concentrate on the rest of his information.

"Earlier today," he went on, "I received a phone call from Jack Haywood. He said Marc had told him to get in touch with me because I had some knowledge of the attacks made on you here in the city.

"Haywood told me that he was willing to testify he overheard his business partner hiring the two men that Val and I apprehended in your hotel room at the Royal York. It seems Sandor Green called in a favor from a long-time friend that the two guys worked for. He also boasted to Haywood that he, personally, pushed you into the path of the taxi.

"Of course, Green refuses to say a word except through his lawyer, but the judge set bail high enough to hold him for a while. We've been in touch with the provincial police in your area and we're hoping to find evidence linking him to the incidents up there."

Uncle Jack had come through for her! As tears of relief filled her eyes and coursed down her cheeks, Cadie mumbled an incoherent thank you. She continued holding the receiver to her ear as Marc quizzed

Willy on the details, but all she could think was that the nightmare was finally over. Sandor Green's campaign of terror had been stopped.

The silent tears were still flowing when Marc rejoined her in the kitchen. A bewildered Vi was fluttering about, anxiously asking her over and over again what was the matter, and, finally, preparing Cadie her all purpose panacea—"a nice cup of tea."

Marc explained briefly to Vi that Sandor Green had been arrested for the attack in Toronto. The only attack that had been mentioned to Vi was the one that had propelled Cadie into the side of the taxicab. He saw no point in mentioning the gunmen who had been captured in their hotel room or the probable connection between Sandor and Sam. He did, however, extract her promise not to tell anyone, not even her family, about the arrest.

Cadie could tell Vi was dying to ask what Sandor would hope to gain by killing Cadie, but obviously Marc had said all that he was going to on the subject. She protested that she could stay on to look after Cadie if she needed her, but Marc shooed her off home as usual at four o'clock.

"Vi," he said to her, as he draped an affectionate arm around her shoulders and led her to the door, "you've been a big help. Cadie's been under such a lot of stress that the good news of Green's arrest snapped her control for a minute. She and I are going to eat that terrific smelling chicken casserole you left in the oven and then I'm going to see that she goes right to bed. Don't worry. I won't leave her side. I promise you."

He gave her a little hug, then watched from the doorway until her old Buick disappeared down the driveway.

"Are you all right?" he asked when he returned to Cadie's side.

"I feel like a fool for falling apart like that," she said with an embarrassed smile. "But, oh, Marc, I can't believe I don't have to be constantly looking over my shoulder any more to see who's lurking in the shadows."

She caught a flash of uncertainty in his eyes. "You don't think jailing Sandor guarantees that Sam will quit, do you?"

*   *   *

He wanted to assure her that all their worries were over, but he had to be honest with her.

"I'm not sure," he said. "It depends on what Sam's arrangement was with Sandor. At least, Green has nothing to gain from your death now. Your uncle's willingness to testify against him tells me that he wouldn't give Sandor control of the claims if he did get them at this point."

"Uncle Jack! He wanted us to call him."

They went into the little den off the living room where Vi had left the message by the telephone on Pop's old desk. The number she had jotted down told them that Jack was still at the Royal York Hotel. Not able to resist holding her any longer, Marc sat at the desk and pulled her down onto his knee.

"You dial and do the talking," he said, nuzzling her neck. "I'll just eavesdrop."

"I can't do anything unless you stop that." She giggled and reluctantly shrugged her shoulder up to protect her neck from his tantalizing, tickling lips.

He chuckled. She felt so good in his arms. And he felt confident he could handle whatever threat Sam Wheelwright presented to her. If, indeed, he did still present a threat.

"Make it a short call," he said, with one final kiss on her neck.

Jack answered on the first ring.

"Katie?" he replied to her greeting. "Your fiancé told me that you hadn't been seriously injured, but I've been worried about you."

When she assured him that she had received only superficial injuries, he swallowed hard.

"Sandor has gone right off the deep end. I couldn't stop him. All I could do was warn you to get out of the hotel. But the next day, when I got back after our talk in the coffee shop, he boasted about having the guts to push you in front of a cab himself. I knew I couldn't hide in the bushes any longer.

"There was nothing on the radio and when I called the downtown hospitals, you hadn't been admitted to any of them. Finally, I thought of calling the ambulance service and they were able to tell me where they'd taken you. When I found out from the hospital that you'd been treated and released, I realized I couldn't count on your luck holding forever. Sandor wasn't going to give up."

"What happened to the evidence he was holding that would send you to prison if you crossed him?"

Jack gave an embarrassed chuckle. "Self-serving low-life that I am, I looked after that first, honey. I had my own piece of luck. While Sandor was taking a shower in the suite before he went out Tuesday night, I went through his pockets and found a key to a safety deposit box.

"First thing in the morning, I went to the bank branch where we have our joint business accounts. I found the man we do most of our business with and talked my way into the safety deposit box area. It didn't take a minute to find the documents Sandor had forced me to sign. It took even less time to destroy them."

"I'm glad," Cadie told him sincerely. He was no saint, but he had gone out of his way to protect her.

"That's when I called Marc, honey. He told me to get in touch with Officer Wilcox. You know what happened then. I still would like to come up to see you, Katie."

"I'll be here."

As she hung up, she looked steadily into Marc's eyes. Their fascinating blue depths beckoned to her. Her parted lips touched his as he gathered her closer. The heat of his large hands on her lower back seemed to radiate right through her skin to add fuel to the already burning fire at the core of her body. She began to undo the top button of his shirt.

"I need you," she whispered into his mouth.

"You have me," he whispered back. He stood up with her in his arms and, with their mouths eagerly tasting and caressing each other, carried her to his bed.

When he set her down on the edge of the bed, she raised her arms and he quickly pulled her sweatshirt off over her head. Standing for a moment, she slipped off her sweatpants and panties. She reached for the front closure of her bra, but Marc took her hands and placed them on his shoulders.

"Please," he said, kneeling in front of her. "Let me do that."

He ran his fingers slowly up from her waist, trailing fire along the sides of her breasts, lightly brushing her armpits and the sensitive undersides of her upper arms. Every nerve ending trembled under his caress, and by the time his fingers had retraced the path to her breasts to undo the fastening, she could hardly stand the torment.

His fingers slowly circled her rigid nipples that ached for his touch, beading the dusky pink aureolae. Cadie had come to the end of her tether. She squirmed around so her breast moved into the palm of his hand. As he kneaded it gently, he leaned forward and took the other nipple in his mouth. She moaned when she felt the suction and the moist heat of his tongue. The sound sent a jolt of hot blood straight to the already engorged organ that had been ready for her since the moment he had pulled her firm bottom onto his thighs in the study.

* * *

It seemed as if it had been weeks since they had last been together rather than merely days. He wanted to plunge himself so deeply into her velvety heat that she would know he was meant to be part of her now and forever. Instead, he replaced the hand massaging her other breast with his mouth and began to suckle gently.

Cadie's fingers that had been roaming restlessly from the thick hair at the nape of his neck, over his shoulders and back, dug into his back. Desire had darkened her eyes to the color of a shaded forest glade. Golden glints of passion gleamed darkly in their depths.

"Now, Marc." Her voice was husky and urgent. "I want you inside me, now."

And that was where he needed to be. Quickly, he lay on his back beside her on the big bed and reached for her.

"I don't want to hurt you, sweetheart," he whispered. His hands moved over her back in long, sensuous strokes. He grasped her hips and lifted her carefully so she could straddle him.

* * *

Cadie was uncertain for a moment at suddenly being given control of their lovemaking, but the sight of Marc, lying tense and fully aroused, waiting for her to make them one, filled her with an excitement like nothing she had ever felt. She inched forward until his erection was resting against the highly sensitive mound under her dark blonde curls, then leaned forward to touch her tongue to a tempting tiny nipple. The rigid pressure against her abdomen made her release a shuddering sigh.

Marc's hips jerked involuntarily.

"Careful, sweetheart," he gritted through his teeth. "I don't think I can hold on much longer."

She laughed, glorying in her power. She quickly gave the other nipple a flick of her tongue.

"Equal time," she explained with a grin, as she raised her hips so he could position himself to enter her.

When she lowered her weight and he filled her, her eyes widened and she cried out at the incredible sensation. He had never been so deep inside her.

"Oh, Marc," she cried, and began to move.

MINE

* * *

Marc had been determined to give over control to her, but he could not help grasping her buttocks and setting the slowly accelerating tempo of their dance. Cadie joined him in the slow, grinding friction that deliciously stimulated every nerve ending and gradually became a hard, driving beat. The sudden disappearance of the cloud of fear that had been hanging over them allowed Marc to open himself to the overwhelming sweetness of his love for her. His ever-quickening thrusts swept them up in a compelling, swirling *bolero,* whose tempo was driven by little cries of joy and hoarse moans of pleasure. He had never suspected the sublime ecstasy that gripped him at the peak of their lovemaking was possible in this imperfect world.

After the dance had spun to its spectacular climax, Cadie collapsed limply on his chest. Neither of them could speak. Marc cradled her in his arms, knowing she would always be the most precious thing in his life.

"You're mine, Cadie," he whispered against her tousled hair. "Mine."

He barely had the energy to pull a sheet up over them before they both drifted off to sleep.

* * *

When he awoke at first light, his left arm was numb and his fingers were tingling. The weight of Cadie's head on his shoulder had caused his left arm to go to sleep, but he did not try to shift her. It was worth the discomfort to look at her sleeping body entangled with his. Her left wrist, which still wore the dark plastic splint, rested on his waist and his thigh was trapped between her legs.

In her sleep, she looked younger and more vulnerable. His arm tightened around her waist as his gaze lingered on the visible reminders of her collision with the taxicab. The bruises on her arm and on her upper body had faded to pale streaks of greenish-purple and the scrapes on her face were almost gone.

The details of last night's loving were vivid in his mind. She was so generous and intense in her passion. Nothing in his life had prepared him for the powerful emotions that had filled him while they were making love. The tenderness that even now had him on the verge of tears, the towering pride that he was the one who could make her want him the way she did, the raw, territorial possessiveness he felt where she was concerned —all shook him to the marrow of his bones. He would kill anyone who tried to take this woman from him. She was his.

He hoped she would not awaken this morning in more pain because of their lovemaking. However, even as he was wishing he had been more considerate, he was becoming more acutely aware of his morning erection. He had better get out of this bed before her nakedness stirred him to make love to her again.

He bent his head and kissed her on the forehead, then slowly extracted his leg from between hers. When she stirred and attempted to snuggle back against his chest, he slid his arm out from under her head and regretfully eased away from her. Without waking, she turned over on her stomach and burrowed her face into the pillow.

He showered and dressed quickly, then, closing the bedroom door quietly behind him, he made his way to the kitchen.

The aroma of charred food greeted him. Vi's chicken casserole that had been waiting in the warm oven had slowly turned to charcoal overnight. Even the dish that it had cooked in was beyond redemption. He opened the windows to air the room, then tossed the burnt remains into the covered trash can outside the kitchen door.

After he fed Lurch, he put on a pot of coffee and sat down to plan his day. He had promised to email his latest manuscript to his editor in New York before the end of the week. He prided himself on never missing a deadline but, this time, a day late would have to do. He could get most of it done while Cadie was still sleeping.

He intended to be right by her side until the question of Sam Wheelwright was settled. They must not allow themselves to become too complacent about her safety. Sam was still at large and they had no idea whether Sandor's arrest had removed him as a threat.

* * *

It was midmorning before Cadie began to surface from her deep, contented sleep. She awoke slowly. Without opening her eyes, she was aware she was in Marc's bed. His scent was still on the pillow and the musky smell of their lovemaking lingered on the sheets.

When she stretched, the cat-like stretch of a woman who had been well and thoroughly loved, she felt twinges in muscles that had been initiated into some memorable new rites of lovemaking. She knew without looking, too, that Marc was no longer in bed with her. Some day they would take their time waking up together. She was enjoying a delightful fantasy about that future morning when her stomach growled loudly.

She hadn't eaten for almost twenty-four hours. They had forgotten about Vi's casserole last night. *Time to get out of bed, have a fast shower, and get some breakfast!*

She was disappointed to find Vi alone in the kitchen when she got there.

"Marc asked me to tell you that he's in his study emailing off his manuscript to New York. He said he should be done before noon," Vi informed her. "Can I fix you some breakfast?"

"I'm starving," she said. "I'll eat what ever you put in front of me." Cadie flushed at Vi's knowing grin. She wondered what had happened to the casserole. "Surprise me. I'll be right back." She headed toward Marc's study.

He turned when he heard her and opened his arms.

"Good morning, love," he said, giving her a thorough kiss. "I wanted to do this when I woke up, but I decided to be noble instead and let you sleep. I hope you are properly grateful."

She grinned up at him. "Give me a few minutes to have some breakfast and I'll be glad to show you grateful."

He grimaced. "Better take your time over breakfast, love. Everything that could go wrong with this invention of the devil has. The computer chose this morning to pack it in."

He pointed to the end of the L-shaped work area. "You see before you a high tech corpse. Right now, I'm in the midst of printing a hard copy that I'm going to have to entrust to the postal service. You may be able to tell by the interesting designs on my fingers that I had an unforeseen problem inserting my last ink cartridge into the printer. And then the paper decided to play a few tricks on me. I think I have everything working fine now, but I'll still be a while."

He swung her back into his arms for another kiss. "But when I get this finished, I'm all yours for as long as you want."

Their eyes met and held. As long as she wanted him. Did he really mean that? She looked away.

"I'd like to go to town this afternoon. There are some supplies I need to get from Betty's shop. All right with you?"

"As soon as I've done this, I'll do whatever you want to do, sweetheart."

He was about to make a few alternate suggestions about how they might spend the afternoon when there was a grinding noise from the printer. He turned back to it with a curse and began to do something with the paper feed.

Figuring that his frustrating task would take him a couple of hours, Cadie decided to go out to the studio. If she told him her plan, he would insist on accompanying her. That would not be fair because he really did need to get that manuscript in the mail.

Instead, she merely kissed him on the cheek and said, "Let me know when you're ready to leave for town."

Vi would tell him where to find her.

CHAPTER 16

By the time she had finished the huge breakfast Vi insisted she eat, Cadie was impatient to get out to the quiet and the isolation of her new studio so she could get started. Vi let her go saying that she would bring a thermos of coffee and a muffin out to the log house in an hour or so. If Marc needed to find her, Vi knew where she was. He wouldn't be pleased, but Cadie felt she was living up to the spirit of her promise to make sure he always knew her whereabouts. Anyway, the real danger was past.

Lurch accompanied her and settled down in his usual sunny spot beside the wide stone steps when she went inside. She loved everything about her woodland studio. The creak of the old wooden floors under her feet was familiar and welcoming. The sharp, yet mellow, scent of turpentine and linseed oil never failed to give her a little shot of excitement and lift her spirits.

The big wooden easel Pop had bought for her years ago stood in a patch of clear north light that poured in through the newly installed glass doors. She lifted a large canvas she had prepared the previous week onto the easel and began the project she had been thinking about for months. The portrait was going to be an important step in saying good-bye to Pop. Her desire to do it here on the land he loved had been one of the main reasons she had decided to come to Nighthawk Lake.

She fitted a photograph of her grandfather into the clip at the apex of the easel, took a deep breath, and proceeded, with bold, deft strokes, to lay paint on the canvas. She was so engrossed in her task that she was startled when Vi arrived with her promised thermos of coffee and muffin. Not quite two hours had passed, but Pop's gentle smile was taking shape.

"Oh, Cadie, child." Vi drew in her breath softly. Her words were almost inaudible. "You've brought him back to life."

"I'm happy with the mouth." Cadie stood back and looked at the portrait critically. "But the eyes are not quite right."

She added a touch of color to highlight one eyelid. "That's better," she said with a cautious smile. "I'm a little unsure about this. My partner, Doris, is the one who does portraits."

"Don't be foolish," Vi said, beaming at her with pride. "The likeness is amazing."

Cadie reached gratefully for the thermos and poured herself a cup of the dark brew.

"No cup for you?"

"I'm afraid I have to get back to the house. I wish I could stay out here and watch you work on George," Vi said wistfully. "But Sam's sitting in the kitchen waiting for me."

Cadie's heart almost stopped beating. She'd thought Sam had left the area.

"You changed your mind?" she asked.

"Not likely! He got his truck back on the road and decided this morning was the time to come down and sign the papers. My lawyer's only been after him to sign them for about six months," Vi went on merrily. "He tells me he's heading out west today and won't be back. Says I'd better catch him while he's in the mood to do it."

Cadie did her best to hide from Vi the tremendous surge of relief she felt at the news that Sam was finally leaving. She wondered if Marc knew he was sitting in their kitchen. She could ask Vi to tell Marc when she went back inside, but Vi would wonder why Marc would be interested. Cadie made a mental note to have a telephone installed in the studio.

"Don't waste time with me then," she told Vi. "Go and get those papers signed. That's a lot more important than bringing my mid-morning snack out here. I do appreciate it though," Cadie said, taking a healthy swallow. "Good coffee. Strong."

"I put a healthy dollop of wild honey in it to give you a little extra energy. Don't overdo now," Vi cautioned as she slid open the screen door. "You're still getting over that accident."

"I won't stay much longer," Cadie told her. "All I can do on this painting today is a bit of work on the hair. The paint has to dry before I can touch anything else again."

The studio seemed strangely silent after Vi left. Cadie could hear the whisper of the wind in the pines and the distant caw of a crow, but inside the log building there was not even the sound of a clock ticking. She glanced out the window and saw Lurch's reassuring bulk sleeping in the sun. Sitting on the wooden rocking chair, she tucked her feet up under her and sipped the strong, hot coffee.

She gazed at the lifelike image of her grandfather. His hazel eyes seemed to dance with golden light and he beamed at her with the same unqualified affection he had given her all his life. She missed him. But today she could look at his portrait without the tearing pain she'd felt only a few weeks ago. Perhaps that was because she could see Pop's dream beginning to take shape. Stephen Travelle had the matter well in hand. She was even beginning to find some bittersweet pleasure in her memories of the happy times she and her grandfather had spent together over the years.

Her mind drifted, as it always did these days to Marc. "Mine," he had said. She smiled drowsily. It wasn't "I love you," but it had sounded marvelous to her.

She yawned. Perhaps she would have another nap when she went back to the house. Last night had been beautiful, she sighed, but not restful.

She drained the last of the coffee. When she got to her feet to put the last few touches on the painting, she felt a bit lightheaded. She must have stood up too quickly. She shook her head and the wave of dizziness passed. She dragged the tall stool she sometimes used when she was working on a large canvas over to the easel and perched on it. Maybe Vi was right. She was pushing herself too hard. She would do the ten or fifteen minutes work that she had planned and go back to the house.

As she mixed the colors on her palette, she found herself struggling to remain awake. This was absurd. She'd slept in this morning. But just lifting her palette knife to blend a streak of blue into the white paint she was preparing for the highlights on Pop's hair was becoming too much effort. She yawned again.

"Sleepy, Miss Haywood?"

The rough voice that came from the direction of the door to the old core shed was vaguely familiar. It took a monumental effort to turn toward it. Sam Wheelwright leaned casually in the open doorway. He looked very much as he had the last time she saw him. He was wearing what looked like the same black baseball cap, baggy denim pants and red plaid shirt. He would have looked quite nondescript, except for the very businesslike revolver he was holding in his left hand.

"Are you planning to shoot me this time?"

The sound of her flat voice, slurring the words was a surprise. Cadie hadn't intended to speak her thoughts aloud.

"Oh, no. You're going to have another accident." His chuckle was devoid of any humor. "I never met anyone so accident-prone as you, lady. Or so lucky."

Cadie thought as quickly as her muzzy brain would allow. She should have kept Lurch in the studio with her. Outside, before Sam entered, the dog would not have sensed that the man was a threat to her, but if Lurch were in here, he would surely sense her fear and try to defend her.

This was not productive thinking.

Sam wasn't too bright threatening her with a gun and, at the same time, telling her he wasn't going to shoot her. Maybe she could outsmart him some way and get away before he rigged his "accident." The only weapon she had was the blunt palette knife she held in her hand. That was ridiculous. Its round-ended, flexible blade wouldn't penetrate anything tougher than oil paint.

Sam apparently didn't see the knife as a threat either. He was not even bothering to point his gun at her. Its barrel was pointing toward the floor.

"But you've run out of luck," he said. "You should be passing out any minute now with all the sleeping pills I put in that coffee while Vi was getting the papers from her purse."

The coffee! She'd have to act fast while she still could. She threw the palette knife at him with all her strength and ran for the door. At least, that was what she intended to do. The true state of affairs was that she could barely lift her feet and Sam easily dodged the limply thrown knife. He caught her before she had stumbled halfway to the door and threw her hard into the rocking chair.

"I should've waited until you were asleep, but I couldn't resist telling you why you're going to die." He waved the gun in her general direction. "Take the laces out of your running shoes," he commanded.

He didn't intend to strangle her, did he? It would be hard to make being strangled with her own shoelaces look accidental. Why hadn't she told Marc that she was coming out here?

Vi was expecting her back at the house any minute. She was such a mother hen she would probably send Marc out to see what was keeping her. If Cadie humored Sam and was slow and deliberate about following his instructions, she might gain enough time for Marc to come looking for her.

When she bent over to undo her laces, she had to wait a moment for the dizziness to ease. She didn't have any choice about the speed of her actions. She tugged ineffectively at the laces with fingers that were losing all sensation.

Sam slapped her fingers out of the way.

"Give me the shoes," he snapped, tearing them off her feet.

He removed the laces. When he began to tie her good wrist to the arm of the chair with them, Cadie tried to strike at him with the splinted wrist. Almost casually, he wrenched her sprained wrist around to fasten it to the other arm of the chair. She moaned with frustration and pain as she struggled weakly against him. Outside, she could hear Lurch's low snarls becoming interspersed with ear-shattering barks.

"Lurch!"

All the volume she could muster was little more than normal speaking level, but the dog began to leap at the glass doors.

"Get down, Lurch!" Sam shouted.

She had to think! Where was Marc? Unless he got here soon, she was going to die.

The dog stopped leaping at the door, but did not cease his barking. Sam shrugged and turned back to Cadie.

"That should hold you," he said.

He focused his attention on the painting of Pop resting on the easel. His fists clenched and unclenched as he leaned over to peer at it closely.

"That's the way you see the sanctimonious, old bastard, eh? You forgot the snobby look that says, 'I'm a big man, but I'll let you do odd jobs for me and be grateful when I pay you peanuts for it.' And where's the smug smile that says, 'You took my woman but you couldn't make her forget me'? He thought he'd get her in the end—but he was wrong."

Cadie pressed her sprained wrist as hard as she could against the arm of the rocking chair. The sharp pain cut through the wooliness in her brain, but she could feel herself drifting toward unconsciousness. However, the impact of Sam's next statement snapped her briefly to full attention.

"He didn't look so smug when he was grabbin' air as he fell down those stairs. The self-righteous old bastard had caught on that I was copying his core log. I'll never forget that beautiful look of shock on his face when the shove I gave him sent him flying into the cellar. He couldn't believe I got the best of him at last."

Sam killed Pop.

Cadie tamped down the burning rage that threatened to erupt in futile words. She'd allowed herself to be trussed up like a turkey—a drugged one at that. Delaying Sam was her only hope. He'd said he wanted to give her reasons. She had to keep him talking. He had put the gun in his pocket once he had her tied up. Marc could overcome him easily. If only he'd get here. Surely, he should be finished with his printing by now and be coming to look for her. Couldn't he hear Lurch barking?

"That is," Sam appeared to be talking to himself as much as to her. "I will have got the best of him when his darling Cadie is dead. I couldn't believe my luck when Sandor offered me ten thousand dollars to do the job. He was damned mad when I messed up with the propane.

"I jumped the gun when I called to tell him that you and Banachek were dead. I was sure that was why the police were at the house. But that afternoon, Vi told me you were on your way to Toronto and I had to phone Sandor back. How was I supposed to know you were going to choose that night to drop your Miss Innocent act?"

"Didn't you know Sandor was arrested yesterday?" Her speech was even more slurred. "He's in jail. There's no reason to kill me now."

His eyes flashed to hers in disbelief. Sandor's arrest was obviously news to him, but after his initial reaction, he shrugged his thick shoulders.

"He paid me half the money. A man doesn't cheat a man like Green. Not and get away with it.

"Besides, there's plenty of reason, girl. You've got the same smug cat's eyes as George did. Every time you look at me as if I'm something you scrape off the bottom of your boot, the way you're doing right now, I've got a reason."

Sam stepped out of her field of vision and moved quietly around the room for a minute. Cadie tried to make her head turn to follow his movements, but her brain was turning to cotton wool and, against her will, her eyelids were closing. When Sam waved a large tin of turpentine under her nose, her eyes opened with a start. He laughed.

"Stay awake! I want you to see this."

MINE

He splashed some turpentine on Pop's portrait.

"Tut. Tut. You're such a sloppy painter. Don't you know you should be careful with turps?" he taunted, pouring several ounces of the volatile spirits on the floor around the easel.

"You're so messy, you dribble linseed oil around, too," he said, suiting action to his words.

He poured some oil and turpentine around the base of the sliding doors and the picture window; then drizzled a path from the painting to the air-tight stove and poured the last of the turpentine onto the pile of paper and sticks that had been laid in the fire box.

"A woman that careless with combustible fluids shouldn't light fires. As soon as you're asleep, I'll untie you and put you in front of the stove. Then I'll light the fire for you."

He gave a dramatic sigh. He was enjoying his performance.

"They'll call it a tragic accidental death. But this time it's really going to happen. You avoided the propane by whoring around, but you won't get away from the fire."

Lurch was pacing back and forth in front of the glass doors, and his full throated bark sounded frantic and insistent.

"Damn fool dog," Sam shouted. "Get outta here."

"George always won," he said, in an almost conversational tone. "Even when I won, I lost. I stole Vi from him, but she never stopped praising him. I got fed up being compared to the great George Haywood, I'll tell you. It got worse after he moved back here. She's been doing his housekeeping and mooning after him ever since.

"He made a big show out of giving me work and letting me graze beef cattle on the land for almost nothing just to make me feel small. But I paid him back. I only wish I could see him crying over losing his darling little Cadie. But when you're dead, George'll be paid in full."

Cadie attempted to struggle against her bonds, but her limbs would not cooperate as her mind finally surrendered to the powerful narcotic. When her eyelids drifted closed, they shut out the sight of the implacable hatred in Sam Wheelwright's cold, black eyes.

CHAPTER 17

The last stubborn chapter was being printed and Marc had just finished fixing the label to the padded mailing envelope when the telephone on the desk began to ring. The dead fax machine and the recalcitrant printer were not the only reasons for his short temper this morning. Something was eating at him. He wasn't sure what. Now that Sandor Green was in custody, the feeling of apprehension should have eased off, but he still had a strong sense of impending trouble. This phone call might cast some light on what that something was. He almost tripped over a chair in his rush to reach the phone.

"Banachek here," he snapped.

"Marc, this is Chuck Fournier. I picked up some information that'll interest you. I've been checking on Sam Wheelwright's movements. That old guy really gets around. You'll never guess where he was last May when Cadie's car went off the mountain. He was in Colorado. Working for NorthAm."

So Sam had been doing Sandor's dirty work from the beginning. That could be good news. According to Jack, the two thugs who had been arrested in their hotel room were not in Sandor's regular employ. If Sam had been the only person involved with Sandor, it was unlikely Cadie still had unidentified enemies ready to pounce on her.

"Have you picked him up for questioning?"

"Not yet. He's not at the farm or at the place he stays in North Bay. We'll keep looking, but you'd better keep an eye out, too."

"Will do. Thanks for letting me know."

He had to tell Cadie right away. He went directly to the kitchen, expecting to see her there, but Vi was alone, looking out the window toward the studio. He could no longer avoid saying something to Vi about what her husband had been up to. Even if she had kicked Sam out, she was still married to the man. He didn't want her to get the news from the police or the media.

"That fool dog must have treed a squirrel," Vi told him. "He's been barking his head off for the last five minutes."

"Where's Cadie?" Marc asked. "I thought she was going to spend the morning with you."

"She's out in the studio doing a painting of George. She's fine. I took her out a snack a little while ago."

The loud, insistent barking suddenly ceased, leaving a quivering silence in its wake.

"Thank goodness," Vi said, still peering out the window. "The squirrel must have got away. I still can't see Lurch, though. Marc," she said sharply. "Come here. Is that smoke?"

After one quick glance out the window, Marc grabbed the small fire extinguisher from its bracket on the wall beside the fireplace and started for the log house at the dead run.

"Call the fire department," he shouted over his shoulder. "And Chuck Fournier."

As he neared the studio, clouds of black smoke were billowing out the open windows on both sides. There was no sign of Cadie. Was she still inside?

From behind the studio, he heard a man's loud, terrified voice cursing and shouting for help. Marc angled his course slightly so he could see beyond the corner of the lean-to core shed. A few yards from the back door of the shed, Lurch was standing, snarling over the prostrate form of Sam Wheelwright. The dog's huge white teeth were a fraction of an inch from Sam's throat.

"Call him off," Sam screamed, his face scarlet and his eyes almost starting out of his head with fear.

"Where's Cadie?"

"Call off your dog."

"Where is she?"

Marc's heart stopped beating while he awaited Sam's reply.

Sam defiantly clamped his mouth shut, but there was a kind of grim satisfaction in his beady eyes.

Good God! Cadie's inside. Marc had never been one to pray, but he prayed now. *Please God, let her be alive!*

With an almost superhuman burst of speed, Marc sped to the front of the studio. He was severely tempted to let Lurch wreak whatever damage he wanted to on Sam, but, over his shoulder, he bellowed the command that would hold the dog in his present position, but should prevent him from tearing out Sam's throat.

At the front doors, he was halted in his headlong dash by the intense heat radiating through the heavy glass. He couldn't see past the bright flames just inside that were licking at the well-aged, dry log walls. Behind the flames, were billowing clouds of low-hanging, oily smoke. He couldn't see her!

After a moment of near-panic, he thought he caught a glimpse of something pale through the flickering flames. *There!* He made out the dim outline of her body lying on the floor.

Grabbing several towels from the drying rack on the washstand, he plunged them into the rain barrel. The few seconds it took to saturate the towels completely seemed to last forever. After quickly winding one around his head and the lower part of his face, he draped another around his neck. The third he wrapped around his right hand. Then, he tried to slide open the door.

It wouldn't move. He gripped the handle more firmly and pushed with all his strength. The metal handle burned his hand through the wet towel and the door refused to budge. He swung the useless little fire extinguisher he was carrying against the glass with all his might. When he smashed through the glass, the flames rushed toward him, hungry for the fresh oxygen outside the broken window.

The intense heat of the flames drove him back a step. But Marc was desperate. He took a deep breath and, heedless of the fire and the sharp points of glass that slashed his legs as he leaped through the hole he'd made, he charged into the room.

Cadie was lying at the base of the blazing easel. The flames were all around her, but had not yet reached her body. He knocked the easel away with the fire extinguisher and stepped across the line of flames that danced between Cadie's inert form and the wood stove. Quickly, he pulled the wet towel from around his neck and wound it around Cadie's head and, yanking a blanket off the day bed that miraculously had not yet been engulfed by the flames, he wrapped her in it. Then, hoisting her over his shoulder, he staggered back out through the inferno.

When he burst out of the blackness of the smoke into the clear air, he tore the steaming towel off his face and gasped for breath. He had to get Cadie farther from the fire. When he reached the knoll where they had sat, not two weeks before, watching Luke pull the old door out of the cabin, he laid her on the ground. He quickly removed the large cloth Sam had used to gag her. She was very still. He felt for a pulse below the angle of her jaw.

It was faint but it was there.

However, she had stopped breathing.

With an anguished cry, he tilted her head back and began to give her mouth-to-mouth resuscitation. The pain from the burns on his face and left arm became agony, but nothing in his life had ever been more important than making Cadie breathe again. Desperately, despairingly, he forced his own breath into her lungs, but her body refused to take up the action on its own.

At least, she did not seem to have been badly burned. Her clothing seemed to be intact. By some freak of chance, the flames didn't appear to have reached her. But what good was that miracle if she couldn't breathe?

He was oblivious to everything around him except the mechanical action of pumping air in and out of Cadie's chest. The fire brigade arrived and tried to take over from him, but he brushed them off. Finally, when his own lungs were burning with the exertion and he was on the verge of collapsing, Cadie's lungs drew air on their own. She coughed and the paramedics pulled him off her.

"We'll look after your lady," one uniformed young man told him forcefully. "You could use a little attention yourself."

They wrapped Cadie in another blanket and sped her on a stretcher into the waiting ambulance. Before Marc could muster the energy to raise himself to his feet, they were attaching an I.V. and administering oxygen to her.

"Wait for me," he ordered them. "You're not taking her anywhere without me."

"We wouldn't dream of it," the attendant said with a tolerant smile. "Besides, those burns of yours need some looking after."

"Marc!" Chuck Fournier came running from the side of the log house. "Do you think you can bring yourself to call off your dog?" he asked, grinning with relief when he saw he was still on his feet. "Sam has told me a few things we wanted to know in the hope I could get Lurch off him, but I don't seem to be having any luck with moving the dog."

Marc wearily returned his grin.

"Good for Lurch," he said.

Grudgingly, Marc gave the command that made the dog release his prisoner. Then he hoisted himself into the back of the ambulance. To the heavenly accompaniment of Cadie inhaling oxygen through a rubber mask, he allowed the paramedic to begin first aid on his burns.

* * *

Cadie lay very still and listened. She had the stench of smoke in her nostrils and a very sore throat. She could tell she was no longer tied to the rocking chair, but she still felt strange and woolly-headed from the drugged coffee. Where was she? She was lying down. She couldn't hear Sam moving. He must have lit the fire. Why didn't Marc come? She slowly opened her eyes.

The room was unfamiliar and dark. The silence was heavy and unnatural. By the dim light that seeped in around a door at the end of the room, a large figure slowly rose and loomed over her.

"Marc!" she screamed. "Marc! I'm in here."

Immediately, a woman in a white uniform pushed the door open and snapped on the overhead light. Simultaneously, the hovering figure became Marc and enveloped her in his arms.

Marc's deep voice murmured in her ear, "I'm here, love. It's all over. You're safe."

She clung to him. She wondered why he smelled like smoke, but she did not have the energy to ask him. All she wanted in the world was to stay in his strong arms.

"Oh, sweetheart," he said. His voice caught in his throat. "I never knew I could love anyone so much. I thought I had lost you forever."

"I love you so much, Marc," she whispered.

"Enough to marry me?"

"Oh, yes." Cadie met his eyes. The love she saw there made her want to weep with joy. "Soon."

"It can't be soon enough for me," Marc said, lowering his lips to hers.

Their wedding vows would not be more solemn than the promise of love and trust in that tender and eloquent kiss.

DEE LLOYD

Award-winning author Dee Lloyd credits her upbringing in Timmins, a Northern Ontario gold mining town, for her love of dramatic scenery and her conviction that nothing is impossible to a person who is willing to work for it. When she was thirteen years old, she told a reporter for the *Timmins Daily Press* that she was going to be a writer. Many careers—ranging from sales clerk in a record store to teacher of literature and creative writing—and years later, she is doing just that.

She is fascinated by electronic publishing and the fresh new settings and story lines, which this new medium encourages. Married to Terry Sheils, EPPIE award-winning author of horror, humorous mystery, and historical novels, Dee states, "Writing is as essential as breathing in our house."

A former Senior Editor with LTD Books, Dee is a popular speaker at Romance and Mystery conferences. She enjoys coordinating her Library In Your Hand workshops in which authors introduce readers to the pleasures of reading novels on handheld readers, PDAs and Pocket PCs.

Dee's *Ties That Bind* won an EPPIE Award for Best Contemporary Romance.

When asked where she lives, Dee says, "We live in Toronto and enjoy the kind of shopping, theater, art, museums and the great zoo that this great city offers. However, Terry and I suspect that we really live on an island in the beautiful lake country of Central Ontario. That's where we get to spend time with our daughters and their families. I'm sure the grandchildren think of us being there. It's our natural habitat."

AMBER QUILL PRESS, LLC
THE GOLD STANDARD IN PUBLISHING

QUALITY BOOKS
IN BOTH PRINT AND ELECTRONIC FORMATS

ACTION/ADVENTURE	SUSPENSE/THRILLER
SCIENCE FICTION	PARANORMAL
MAINSTREAM	MYSTERY
FANTASY	EROTICA
ROMANCE	HORROR
HISTORICAL	WESTERN
YOUNG ADULT	NON-FICTION

AMBER QUILL PRESS, LLC
http://www.amberquill.com

Made in the USA